HER

Unbreakable
Protector

ALESSA KELLY

"I'm not your knight in shining armor. I'm just a man who stands between you and hell." ~ Samuel Redley Kelleher

1

CASSIDY WINTER

I've lived long enough to know that nightmares do come true. But I never imagined that the one I fear most—the terror that has haunted me for years and has me gasping for air long after I wake up—would grip me like this.

I'm drowning.

Yet I'm not in the water.

"Where is the money, Cassidy?" one of my captors repeats, snatching the drenched towel off my face.

I cough and gasp, trying to catch pockets of air through the water clogging my throat.

The drug they shot into me had worn off, but somehow I wished I was still under the influence—so I wouldn't have to live this nightmare.

I was tied to a rigid board, my feet slightly above my head, creating an incline. My arms stretch down low, my wrists secured.

The two men keep pouring cold water into my nose and mouth over a thick towel spread across my face. At this stage, I'm too weak even to entertain my panic. Every dollop of energy goes to keeping my lungs going.

Professionals like them don't kidnap and demand money from a single mother who makes ends meet by working at a bar and running a small brewery. Harvey, my ex-husband, is the only man after me, and I have no doubt this debacle somehow links to him. This won't be the first time.

I choke. "I don't know what you're t—"

He slaps me.

"God, I hate that answer! I've heard it many times before. And you know how many changed their minds after I finished with them?"

The man squeezes my chin. "Eight out of ten. The other two didn't even have a chance." His round eyes are only inches away from mine when he leans down to me—it must be what an executioner's stare looks like. "So don't play dumb with me, lady!"

I swallow the remaining water, and for the first time in ages, I manage to take one full breath.

A bitter smile crosses his face. "Unlike your husband, we wouldn't care if you live or die. We'll get the money sooner or later. It'll just be easier if you cooperate."

I fucking knew it.

Damn you, Harvey Whitlock!

But the money matter is still puzzling me. If my ex had sent these men to find me, his only goal would be to take our daughter and me back. He should know I haven't gotten enough cash to entice a small-time gambler, let alone a pro like him.

I give my captor a fuck-you stare as if he was my dickhead ex himself. The man then swings his arm hard. I wince, bracing for his fist. But his accomplice stops him. Obviously, despite declaring they wouldn't care if I live or die, they seem to need me alive—or at least conscious.

"Cassidy, listen to me." His accomplice takes over, leisurely walking around me. He might as well be the same man, for he looks identical. I'm sure they're twins. When they speak, it sounds like the same person talking to himself. The only distinguishing feature among the brothers is the gunshot wound I inflicted on one of them on his arm. He's the one talking to me now.

The injured twin circles me one more time, running his fingers on top of my soaked shirt. I don't have my bottoms on; the two men captured me when I was changing after a shower. They want nothing of me that way—which I'm thankful for.

"You're not on our death list," he adds, "but we know how to hurt. We've studied you. What can I say? We like to know who our employers are, including their families."

"Harvey Whitlock is my *ex*-husband," I emphasize. "I haven't seen him since I left him three years ago. If he promised you money, I don't have it!"

"Well, Cassidy, we like to keep things simple. Ex-husband, husband, what's the difference?"

His brother soon flanks him. Now I notice that the unwounded one has a relatively large mole just under his right ear. I'll call him the mole man.

"If you're thinking about protecting him, just don't," the wounded one carries on. "Your husband told us a long time ago that you're afraid of water. We intend to use it until we get results. So one last time, where is the money?"

"I don't know!"

Soon the towel is back on me. Like the first round, water enters every cavity it can find on my face. I gyrate to no avail as my cry turns into nothing but helpless gargles.

My drowning nightmare was a reality once—an ordeal I'll never forget and keep being reminded of by the night terrors that follow. I was barely fourteen then.

Now, as a grown woman, in the hands of two strangers, I'm

transported back to the place on earth where I should've died. It was the dead of night, as if I had dived into a black hole. Only it wasn't hollow. The water was thick. I couldn't inhale or exhale. As my airway closed, I heard my struggles amongst the sloshing water.

Just like I am now.

And the sensation keeps going. For sure, the brothers have gone on longer than the first round.

I thrash around, imploring the men to release me. But they thrive on my struggles. The time slows, but eventually, they seem to have had enough, and they let me off.

After coughing and retching violently, I beg. "Please... I don't know!"

"A couple of days after we reported your whereabouts to your dear Harvey, he was at your house." The man shows me a photo of that scumbag.

"If you saw him, then why didn't you ask him about the money?" I huff, wincing to counter the sting in my lungs. "He hates me. Why would he give me his money?"

"If you're not dumb, you would've figured out by now that he hasn't paid us."

As always, Harvey has left me to deal with his mess.

"I swear, I don't know where he is. I'll pay you the money. Just let me go."

The mole man appraises me. "We're not queuing up for our wages here, Cassidy."

Maybe the men were still on good terms with my ex when they last saw him, or they hadn't found out about Harvey's newfound wealth—if it exists. Something must've gone astray. Now Harvey's minions have turned on him.

"Then go fuck yourself!" I blurt.

His face reddens. Releasing a nasty bellow, he slaps the towel back on my face.

This time the water comes down like a fall.

The unforgiving passage of time forces me to draw everything I have—to defy death, to deny them a win. My stake is higher than riches. I have my daughter, and I have to stay alive for her.

Second by second, my defiance is crushed by the relentlessness of my torturers.

There's only one person who can turn this around, and he's not just a man.

He's Sam Kelleher—a former Navy SEAL, a rescue specialist.

A lover who made me break my own rules.

And he's the only one whom I would trust with my life.

But I don't even dare wish that he was somehow thinking of me. He's in the middle of a dangerous assignment and can't afford to be distracted. The missing little girl needs him more than I do.

Yet, when there's Sam, there's always hope.

And I'm clinging to it no matter how thin the thread is.

2

CASSIDY

Three days ago

The Slick Smugglers' fast-fiddle number gets the crowd cheering and clapping. It's country fest at the Thirsty Fox, and the bar is as busy as it can be for a Monday night.

After helping my Fox boys fix a clogged keg in the back room, I return to the floor, chatting with our regulars. The bar is only a couple of blocks from the Montana State Capitol, so it's no surprise that many of our patrons are politicians whom I know well.

People nickname me 'Hardy Cassidy' or 'The Sarah Connor of Helena'—depending on whether they see me as the manager or as a chick who's not afraid to do boys' work.

Most of the time, though, what I do is juggle fun, firm, and friendly. I'm twenty-seven years old, younger than the average age of bar managers in the country (which is thirty-eight, apparently). But when someone crosses the line, I'll be the first to say, 'fuck off.'

Tonight I've been keeping an eye on a potential pest. He's the new city treasurer, and he's been ogling my new barmaid since the minute he got here.

"You know, in Helena, by law, a woman can't dance on a table in a bar unless she has on at least three pounds, two ounces of clothing," he slurs to the room over the live music. He then gets closer to my barmaid when she passes him by. "So if you wanna dance for me tonight, darling, I'll get us a room." He extends his arm, ready to ransack her bottoms.

I swipe at the man, yanking the back of his collar. "Out!" I drag the drunken mess outside.

"You yourself ain't bad," he giggles, eyes down at my cleavage.

"You're banned!" I bark as I let him go, almost throwing him to the ground.

"Cunt!" he spits out. "You don't know who I am!"

"Oh, I know you. And I know your boss very well. If I see you step foot on this bar again, I'll make sure the mayor will be the first to know what you've been up to."

"Fuck you!" The man points at me as he steps backward, almost losing his balance.

I leave the prick and return inside, where my barmaid is now serving other patrons as if nothing happened.

I pull her aside. "You okay?"

"Yeah," she replies.

"We've got this, boss," Lisa, Fox's longest-serving barmaid, and my friend, assures me as she serves alongside her.

"I'll be at the back if you need me," I say and head to the kitchen, exiting the bar through the back door as I try to cool the hell myself down.

God! Those bawdy pests really irk me. Sometimes I wonder if the likes of that city treasurer are an outcome of some sort of an evolution-gone-wrong—that they were supposed to belong to a different subspecies. Truly, some men are just born Homo sapiens assholus.

"Lisa said I'd find you here." A man comes out of the darkness of the alley.

Now he, I can categorically say, isn't one of the asshole-kind.

He's Sam Kelleher, the co-owner of Red Mark Rescue & Protect, and a man who has me in knots every time he turns up. Maybe it's because of who he is. Maybe it's because of what he does. Or both.

"Look who's back." I step closer to the man whom I fondly call 'Mr. Gray Diamond' because of his gorgeous gray eyes.

Sam and his business partner Mark Connor are Montana heroes by day, putting their lives on the line to rescue missing kids. And by night, they're the perfect gentlemen who keep a low key, stay pro no matter the situation, and tip generously. So, the Red Mark guys are definitely the opposite of assholes, or may I say, the crown jewel of human evolution.

The pair settled in Montana from New York just over two years ago. New York's loss is Helena's gain, even though men who are the epitome of sex and danger are naturally trouble for girls—especially in this city where you can count on one hand how many eligible bachelors are worth pursuing.

But Mark and Sam have proven that they are a rare breed who's not the trouble kind.

Since I work at a bar, gossip flies my way all the time, whether it's political or not. Mark doesn't date—full stop. And Sam? Well, he's technically single, but he and I usually hook up when he's not away on assignment. 'Hey-I'm-in-town' kind of hookups.

And he never disappoints. The man is a concoction of the sought-after danger and sex. So far, sex is the only ingredient that I've tasted in him. He wears danger like a suit, but when he's with me, he sheds it. And I'm only too happy to be tangled in his nakedness—literally or not.

"You've kept the city as I left it," Mr. Gray Diamond quips, looking around the alley. He has come with his canine companion—Retired Staff Sergeant 'Tripawed' Maximus—who is tugging at him to get to me.

I kneel in front of the German shepherd and pat him rigorously. In response, he lifts up his right paw to give me a high-five, but in the absence of his other paw, he collapses onto me—his well-known strategy to get a hug from his human.

The mutt's still eager to have me for himself, but I let him go. There's only one thing in my mind now—Sam's lips, and I waste no time plundering them.

He still tastes as divine as I remember, although the last kiss I had with him was to say, 'see you soon, stay safe.' Now welcoming him home, his response is that of a man staking his claim—valiant and sexful, if that's even a word. My imagination runs riot, spitting out possibilities of where that luscious pair may land other than my own lips.

"My dog first, then me?" he complains over my puckering mouth.

"He's your alpha," I whisper back. Sometimes I just like to make my man wait.

"Don't encourage him." Sam tries to control his dog, who refuses to be ignored. "Down! Maximus, down!"

Maximus lost his handler in a blast in Iraq, and he himself lost his right leg. Since Sam adopted the mutt, Max has had a tough time transitioning into civilian life, giving his new master a handful.

I survey Sam from head to toe. Despite being off-duty and slightly upstaged by his canine companion, he looks every bit the hero. His biceps stretch his shirt sleeves, which are rolled up just below his elbows. He usually combs his fringe back, but tonight he lets it tumble over his forehead messily as if he had just saved the city.

"What are you doing back here? Reminiscing our first meeting?" He teases me after he finally manages to get his dog to sit.

"I just need fresh air," I deadpan.

"Should I remind you?" He insists on being nostalgic and moves right next to me as if I'd forgotten where I was when his dog found me that afternoon. "You were right here." He points to the ground.

Suddenly he drops himself on the dirt, lying flat right next to my feet.

"Sam, what are you doing?"

"I found you like this, didn't I?" He looks up at me comically.

"Sam, get up!"

He ignores me. "Max, come here!" He taps at his chest, and soon Maximus pounces at him, growling playfully. "I found you like this, Cassidy Winter." His eyes flare, and his mouth gapes.

I laugh at the reenactment.

Indeed, Sam crashed into my life six months ago in this very alley. That afternoon Maximus decided to change his master's life—and mine—by pouncing at me, acting as if the dog had won me in a 'catch the baddie' game. I was lying like Sam is now, but he's nowhere near as stunned as I was, no matter how much he exaggerates it. I was frozen by a presence that I thought was a dream. With the Helena sky spreading above us, he stooped over me, checking if I was okay. Never mind his handsome face and overall hotness, his eyes sparkled like gray diamonds—a first encounter that I'll never forget.

"Come on, play time's over," I assert. "Max, sit." The mutt gets off his master and sits next to me.

I cock my head at the hunky horizontal frame that's still left lying on the ground. I can trace the contour of his muscles underneath his shirt, reminding me that despite him acting like a clown, he was a Navy SEAL—one of the military's most lethal weapons—and his lethality hasn't diminished just because he's a civilian now. A lot of his assignments make the news, and most of the time, he tries to avoid cameras. But when he's in view, in his full gear—covered in sweat, full of testosterone—God, even a full-grown lion would not want to mess with him.

"He listens to you, you know," Sam remarks as he gets up and dusts off his shirt.

This man never hesitates to show that he's happy to see me when he returns from assignments. But after an upbeat start, he's usually turning serious just about—

Now.

"Your place? My place?"

I frown—not the kind of seriousness I was expecting. Usually, he would hint that there's a thing or two about his assignments that he wants to share with me. At other times, he'd look at me and beg *please don't ask*.

He might have a different agenda tonight because his question about our rendezvous logistics is surely out of character.

"What do you say?" His smile disturbs the ebony scruff wrapping his square jaw. The scruff is studded with sporadic sprouts of silver. He said he was getting old, but for me, he has simply experienced life—too fast, too dangerously.

"You're kidding, right?" His place is by the creek. The first time I went there, I had a panic attack, and I never returned.

And my place? I have little Grace at home with her grand-mother. "What happens to a hotel room?"

"Just trying to up the ante."

"Hotel, Sam."

"Okay. Join me when you're ready," he says. "You don't mind a bit of a drive?"

I hook my index finger under his chin, keeping his head still. "No. Wherever you are, baby, I'll be there."

I lock my gaze on him, and I gnaw my lower lip.

He draws me into his embrace, breathing hard like we're already in our room. "Goddamn, you're sexy like that."

"Later," I murmur.

He slowly lets me go and turns away. His perfectly rounded ass sways as he disappears into the night.

God! I can't wait to have him.

If I was me six years ago, I'd take the plunge headfirst with this man. But for a single mother on the run, for now, our 'Hey-I'm-in-town' hookups are as far as I would go.

THE HOTEL that Sam has picked tonight is a beautiful forest resort a couple of hours outside Helena.

I don't even have to knock. As soon as I arrive, Sam presses his palm into the small of my back and leads me into his room, or should I say, his suite. It's past midnight, and he's still wearing the same clothes. It looks like he's been working.

Not anymore, though.

He showers me with ferocious, lusty kisses, sending the room temperature to soar above the work-friendly threshold.

I meet that lust by parting my thighs, and he wastes no time in filling the gap.

That is some serious wood.

And he knows it.

"How do you want me, sweetheart?" he murmurs, very gentle for a man of his caliber.

Yes, that's the kind of lover Sam is. Always asks, always puts me before him.

"You wanna be my cowgirl?" he teases me about the position I usually opt for.

Not tonight.

Toe to toe, I nudge him back, all the way to a wall. As he grunts in anticipation, I get my muscle to work and rip open his impeccably-ironed shirt.

Serenaded by the sound of plastic buttons hitting the wooden floor, I press myself against his bare chest. Then I ditch the ruined Armani shirt off him. Well, I'm sure he has plenty of them.

"You missed me?" he growls. "Or do you simply want to kill me?"

"The latter," I moan and attack his lips, my tongue pushing in, demanding access. Meanwhile, my hands haven't stopped stripping him. The clinking of his belt buckle has conditioned me that pleasure isn't far away.

"Liar." He breaks the kiss then exposes my chest, a little more civilized than how I did it to him.

"You don't mind either way, do you?"

I strip to my underwear and rub my crotch against the strain behind his white boxer shorts. The sensation seems to drive him on. He forces himself on me, hitching my breath. As our lips collide once more, he blows warm air into my mouth. Who needs to breathe if a man is doing it for you?

Sam works his lips along my neck, planting harsh kisses down to my cleavage.

"Jesus, Cass." He hisses at my bare boobs. I don't even remember how my bra is now on the floor.

Slowly he dips, and his tongue soon toys with my nipples. His beard abrades my skin as he sucks them rigorously. At the same time, he slips his hand under my panties, poking a finger in to find my clit.

"Fuck, you're wet." His voice is hoarse. It sounds like he's as short-winded as I am now.

I writhe from the sheer ecstasy, and he prolongs it by sliding my panties down slowly, heightening the contact between the fabric and my skin. Primed for Sam's stimulation, my thighs shudder as the tips of his fingers trail along my leg.

He then gives his cock a few shakes. It's already raging behind his underwear. If it grows any bigger, it will spill out.

I fling my arms around his shoulders and jump up to straddle him. He spins us around, pinning me against the wall. My heels perch at the small of his back, digging into the elastic band of his boxers, desperate to expose him. Responding to my struggle, he renders his help to complete the job.

His cock taps against my center as soon as the garment leaves his hips. I can feel the roundness of the tip rubbing my opening, so tantalizing I almost let myself go. His bare flesh in me? Fucking beautiful—if only reality wasn't so complicated.

But I haul myself up, allowing Sam to suspend me above his waist so he can sheathe himself. Then, like the great lover he is, he enters me, making every inch count.

My body tightens as he cages me in. The man is safety, pleasure, beauty, and power in one.

"God…" I moan as he keeps thrusting.

Tack-size pain points scatter around my back thanks to the log wall behind me, while in front of me, the friction between my nipples and his chest sharpens. I rise up and sink down hard, over and over, sending me to a familiar place—a place of bliss that is only reachable when I'm with him. "I'm close."

"Just how I like it," he murmurs against my lips.

I'm burning. It's hotter than fire—it's a friggin' furnace. "Bed," I huff. "Sam, I want you in bed."

He scoops my ass cheeks and carries me. All the while, we stay connected.

My back bounces against the soft mattress, and soon Sam blankets me. I know missionary is his favorite—a no-frill position that often gets unfairly labeled as boring. But I've had it with Sam enough that I can guarantee he'll deliver it on a silver platter.

Sam glides long, creating steady friction between his cock and my core. Comforting, lingering. And just like that, he slows the tempo as if tempering the heat, so our passion doesn't burn off prematurely.

Battering my face with his breath, he then takes the time to appraise me.

It takes two to tango, and I rein in my desire to go all-out again.

His solemn stare tells me that he needs time.

He needs closeness.

He needs to be in me—with me—to reset himself from whatever he has seen out there.

So I give myself over to him, granting him a moment to lose himself in our togetherness—his way.

My arms slink behind his back, steadily massaging his spine. His way is now my way. *Our way.* Every now and then, he moves his shaft as if reminding me that he's still highly aroused.

"Sam," I whisper.

"Yes, sweetheart?"

I tighten my walls slightly. "Do you feel me?"

He sighs in my ear, "Every damn pulse."

Right then, he crawls up, nudging his hard erection deeper.

The impact sends my pussy clenching.

His abs contract and relax repeatedly as he changes gear, gliding faster.

He's ready for me. Oh, he's always ready for me, but this is Sam's cue that he's about to take me to the peak. His straight arms bend and he drops just enough weight on my pelvis, knowing how I like it—tight, painful, and deep.

His kiss is venom, yet it's what I feed on.

The way he makes love to me is murderous, but it's the only way I'd rather die.

Sam grinds his hips faster. His pecs descend on me, giving my breasts a good rubbing. The tightness creates balls of pleasure in my core, along with his relentless thrusting.

Something's got to give.

The balls of pleasure burst as Sam releases in one long glide.

A damn beautiful climax.

And he makes sure I know he's responsible for it. He lets out a grunt—so masculine, and sexy as fuck.

My body stretches, absorbing the euphoria.

"Sam…" I squeeze his traps, trying to cling to the sensation. My pelvis raises to his, hinting that I'm still enjoying him inside me. The swelling of his cock has eased after the release, but it doesn't mean it's not hard still.

Reading my signal, he helps me milk the last aftershocks of my climax by driving his length just a step deeper.

I release an exhale, letting the onslaught of pleasure shut my system down.

Sam hurls himself next to me, and I climb onto him, not wanting to be apart. My system might be down, but I don't even dare close my eyes. I ought to indulge in his company for a while longer.

My breath reflects back on me as it hits the surface of his skin. I watch his Adam's apple bobbing up and down as he pants.

Then I hear him say, "I missed you, Cass. It's only been three days, but it felt like weeks."

Since I met him, Sam has been on longer missions—up to two weeks at a time. Three days should've felt like a breeze, but I must admit it has drained me just as much, if not more. Perhaps duration has nothing to do with it. I've been keeping my feelings behind my never-miss-you stance, but the fact that Sam is away creates a storm within me, knowing that anything can happen no matter how long or short he's out there.

I look at him. While I'm still dealing with the afterglow, the man is fighting with something. If pain has a color, it will be that tinge that darkens his gray diamond eyes.

Something happened during the assignment.

"Tell me, Samuel."

He sighs deeply, grimacing.

After staring at the ceiling for a few moments, he turns to me, running his fingers through my hair. "Never mind."

I caress his cheek, telling him with my eyes that I've got him—whether he wants to share the pain or not.

He finally explains, "We rescued the boy, he was safe. The ransom his parents paid was returned. What disturbs me, though, Cass... The boy just smiled as if nothing had happened. His kidnapper was a total stranger. But there was no cry, no sign of fear. I should be relieved, but somehow I just couldn't get that smile out of my head."

Sam closes his eyes as if the smile is hounding him.

He sighs. "It was like what he went through was an

everyday thing. He's nine—a bright, active student. So he understood what was going on. He should've been scared. He should've."

I caress his cheek. "A smile can mask a thousand things."

He nods, pulling me close as if that was exactly what's on his mind—the boy's coping mechanism at the time might have long-term implications.

"He's got his family who will do their best, I'm sure," I say.

"One should hope so."

Sam is highly trained. Anyone who passes Hell Week in the BUD/S training is equipped to thrive in any kind of situation. But he's no Atlas. He can't bear the world on his shoulders.

If he falls apart, he won't be the one to blame.

If he falls apart, I'll be there for him.

"It's so messed up," he sighs. "The world is so messed up."

God creates assholes because he has a bad sense of humor. But the people that Sam is up against as a Red Mark are as good as proof that evil flourishes on earth.

I shift myself up and then encircle one arm around his shoulder. My other hand stays on his cheek. "It is messed up —so badly that even a slither of kindness or care can make a big difference. That's what people like you, and Mark, do in this world. I'm not saying what you've achieved is small. For that boy and his family, what you did was huge."

"How do you know?"

"We've both lost someone." My fingertips trace the contour of his cheekbone. "Saving a family from a tragic loss is one of the greatest things a man can do."

Sam nods, drawing my hand off his cheek, and then kisses it.

"Kids are resilient, Sam. Maybe more than you think."

"I guess it's the adults who can't handle it, huh?"

Including him—that's what I interpret in his remark.

And his parents for that matter.

The way he folds his hand around mine, and his distant gaze, tell me that he's thinking about his missing brother. I'm still learning the details of his disappearance, but enough to know that the family was torn apart—to the point that Sam and his father have become estranged.

Following a moment of silence, a soft kiss lands on my forehead. "Cass..."

"Yes, Sam?"

He breathes into my skin, then his lips slowly part. "Suppose I moved out of the creek house and found a new place. Would you move in with me?"

I feel a nervous whir behind my chest. "Sam..."

"Suppose. Hypothetically."

He might still be shattered from his assignment, and I have promised myself that I'll be there to comfort him, but not by saying yes just for the sake of it.

His gray eyes pierce me.

It hurts.

But I have to tell him as it is.

"No. I wouldn't. I can't, Sam."

He sighs. "Okay."

I take his hand. "I'm here for you. But you've got to understand, I have Grace."

"So you don't want us to be *together*-together?"

"What's wrong with how we are right now?"

"I want you and me to be more than—this." He gestures at the hotel room. "When you said Grace, is it about your ex?"

Yes and no.

Grace barely knows her father—I've kept it that way for good reasons.

So *yes*. Because my daughter has had her share of instability and chaos, and I have to protect her from any further life disruptions.

As a mother on the run, I vowed not to introduce a man into my life again. That went out the window when I met Sam. He's the most genuine man I've ever known. Being a specialist in missing children, it's well-documented how well he handles kids. So if Grace had tasted Sam's love and care, and if my relationship with Sam fell apart one day, I wouldn't want her to bear the heartbreak.

And *no*, because there's something bigger than my ex. It's not an enemy you can touch—it's real and unreal at the same time, and I've kept it locked behind the Hardy Cassidy fortress that people see.

I've made a rule never to fall for a military man. Separation and loneliness aren't my problems. *Possibility* is my problem. The possibility of him not coming back, the possibility that he might come back as a mangled, lifeless body beyond recognition. I have lost someone I loved that way, and I'm not about to test whether I have the courage to face it again. And there's no way I'll let Grace go through what I went through.

But goddamn, Sam has forced me to break that rule. And before things get out of hand, I've got to set boundaries. Going back to the danger and sex thing—I'll stay on the sex side for the sake of stability.

"Well, my ex—it's over between us. I mean, I haven't seen him in years," I say, emphasizing 'years' as I try to play down the scumbag's possible return. "He's gone, but we're still dealing with the aftermath of our divorce."

Sam pulls me closer, his lips hovering near my ear lobe. The fire he kindles melts me, but he's not going to change my mind.

I add, "Grace doesn't deserve more disruption."

He nudges himself up, so he faces me. "So I'm a disruption?"

I shake my head. "Not like that."

"So what are we doing here?" he asks.

"What do you want us to be, Sam?"

Just as he straightens himself to explain, his phone rings. It's Mark.

"Sorry, Cass. I have to take this."

I glare at him, telling the man silently that *this* is exactly why we can't be *together*-together.

3

SAMUEL REDLEY KELLEHER

Out of any night, last night, I had chosen the furthest hotel from downtown Helena for our tryst.

The distance doesn't bother me. In fact, it gives me time to mull over my night with Cass before I enter the twisted world once again. I don't usually allow myself to think about the shit that's happening in my personal life before an assignment, but I'll always have time to think about Cass. She's never a distraction.

She's the reason I'm happy to be breathing.

I'm not one to fall for the sweet type, and Cass is anything but. I want stubborn, wicked, deep. She's composed most of the time, but when she wants me—damn, she's wild. First, her scent gives it away. Then, she turns into this spitfire that I have no hope of escaping from.

But what brings me to my knees is her gentle strength.

She has beautiful blue eyes, sharp, penetrating. But when they soften, you know she's opened her heart to you unconditionally. And that's when I love her best.

She props me up in a way that nobody else can—and she doesn't even know it. It's amazing to realize that Cass is almost seven years younger than me. It's just in her—and it's not just one thing that she does, or it may not even be a thing at all. It's in her touch, her closeness, her presence.

Whatever my mood, I can simply be myself when I'm around her.

I've been with enough women to say for certain that nobody else can do what Cass does. On the other hand, I've been without a woman. And from that experience, I can declare that Cass is the one I need.

Tonight, though, I was reminded of another side of her— she doesn't sit on the fence.

No, I wouldn't. That was her response to my hypothetical question about her moving in with me, leaving us with no room for talks.

Damn, she's a tough nut to crack!

And that makes her even more irresistible.

The truth is, my question to her wasn't hypothetical.

I've jumped the gun and bought a tidy country house with twenty-acre land in East Helena. Needless to say, it's away from any kind of body of water. I wanted her and me to go steady, and I couldn't let the creek house get in the way of our relationship. And more importantly, I want to show her my commitment—that I want us to be more than just great sex.

Trysts.

I kept saying our nights together were trysts because I didn't know what else to call them.

But hell, that's not us!

That's not how I see Cass.

I want her to be my partner in life and love.

I understand that she needs to put Grace first. I'm up for raising kids—I'm up for anything as long as she's beside me. Tonight, her outright 'no' told me the road between who we are now and what I hope we can be, is a long hard one.

Is it the price of love?

No. If we ever get there, her love will be priceless.

It's a price that a man has to pay to prove his worth.

Nothing is easy when it comes to Cass—and that's how I like it.

If Cass isn't the one, no other love is worth pursuing.

As the 'Helena City Limits' sign comes into view, my business partner and friend Mark Connor calls me.

"I'm almost there, buddy," I answer.

"Easy, brother. I'm not trying to hurry you up." Mark's crisp low voice switches my brain to Red Mark mode. Just in time. "I wanna check that you're okay. I know I've ruined your night."

"Mark, I'm still alive."

"We'll recruit more men, so it's not just us in the frontline. Or I can go solo every now and then, giving you a break."

"We talked about that. And you know my answer."

Not that I don't trust him going in alone—he was a Green Beret, and he's the most capable soldier I've ever known. But two is always better than one—if not critical.

"Well, we've got time to plan our future, brother," I say. "For now, let's find Chloe."

WHEN I GET to the Helena PD, Mark is already waiting in a conference room.

I take a seat next to my partner, facing the open door where I have a clear sight line to Captain Zander's office. He's tensely conversing with the attorney general of Montana, Ivy Cavanagh. Another man, perhaps in his early forties, is sitting next to her.

"The dad?" I ask Mark, nodding in the direction of the man.

"Yeah."

During his first phone call to me at the hotel, Mark filled me in on the missing girl. She's twelve-year-old Chloe O'Rourke from Lincoln. Doctors describe the girl as having a brain of a six-year-old due to her learning disability. Her father saw her last two nights ago, tucked in her bed. He found out she was gone when Chloe didn't wake him up at around midnight—because she always does, to go to the toilet and have a glass of warm milk.

"Mother?"

"Died of cancer two years ago," Mark replies. "Caught up with Brand earlier—he's leading this one."

Politics is not my strong suit, and it's usually Mark who deals with inter-agency matters. But working with the authority is a necessary evil, sometimes vital. Captain Zander has been our man since day one, and we're close. But Mark and I only know Brand fleetingly. I wonder about what kind of a detective Brand is as a team player—or in my dictionary, his DH level, or 'Dickheadness' level.

Mark continues, "Brand talked to O'Rourke's neighbors and friends. Apparently, the old man is the reason Chloe can speak, eat, shower, and take care of herself. Well, to a certain degree."

Father of the Year in my eyes.

Mark watches the Captain's room as closely as I am. I ask him, "Why's Ivy here?"

"Our suspect killed a trooper on the wrong side of the Idaho border. So there's an interstate talk going on," Mark explains. "Besides, the father almost took matters into his own hands with the wrong guy."

"Shit." Father of the Year, he may be, but he's gotta know that being charged with assault was the last thing his daughter needed.

Desperation might've led him to take that stupid action, but it's better than weakness. I wish my father would've gone all out like him when my brother went missing.

"Maybe she's here because the case needs a woman's touch." I wink at Mark.

The recently divorced Ivy Cavanagh is legit in love with him. As intelligent as he is, Mark, taking his job seriously, has become a victim of his own stoicism. Mark has sworn off women since his once fiancée walked out on him the day before their wedding. But there's something about Ivy that sets her apart—if only Mark isn't so stubborn.

My partner cocks his head. "Maybe not the 'case' per se. I think it's the dad who needs her."

"I think you're right." Look at the old man's face—it's sunk as if his expression had been eroded by grief and hopelessness.

Captain Zander and AG Ivy Cavanagh enter the room, along with a suit-clad Detective Brand.

"Gents," Captain Zander starts. "Following the discovery of the body of Elsa Jones two days ago southwest of Ripley, this morning we found another body, which we've identified as missing girl Vera Clark. Both victims were strangled.

"We believe these murders were carried out by the same man as the one who took Chloe O'Rourke. The suspect, Neil Parr, was last seen around an RV park in Libby. Unfortunately, no sign of Chloe. But we're hopeful that she's still alive."

"As we've already informed you, Parr has killed an Idaho trooper during a routine check along Highway 200. Execution style," Ivy says, looking at me, then at Mark.

"We're dealing with a child kidnapper who's not afraid to shed adult blood," Zander warns.

"Although we believe Parr has come back to Montana, it's not out of the question that we may need to cross borders," Ivy advises. "Zander and I will worry about jurisdiction. Your job is to find Chloe. Safe."

Mark and I nod.

She then adds, "It's a delicate matter, gents. Please proceed with care."

She doesn't have to say that. We've proven ourselves with our impeccable record— including rescuing her own son.

Perhaps Ivy did it simply for formality. As an attorney general, she's well attuned to protocols, but I can't help thinking she has remained formal because Brand is here. Zander, Ivy, Mark, and I are tight, but she refrains from showing it. It's a good thing—the last thing anyone wants is friction between Red Mark and the case's lead detective because he assumes favoritism.

"I'm gonna head to Libby next," Brand announces. "I've already sent my men there, and I think they're closing in on him. Our focus is Parr, and yours—Chloe." His poker face remains. Whatever causes the detective to maintain that look, so far, he doesn't seem to be the precious type who likes to show who's alpha and treat people like his doormats— medium-low DH level, I'd say. "You coming?"

"Let us talk to Mr. O'Rourke first," I say to both Ivy and the captain.

Zander agrees.

"Can we please speak in private?" Mark requests.

"Of course." The captain gestures to Brand and Ivy to leave the room. "I'll get O'Rourke."

Before Ivy steps out, she asks Mark, "Can I talk to you for a second?"

Mark and Ivy head to a quiet corner. From what I can see, Ivy's face is almost like a mother worried about her child going away. Granted, she's five years older than Mark, and his baby face exaggerates the age gap between them even more. But her concerns simply show the gravity of the case.

Seconds later, Mark returns, followed by Zander, who introduces us to Chloe's father, Harrison O'Rourke. The old man clutches a cup of water. If he squeezes the plastic cup any harder, he'll break it.

An officer offers us coffee or water, but we decline, and now we're alone with the old man.

"Mr. O'Rourke, thanks for talking to us," I say. The first time I noticed him in Zander's office, I saw grief. Now, up close, I'm confronted by an expression so close to home it feels like I was back at Syracuse PD when the detective in charge of my brother's kidnapping told my dad that he was sorry, that there was nothing more the police could do.

"So you're the specialists?" O'Rourke says.

"Yes," Mark replies. "I'm Mark Connor, and that's my partner Sam Kelleher."

"I want my daughter back. Do you hear me?" The old man rises from his chair but still holds on to his cup of water. His face strains as if trying to exert whatever is left behind those bloodshot eyes to make sure we get the message. "Do you hear me?"

"We'll do everything we can, Mr. O'Rourke," I say.

"Hmm... of course," he sighs hopelessly, sitting down as if he's heard that many times before. He takes a couple of deep breaths. "Sorry. It's just been hard—you have no idea."

"I understand," I say, looking the man in the eye.

He shakes his head. "No, you don't. But I guess you're used to dealing with desperate parents."

The man sips water off the out-of-shape plastic cup. His agitation still shows, but the guy chooses respect over rage, letting us speak.

"We're here for you and Chloe," Mark assures him.

O'Rourke said I didn't understand, but I did. He's a father, and he'll do everything he can to get his daughter back. Different from my old man. When the police told us their investigation was over, that Jack was presumed murdered, my father simply nodded. There wasn't a shred of curiosity or will in him to at least challenge the police's findings. I insisted on going on our own to find my brother, but it was like shouting at a wall.

Harrison O'Rourke nods a few times as if trying to shoo away his exhaustion. "I heard you never failed. That was why I said yes to Ms. Cavanagh when she mentioned Red Mark."

I examine his expression—sensing he has another reason. But I acknowledge him anyway. "Thanks for trusting us."

"Well, actually, I said yes to Ms. Cavanagh because of something I found about one of you. So maybe you do understand what I'm going through, somewhat," O'Rourke leans forward, eyes on me. "Your brother went missing?"

I meet his stare, trying to judge where he wants to lead me with his question. "Yes," I reply.

"What was the outcome?"

I narrow my gaze. "I'm still searching for him," I assert, letting him see a glimpse of my emotion when I think about Jack. Hell, yes. Everybody else, except Mark and Cass, thinks I'm delusional. Everyone assured me Jack was dead because the police had recovered his blood-stained clothes. Twenty-two goddamned years have passed, and they keep reminding me. But there's nothing delusional about what I believe.

Because Jack's body was never found.

I maintain eye contact with Harrison O'Rourke, silently telling him to rein in his questioning. I know he has his doubts about us. Red Mark has never failed, but no one—not even God—can guarantee anything. But what I can guarantee, I will exhaust every single breath and every single drop of blood I have for the safe return of a child.

I straighten myself. "Tell me, what's the one thing that will make Chloe trust a man?"

O'Rourke exhales, staring at the now empty plastic cup as if trying to focus. "Well, she hardly trusts anyone, so I don't know how that prick took her and moved her around without raising suspicion."

"She could've been drugged," Mark argues.

The old man grimaces, rubbing his arms as if something was crawling under his skin. "She was drugged?"

"It's a possibility."

"So, how should we talk to Chloe?" I question. Apprehending the perpetrator in a rescue effort is one thing, but what you do when and after you find the child is what makes or breaks the rescue—it's what sets us apart from other agencies.

"Well, Chloe... little Chloe..." O'Rourke clears his throat. "Um... she responds to a soft tone, but it must be reassuring. Yes, reassure her that you don't mean any harm, but... but at the same time—" He pauses, apparently searching for the right words. "Well, you need to show her that you have the authority to tell her what to do so she listens to you. I'm not sure if that makes sense."

"That makes perfect sense," I acknowledge his explanation.

"And eye contact. Don't stare, just frequent eye contact," O'Rourke adds.

"What does she like?" Mark asks.

The father smiles. "She likes drawing. Crayons are her thing."

Mark and I smile back at him as he chokes back tears. My

partner glances in the direction of Zander's office. We know they're watching proceedings.

"Anything pertaining to her disability that we should know about?" I ask. "What would trigger her anxiety?"

"Um... Don't touch her ears. Well, she doesn't like to be touched anywhere, but particularly her ears. And um... I guess she's afraid of strangers, strange places... being far from me... Oh, God!" The old man puts his face in his hands. "She must be so scared right now."

Ivy immediately comes in.

I may have made Harrison O'Rourke cry, but we had to ask tough questions. Especially in Chloe's case, as her disability might amplify the need for us to take extra care.

"I'm okay, I'm okay," O'Rourke tells Ivy, gathering himself.

Mark glances at Ivy, gesturing that we're done with the interview. He then turns to the old man. "Thank you, Mr. O'Rourke. That was very helpful."

Ivy escorts the man out, but not before she gives me a nod —*be careful out there*—and grants my partner a soft glance—*I love you, come back safe.*

"Gents!" Brand storms into the room after Harrison O'Rourke has left the building. "We've got a hit on Libby. You won't believe what the guys found!"

4

SAM

Libby is almost three hundred miles northwest of Helena. We're hoping to get there before midday.

Mark takes us north along Highway 83. "So, O'Rourke went ahead with us because of you."

"Nah, man! It was your Ivy," I argue. "You know how persuasive she can be."

Mark gives me a side smile with a glare—he's agreeing with me but also not impressed that I brought up her name. I guess the attorney general isn't persuasive enough to change his mind to take a chance on her.

"Well, it's not her," Mark denies. "O'Rourke chose us because he knew we don't do bullshit. You know, when we take on a case, we're not just on it, but we're *in* it." He glances at me. "And a big part of that is you, Sam."

It bothers me that my missing brother sometimes becomes the reason people trust us over other agencies. Before Red Mark became child rescue specialists, when Mark and I were still bodyguards, nobody knew my backstory. But as our profiles become more public—after all, our rescues are about everyday citizens, and they often make the news—inevitably, people do their research.

It's not the way I would've liked it. Regardless, I'm who I am today because of my brother Jack. And I'm grateful—for the children that we've saved, the families that we've reunited.

"Well, there's no Red Mark without you, buddy." I pat Mark's shoulder. "You're Yoda, and I'm Luke."

He chuckles. "That's the best thing you've said about me. Even though technically you're older than me, and I'm not nine hundred years old."

I chuckle at Mr. Stoic.

I'm thirty-four, and he's thirty-two, but he's more than my Yoda.

Mark and I go back a long way since our military days, even though we were in different branches and never had a tour together. But we trained together when off duty. The assignments we've completed as Red Mark's founders have brought us even closer—we've always had each other's back.

"Well, in my universe Yoda is younger than Luke," I tell Mark. "Time is a dimension, and dimensions can be manipulated."

"Gee, you're deep," he deadpans.

We stop for a quick coffee break. Libby is now only a couple of hours away.

"Talking about Jack, you haven't told me much about your progress recently," Mark says as I take over the wheel for the rest of the journey. "Anything about the sidewalk boy?"

In one of my recent investigations, a photo came up from a cold case in Georgia. It's a photo of a boy squatting on a sidewalk—subject unknown, location unknown.

The quality of the picture was poor, but it hit me.

It just hit me. Even in all its blurriness, I see Jack in that boy—his face, the shape of his head, the way he crouched.

The archive note says the photo was likely taken around eighteen years ago. If so, the age of the boy would've matched Jack's age at the time—about ten or eleven.

In our line of work, we use logic and training, but we never discount our instincts. This is one of the occasions where I can only rely on my gut to decide if the lead is worth pursuing.

I've sent the photo to a friend of mine who's an expert in photo restoration.

"I should receive the enhanced version of that photo soon," I tell Mark.

"Good." He appraises me. "How do you feel about it?"

"I've been there before, Mark. Thinking I'd got it all figured out, but came back empty-handed. It fucking sucked. So I don't want to get my hopes up, but I'm, well—encouraged."

"I think you're starting to sound like me."

I know he senses that I'm approaching things pragmatically this time. I try to process if it's a good thing or not. He's my Yoda—so it can't be that bad to be sounding like him.

I slow down as we enter the town of Libby.

"When we know the girl is near, leave her with me, okay?" I tell my partner. There's no one I'd rather be with in any kind of mission than Mark. But some of our rescues have exposed that the baby-faced soldier isn't as popular among kids—a mystery more intriguing than the legend of sasquatch.

"Noted," Mark assures me.

"Let's see what's behind those walls." I examine the façade of the weatherboard cottage that is supposed to be Neil Parr's hiding place. Its windows have been blocked by yellowing newspaper sheets.

Police and forensic personnel going in and out of the property freely can either mean Parr and Chloe aren't in there or something terrible has happened.

Detective Brand approaches us. I can't trust his poker face, but judging by his casual stance, I don't think they've found a body in there.

"What do you make of this?" Brand opens the door for us.

The house smells of cleaning products, but there is something more persistent inside the stuffy interior—PVC. And we know where it's coming from.

Dolls in the living room.

Dolls in the dining room.

And more dolls everywhere.

"Shit..." Mark gripes.

"Any sign of Chloe?" I ask.

"Only these." Brand presents us with some drawings.

I peruse them. They're crayon drawings—three have the word 'Peace' written on them.

"Sam!" Mark reveals the foot of one of the dolls. There's a name scribbled on it. "All of them on this row are named Paige." Then he checks a few others from the next row. "These are named Patrice."

"Any of those names relate to our victims?" I ask.

"Not as far as I know," Brand answers. "Maybe he's just infatuated with the letter 'P'—for Parr?"

"Hmm..." I purse my lips, scanning the shelves of dolls lining the four walls around me.

Humans are creatures of habit. We seek patterns, we operate on patterns.

Criminals included, most of the time.

My brother's kidnapper, although he was never found, was known to use properties in a vicinity of a church to hide his victims. The man was believed to be part of a child-trafficking syndicate. His operations never had a base per se, as he moved around the country randomly, but the church pattern remained constant.

Neil Parr's pattern is his dolls.

But what the hell does it mean?

I come back to the stack of drawings, studying them one by one. After comparing them a few times, I pull three of them into a separate pile and then alert Mark.

I point at the word 'Peace' written in the three drawings.

Mark immediately grabs one of the dolls named Patrice.

"Fuck me," he sighs.

The handwriting on the doll and the drawings matches.

"Mark, these aren't Chloe's. These are *his* drawings!"

"Son of a bitch!"

"Brand!" I call the detective as I spread out the three drawings on the table.

"Look, a doll near a well." I point at the first. The well looks insignificant in the drawing, but it is a well. "Elsa Jones was buried next to a well, right?"

"You're shitting me!" Brand's eyes widen. It's the first time he ditches his poker face.

"A doll near a treehouse." I point at the next drawing.

"And this..." Brand looks closely at the last one. "Is this supposed to be a forest?"

"Looks like."

"There's no doll." Mark notices.

We look at each other.

"She's still alive!" I claim.

"This forest could be anywhere!" Brand shakes his head.

"What's this supposed to mean?" Mark points at an object placed in the same position on the paper as the well and treehouse in the other drawings.

"I don't know. Looks like a ball?" I think hard.

"It is definitely a ball," Mark agrees. "Floating on a river or something?"

"It's a long shot," Brand says. "But there's a Ball Creek in Idaho."

My fist lands in the middle of the drawing. "Let's get that son of a bitch!"

WE ARRIVE at Ball Creek in less than a couple of hours. The Idaho police are leading the search this time, but as Ivy Cavanagh has promised, Red Mark joins forces with them without any jurisdiction issue.

We spread out. Mark and I are in our full hiking gear, heading upstream, canvassing the bank and the forest around us. As a former SEAL, I've always preferred deep water, but Mark looks very much at home. Having been a Green Beret for four years, most of his missions were inland, where the terrains were unforgiving, and the vegetation was punishingly dense.

But in the water or not, we're always in our element when the situation calls for it.

"Sam," Mark whispers, eyes shooting straight at a head protruding out of the bushes. It's clearly a kid's head with long blonde hair.

We radio in the others and give them our coordinates.

"We're going in," Mark advises the team.

I give Mark a signal to cover me as I move on to approach our target. The kidnapper seems to have chopped off some bushes to create a space like a picnic area.

"Clear," Mark declares.

I move slowly as I show myself to the girl. She's drawing. A crate has been turned into a makeshift table, and she's sitting on a chair that you'd find in any kindergarten classroom.

There are finished drawings and also blank sheets, while a set of crayons is scattered all over.

"Hey..." I say softly, staying low so I'm not towering over her, still keeping a distance. "Don't be scared. My name is Sam, and that's my partner, Mark. What's your name?"

Chloe stares at me. The red crayon trembles in her hand. Her grip reminds me of O'Rourke's grip on the plastic cup back in the Helena PD conference room. Like father like daughter?

I check the ground around the 'picnic square' that Neil Parr has created—looking for signs of buried trip-wires or traps.

The immediate area is clean.

I take one step closer toward Chloe. Meanwhile, my partner is watching my surrounding with tiger eyes—pivoting three-sixty-degree with his gun firmly in his hand.

"What's your name?" I need to hear it from her.

She shrugs, dropping the crayon to hug herself. She's wearing a sleeveless dress, revealing multiple prick marks on her arms.

She's been injected with drugs, no doubt about it.

Monster!

While I wish Neil Parr was here so I could send him to hell immediately, I take a deep breath to set aside my emotions. The girl might have a learning disability, but with that, her sensitivity to others' emotions could be heightened.

I remember what Harrison O'Rourke said. I have to show Chloe that I mean no harm and that I have the authority to tell her what to do.

"Your dad is worried about you. So he sent us to come and get you."

Chloe's breathing hastens as I close in on her. She wraps her arms around herself even tighter now.

I turn away from her to ease my eye contact. From the corner of my eye, I can see her releasing her arms.

Slowly I face her again, with a small smile this time. I kneel just two feet away from her. "Are you cold?"

She nods. I haven't forgotten that her father told me she doesn't like to be touched, so I keep my distance and rely on my stretched arms to wrap my jacket around her. Fortunately, she remains calm.

"Comfy?"

She nods again.

"What's your name?" I want her to say it.

"Chloe."

"What are you drawing?"

"Dolls."

I nudge myself closer and scan the drawings. They mimic Parr's three drawings: doll next to a well, doll next to a tree, and lastly, a forest with a ball floating in a creek. There is no 'Peace' written in them, but I feel chills in my bone. In Parr's forest drawing, the doll was absence. But here, I can see that Chloe has just started drawing the head.

"Who told you to draw these?"

She shrugs, but her eyes drop to the ground. A blank sheet lies next to her feet. I pick it up—it isn't blank. There are three black Xs in the top right corner, drawn in a stack like a tower.

I look at Mark, and he immediately warns Brand about a possible fourth victim. Through the radio, I can hear Brand acknowledging it, also announcing that his men and the Idaho police team are approaching us.

"Chloe, would you help me?" I ask her.

She nods her head.

"The man who took you here, do you know where he is?"

She shrugs.

Brand and the others finally find us. Their presence sends

Chloe to flee from her chair, shrieking, with her hands covering her ears.

I catch her.

"Sweetheart, I know you don't like this, but I'm going to carry you, okay? Then I'm going to take you to your father. I promise."

It's obvious the girl hasn't cleaned for days—there's more than mud clinging to her skin and clothes. But I don't care. I take her in my arms and hug her. Her dad isn't here, but I'm making sure that I'm the next best thing to her.

Suddenly Mark takes a giant step to cover Chloe and me, pointing the gun into the bushes. Mark and I know each other's moves like the backs of our hands. Everyone else would think it was the wind, but there's no doubt in my mind he saw Neil Parr.

"Brand!" Mark alerts the detective. It's far, but now we all can see that someone is running away.

Mark and two troopers stay put while everyone else runs in pursuit. But as they barely move a few yards—a scream.

There's no gunshot, no nothing, and one of Brand's men is down.

Then—

Click.

Right next to my ear.

I crouch, shielding Chloe as I see an object flying toward us.

Fuck!

That must've been what has hit Brand's man too. Parr knew that there'd be more than just one person pursuing him if he ever got caught. A trigger on one trap inside the bushes seems to have triggered another.

"Sam!" Mark runs to me.

Sensing the chaos, Chloe's cry escalates.

"Everything will be okay, Chloe. You'll see your dad soon," I whisper, ignoring the sting in my side.

A trooper hauls the injured man toward us, and I cocoon Chloe furiously to shield her from the scene. I see an object like a spearhead lodged in the man's thigh, it must be what has got me, and I feel it penetrating deeper into my flesh.

I keep standing, trying to soothe the trembling girl in my arms. Luckily I'm wearing all black, so she doesn't see blood streaming down my waist.

Mark steadies me as my legs start to give up.

"God dammit, Sam!" he whispers, pressing at my wound.

"Take Chloe," I direct Mark. She might cry harder in his arms, she might protest, but it's better than her collapsing with me.

Mark takes over Chloe while I hide behind a tree to strip my body armor.

The wound is right below where the hem of the vest would've been.

"Son of a bitch!" I whisper-curse, observing the mess.

There's lots of blood, but the object has disappeared— somewhere inside my abdomen. Every breath I take stings like a motherfucker.

I retrieve my IFAK, individual first aid kit. It's more compact than the one I used to carry in my SEAL days (which also included extended-care items hidden under my body armor). They say it's the kit and your wit that will give you a chance to survive, but right now, I just need to patch myself up.

I apply combat gauze to my wound, followed by pressure dressing. Meanwhile, my partner is interacting with Chloe—a heartening distraction. He learned that from me! Look at him. He carries her and talks to her, just like I did.

But it's no time to be cooing over my learning Yoda.

I gather my strength and push myself up. "Gimme Chloe." I hobble toward my partner. "Go get that prick!"

"No, Sam."

"If anyone can find Neil Parr in this jungle, it'll be you!"

"No! We've found Chloe safe. Parr isn't ours to catch."

"We need to know where his fourth victim is!" The drawing of the three Xs flashes in my head. It's impossible to figure out what it is. We need Parr to tell us!

But Mark the stoic ignores me.

Probably with good reason, because once again, I find myself swaying. The slimness of the spearhead has allowed it to slip deeper after the impact, and I'm not helping myself by standing up.

Paramedics arrive, only two of them, and Chloe starts to sob when one tries to take her away from Mark.

I lean on my partner, making myself look as normal as possible. "It's okay, Chloe." I smile at her. "These are the paramedics. Like doctors and nurses. They will take care of you, and they'll take you to your dad."

"Promise?" she sobs.

"Yes. I promise." My breath starts to hitch.

A female paramedic carries Chloe as Mark catches my collapsing body.

"Sam! Jesus Christ!" Mark helps me lie on the ground, checking the bandage. "Let's get you to the hospital." He slings my arm across his shoulder, and we get moving.

I'm glad he's not the one who got hurt, and he was right not to pursue Parr.

Right now, I can only leave things to my partner's capable hands—including my life.

5

———

CASSIDY

I sit up, drenched in my sweat.

As the wall of sleep around me crumbles, the river disappears. The ghastly figure I saw crawling over a rock, calling out to me, is slowly replaced by reality.

I'm only staring at a pile of clothes draping over an armchair in the corner of my bedroom.

This nightmare has haunted me since my father died—actually, since I learned about how he died. But since I met Sam, somehow, the terror has morphed to include him. Two Navy officers knocked on my door, announcing that Sam had fallen.

I haven't heard from him for days. But I pray, to whoever is willing to listen, that this time my nightmare was just that—a nightmare.

Not knowing, or getting news about Sam from someone else, is like walking behind a thick black curtain that has no ending and beginning. You're going blind, you figure out where you are only when you hit something.

His absence and silence send me crumbling like a sandcastle being overcome by crashing waves. But I'll take it, I'll build myself up again when he's here.

I'll endure anything—as long as Sam is safe out there.

As long as he's safe.

I swing out of bed, and my feet curl as they touch the cold wooden floor. I make my way to the front door.

Everything is quiet and normal, except for a whiff of rock jasmine in the air—the smell of sorrow and demise. Only, there are no flowers around me. It must've been the residue of my nightmare.

I tilt up my face at the sky. The moon is shining just like the night Mother received the news about Dad in our Kalispell home.

Still reeling from my appalling sleep, I walk around the porch, striding from one spot to another where the two Navy officers appeared in my dream. And in that dream, I ran to the Black Crow River, wishing the water would wash away the bad news. I did get away from it, only to be greeted by the sight of the ghastly figure.

I go back inside and close the door softly, not wanting to wake Grace and my mother. But inside me, my heart is still slamming at my ribcage. Only one thing can give me some kind of solace right now, just like what I do whenever I miss Sam.

I take my laptop to bed. I don't have selfies with him, and I don't have mementos, but I saved a newspaper article reminding me of the time Mr. Gray Diamond crashed into my life.

Forbes boy safe after rescue effort.

Look at that figure dressed in a black suit and bulletproof vest. Sam and Mark saved the attorney general's son only a few weeks before I first met Sam. She was still Ivy Forbes then. She bravely went ahead with her divorce—which is usually a death sentence for a politician, especially a woman. But she survived the turmoil to hold her position.

You can't see Sam's eyes clearly in this photo, but I swear, I'd never seen such a beautiful gaze.

Sam is the best I've had, not that I've been with many men. But he knows how to love me, and he knows how to calm me —my soul rests when he's around, relinquishing the need to be logical and prepared. With him, everything feels the best— the connection, the joy, the companionship, and yes—the sex.

Sex can be good with anyone, but it has to be meaningful to be the best. And only with that someone special will you find meaning.

His battle-hardened muscles, his shuddering growls, the way he calls my name. Everything stays with me, trapped inside my soul, attaching themselves to me—attaching Sam to me.

Attachment is a double-edged sword. It creates a beautiful bond and, at the same time, a deadly dependency. My attempt to dismantle my attachment to Sam has been futile. How could I? When all I've dreamed about a man is coming true?

It hurts that I can't turn that attachment into a true relationship, but Grace is my priority.

My finger traces the outline of him on my laptop screen.

Yet, he's the kind of man I've sworn not to come near.

The pitter-patter of little feet arrives at my bed, followed by a weight falling on my belly.

"Grace, honey. It's four in the morning."

"I can't sleep."

"Come here." I close my laptop and then pull her to my side.

"You're looking at that guy again?" she asks, her tiny hand reaching to flip open my laptop.

She hasn't seen my screen, and the mother in me wonders

about what else Grace might've known that I don't notice. Evidently, my daughter has been observing me musing over Sam. These days, hiding things from her is almost impossible.

"What guy?" I shrug in an effort to act cool.

"The hamn-sum one."

I let out a chuckle. "Which handsome guy?" I challenge her, at the same time correcting her.

"From the news."

"You didn't even see what I'd been looking at."

"You were touching your screen."

"I was just wiping off some dust." My fingertips tingle. It's not dust I feel; I'm just longing to touch Sam again in the flesh.

Many wives, girlfriends, and partners of military personnel have what it takes to deal with time apart. Shamefully, I don't. Not after what happened to Dad—and Mother, for that matter.

"You say you're not supposed to lie," Grace argues.

I toss her a side smirk. "Okay. I was looking at him. He's a hero. He saves people."

Once again, my daughter shows her eagerness to handle my laptop. "Show me?"

I open the computer but still maintain control. Grace is smart. She knows how to operate my phone, and she's not far from being able to meddle with my laptop expertly. Curiosity might not kill, but it could hurt. I won't let her inadvertently see anything she shouldn't see—just like me, discovering something on my mother's laptop that changed my life forever.

Grace observes the picture on the screen, which I've blown up to almost two hundred percent. "Yeah, he is *hand*-some," Grace affirms. "What's his name?"

I zoom out of the image and point at Sam's name in the description under his photo.

Grace looks closer, focusing. "Sss... Sam Kel... How do you say it?"

"Sam Kelleher."

"I won't remember that. So difficult." She scrunches her face. "Wait... it sounds like the lion place in Africa. Remember, Mom? We watched the show together? The desert—Kali... no, Kalahari!"

I laugh, admiring her logic.

Grace has a great memory, especially of places. My mother used to say she might discover a new territory one day. Because of that, sometimes I teach Grace to remember difficult or foreign names by associating them with places. Once I helped her remember the name of a family friend. It's an Italian name—at the time, we used the River Jordan to help her remember Uncle Giordano. Now she's using the Kalahari Desert to remember Sam's surname.

"Do you love him?" Grace asks.

"Grace!"

I earn a giggle from her. I pull her into my embrace, and my fingers thread into her soft hair. "What do you know about love?" I ask her softly.

"Well, boyfriend girlfriend?"

"Honey, you're five. You shouldn't be worried about such a thing."

"I'm five years seven months," she corrects me. I know she tracks her age every month.

I kiss her crown, pondering.

Do I love Sam?

Answering 'no' would mean I'm lying. So I give her the standard answer when you don't want to commit or admit it. "Sam is a friend. He and his friend often come to my bar."

Grace falls to my lap, yawning. "Will grandma drive me to school today?"

"Yes. You'll be good, won't you?" The school's summer camp starts today. Grace and her class are heading to an artificial wilderness park near Lake Helena, a place that gives young kids an opportunity to learn survival skills in a safe environment.

"Yeah," Grace sighs.

Grace is a sweet girl at home. It's only at school or daycare that she sometimes shows her attention-seeking behavior. Mother will always argue that my daughter needs a father figure, while I blame myself for not being good enough for her.

"Why don't you drive me to school today?" she asks.

"I have to go to the brewery." There's a massive order from a supermarket chain that has fallen behind. I have to be there. Besides, Grace won't throw any tantrums with Grandma even though she's not keen on joining the camp. "I'll pick you up tomorrow morning."

"It's Wednesday, so I will miss swimming class this afternoon then," Grace complains.

"That's okay. It's only for this week. The camp will be fun," I encourage her. "Hey, remember, there's horse riding too."

She nods, a bit convincing this time. Then she raises her eyes to mine. "Mom, why do you never take me to swimming classes?"

This isn't the kind of question I'm keen on answering before dawn. Having a bath is my limit regarding water, but sooner or later, I have to tell Grace.

Water was my friend until it became my nightmare. The Black Crow river was a place of memory, but it was never the same without my father.

A hand sweeps at my chin. "Mom?"

"Promise me you won't tell anyone?" I say, recovering from my thought.

"Can I tell Grandma?"

"Actually, Grandma knows."

"How about Uncle Ben?"

My brother Ben was the one who saved me that night. He was the first one to notice my water phobia after the event, but I've never told him about my nightmares.

"Uncle Ben knows."

"Everyone knows. So why?" She narrows her gaze, apparently thinking of a plausible answer to my pool evasion syndrome.

I caress her hair while trying to compose myself. "I'm scared of water, Grace. So you're braver than me."

"Oh..." She frowns. Perhaps recalling the many invitations to events involving a body of water that I've turned down. "That's strange."

"I know."

"You are honest, Mom."

She never ceases to amaze me with her intelligence and wit. Kids grow up fast—too fast—these days. Their levels of comprehension often surpass what adults expect. I once watched an interview with a boy who became a millionaire at five. Jesus, he would've given Bill Gates a run for his money.

"Thank you, Grace. It's good to admit your weaknesses, things you're not good at. But don't be like me, okay? Water is good." I caress her hair. "Come on, let's get back to sleep."

While Grace falls asleep immediately, I keep myself awake. The last thing I want is for her to see me huffing in sweat, mistaking that the pile of clothes on the corner chair is a dying man calling for me.

6

SAM

The doctors at Idaho's Boundary Community Hospital managed to remove the spearhead cleanly from my abdomen. It was apparently a couple of millimeters away from piercing my kidney.

They've kept me overnight, turning me into a nocturnal grump. But I curbed my urge to escape, and I deserved a fucking medal for that, considering how much I hate hospitals. Besides, Mark is watching me like a hawk. I might as well have been cuffed to the bed.

A nurse comes in with a breakfast tray. "You're lucky. It's Wednesday, which means cooked breakfast."

I thank her despite the dismal spread of food in front of me. I don't know where the term 'a dog's breakfast' came from, but I swear, even Maximus' morning meals look ten times more appetizing than that.

"Would you like me to adjust the volume?" The nurse grabs the television remote, perhaps seeing the sound is muted.

"No, it's okay, thanks."

"Let me know if you need anything else." She smiles and leaves.

"You heard from the doctor?" I ask Mark, putting away the tray in front of me. I never eat this early anyway.

"There's a reason why people admitted to a hospital are called 'patients.' He'll be here soon."

"If I'm still here after *Good Morning America*, I'll kill someone!"

Mark grins at me.

"Any news on Parr?" I'm still occupied by Chloe's fourth drawing, the three vertical Xs.

My partner shakes his head. "But Brand is screening a list of missing girls who might fit Parr's victim profile."

About half an hour later, the doctor turns up.

"How are you feeling, Mr. Kelleher?"

"Good, fine, yeah."

He checks on my vital signs and then asks me to take a breath, watching how deep I can draw my belly in.

"Looking good, Mr. Kelleher." He assesses me as I keep my expression flat—no grimace, no wince. "But I'd like to keep you here for one more night.".

Fuck that!

I throw a glare at Mark. I can't be held responsible for what I'm going to tell the doctor, so I decide to shut up. But once the doctor leaves, I swing out of bed and get dressed.

Mark grunts at my action. But he knows better not to be my mother hen this morning. He's aware when I *really* want out—nobody can stop me. *Nobody.*

"Sam," Mark follows me to the parking lot. "I'll let you off, but once we get to Helena, you stay home!" he orders.

"Try me!" I perch my bum on the passenger seat and push myself up. Jesus! It stings. Clearly, the morphine has worn off.

"Leave Red Mark to me," my partner says. "Spend time with Cass."

"Since when did you become a couples therapist?"

"Seriously, get some rest and talk to her. Have you even called her?"

I bow my head. He knows I haven't. My head is a mess, I can't talk to her right now even though I'm dying to.

Mark carries on, "I'll work with Zander and Brand to find our possible fourth victim. When we get a lead, I'll call you."

I sigh—maybe not a bad idea.

As Mark drives out of the hospital carpark, I confess, "I asked Cass if she'd move in with me."

"And?"

"She didn't even want to entertain the idea."

"Dang. What are you going to do with the house?"

I lean back, watching the trees passing by alongside the highway. "Don't know. But I'm not gonna let her go. No way in hell."

"That's the spirit! And that's why you need to spend time with her."

"Maybe." I keep following the rows of trees. "I guess I have to come up with something soon. I can't be you, staying married to the job."

"No. You tried, and you almost died." Mark smirks. "I mean, you just can't survive without a woman. You'd need CPR every day."

"How do you do it, Mark? Living loveless?"

"I choose not to love. Never give myself a chance to even think about it."

"That sounds sad," I drawl.

"Why?"

"I don't know. Call me conservative, but a man is meant to be with a woman."

"If a woman doesn't need a man, she's independent. If a man doesn't need a woman, it's sad. Is that what you're saying?" Mark argues.

"Kind of, yes. Women are way stronger than we are."

"I guess you're right." He keeps his eyes on the road. "Anyway, I meant what I said. Rest your ass when we get back to Helena. In the meantime, I'll work with Zander and Brand. And I'll start advertising jobs and sifting through resumes. We really need more men."

As I ponder about what Red Mark will look like with more personnel, something in my peripheral catches my attention.

"Mark, stop!"

I pull up my binoculars, observing the length of a dirt road off the highway. A trooper's car is parked sloppily, and there's no sign of the driver. I hand over the binocs to Mark.

As I gaze further, I notice something—an everyday thing that is not so everyday when you are looking for clues.

There's a cell tower behind the rows of trees lining the highway.

It could be any tower, but I'm sure that is what Chloe's fourth drawing depicted—the three vertically-positioned Xs.

7

CASSIDY

Why am I staring at my phone? Not that Sam usually calls during assignments, but I can feel my 'Hardy Cassidy' effort to deny the possibility of him getting hurt or killed is unraveling fast.

I don't want to stop him from saving lives, but his consistent, sudden goodbyes and lack of communication affirm that my decision to stay off being together-together has been the right one. I may be able to keep my fear of possibility to myself, but if Sam ever enters Grace's life, there'll be no turning back.

I told him kids are resilient. It's true. But when it comes to my own daughter—I admit it's easier said than done, especially after what happened to me and my ex. I'm her mother, I can't just let someone in and say let's give it a go and see what happens.

I swear I'll be there for Sam—there's no way I'll forsake him and leave him high and dry. Mark is always there, but I know firsthand the love of a woman can keep a man alive.

My dad had survived many ordeals in his military career, many of which he owed to my mother. Knowing that he had her love, he fought and came out winning—from escaping an ambush, surviving a bullet to his heart, and a hundred grand on his head for killing too many high-ranking Iraqi insurgents.

If only his winning streak had never ended.

I'll be there for Sam as a woman who loves him, not in a traditional context of wives or girlfriends, but as a woman who will be by his side and hold his hand when his heart needs me. I have no interest in pursuing another man, so I'm always here for him.

I tuck my phone inside my pocket and check on Grace, helping her to correct her T-shirt, which she has put on back-to-front.

"Now put on your shoes and then come down for breakfast, okay?"

"Okay, Mom."

Swinging lazy steps, I head downstairs.

"You look awful," Mother greets me when I join her for coffee in the kitchen.

"Thanks, Mom," I drawl.

"Have you heard from Sam?"

"No," I sigh as I grab the jug of coffee for a refill.

Mother holds my hand. "He'll be okay."

"Of course." I say, contradicting the thought that's running in my head.

"You've been seeing him for a while now. Don't you think it's time to introduce him to Grace?" she glances at the ceiling, where we hear Grace's footsteps moving erratically from one corner to another.

Now I regret ever telling Mother about Sam.

"There's nothing serious going on between us. I mean, I met him six months ago. But you know, he's away a lot. So no. It's not a good time to introduce him to Grace."

I plod toward the staircase as I hear more noise upstairs. "Grace, honey, are you okay?"

"Yeah. I'm just putting on my socks."

I stare at the ceiling as if I could see Grace. "Don't you need to sit down?"

"I've got it, Mom!"

I go back to the kitchen, mixing pancake batter. I tell my mother, "The more I spend time with him—well, the more I don't spend time with him—the stronger I feel that I can't live without him. You know firsthand it's a dangerous thought. I *can't* depend on him!"

Had Grace known him, she and Sam would be best friends. He would become part of her life, loving her, protecting her. But I know what it's like to have love and protection only for it to be taken away.

"I don't want Grace to experience what I did," I tremble. "And I don't want to be..." I get up and turn back to the batter bowl, stirring it aimlessly.

"You don't want to be me?" Mother completes my sentence.

I sigh out my guilt. "Not like that, Mom."

"Cass, honey. You haven't said it out loud, but I can hear what's going on in your head. You've made it your duty to stay away from military men. I'm telling you again, it's absurd. Look who you ended up marrying."

I blow out air.

My ex-husband, Harvey Whitlock.

He was a businessman—never picked up a gun, never put himself in danger to save anyone. He had been in danger, but he'd save himself and put *me* in it.

I'd escaped him, and there hadn't been any sign of him resurfacing. But I know his danger will come back to haunt me.

Someday.

"Mom, I know Harvey was a bad choice, but it doesn't make my aversion to military men a bad choice either."

"Losing your dad was the hardest thing I'd ever had to go through. We weren't exactly young, but we always thought of ourselves as a young couple," Mother says. Her statement reminds me that Dad died at about Sam's age. "I shouldn't have let it show. I shouldn't have—"

"Mom... it's not your fault."

My mother gets up and puts her arms around me. "I wish I could be stronger for you," she whispers.

Alice Winter—bless her. She has tried her best, and I know how much she wants me to find happiness again. But being with Sam has had me fighting with myself. There's the dependency—which I'm determined to banish, yet it's growing every time he kisses me goodbye.

Grace finally joins us in the kitchen.

"I'm impressed." I assess her summer camp uniform.

I serve her a couple of blueberry pancakes and a glass of orange juice.

"Mom, can I bring the *Imaginary Places* book to the camp?"

"No, honey. You will join the activities there and have fun. You can read at home," I say. "Besides, the book might get wet or damaged."

Grace tosses me a toothy grin. "Okay, Mom."

I pour myself more coffee, to which my mother rolls her eyes.

"Trust me, I need it," I quip. I know I will be jumpy all day —but that's a fact whether I have excessive caffeine or not. It's the Sam effect that I can't control.

"I'll go straight to Kalispell after dropping off Grace if that's okay," Mother says.

"Of course. Say hello to Ben and Uncle G."

After breakfast, Mother and Grace make their way to the car. I kiss my daughter, hug her, and wish her well.

Mother suddenly turns around, motioning for me to take a couple of steps away from the car. "I think you're in love with him. Well, actually, I take that back. I know so!"

"Oh, Mom!" I hug her.

She scans the façade of the house. "Perhaps once you're going steady, he can start bringing you some pot plants. Peonies and lilies are beautiful and hardy, and low-maintenance too."

I smile. "Come on. You don't want Grace to be late."

The front of a maroon GMC truck catches my attention. It has stopped abruptly. Most of the time, we only have local traffic here, and I haven't seen that truck before. The driver reverses and makes a quick U-turn. Perhaps he didn't want anyone to catch him getting lost.

I wave goodbye to Grace and Mother. Meanwhile, Mother's remark starts sinking in.

Maybe I am in love with Sam—the man, the protector, the lover. It's a beautiful thought. But I'm frightened by *the idea* of Sam—what he does, what I hope and want from him.

I return to the kitchen, determined to finish what's left in my coffee mug. But still tingling with the thought of Sam, or perhaps from my lack of sleep, my hand decides to do its own thing.

The mug slips.

"Just fucking perfect!" I stare at my coffee-drenched shirt. Smelling like Arabica beans won't make a good impression when you're a brewery owner trying to negotiate a delivery extension.

I dash to the shower—in and out in three minutes.

I smell myself, ensuring that any trace of my morning disaster has gone.

The quietness outside breaks as the sound of a heavy vehicle approaches. I peek out—it's that same maroon GMC stopping by.

Something isn't right.

I use my camera phone to zoom in on the registration—a Washington plate.

"Son of a bitch!" I think my ex has found me.

Dread piles inside my head like a stack of steel beams.

I take photos of the plate, and the whole vehicle, just before the truck drives away again.

I've only managed to put on my underwear and shirt when I hear noises downstairs. There's more than one person, and their steps are heavy.

My pants can wait. Right now, I have to grab my gun.

I tiptoe to reach a box in the wardrobe. I can't remember the last time I fired a gun, but it's always been there—as Mother used to remind me of this situation. I still hope that I don't have to use it.

I plod down, stopping halfway through the stairs.

"Hold it right there!" I point the gun at one of the men.

Seeing him armed and pivoting to face me—I fire. But soon, the other charges up. He lands on top of me in less than a second, disarming me as I struggle to set myself free. I elbow my assailant's face and stretch to retrieve my weapon, but the man I just shot comes to his partner's aid. It seems that I only got his arm.

Dammit!

"Get the hell out of my house!" I yell as I fight them. But two men almost as big as Sam are proving too much. Still, my struggle has forced them to subdue me even further.

I feel a prick on my arm, and I pass out.

8

SAM

That tower is the three Xs that Chloe drew, alright!

We find the trooper lying lifeless under his car. He was shot in the head, just like the first one Neil Parr killed.

That prick is not far away.

I can smell his filth.

Mark is on a call with Brand, who is probably scrambling to get back here. I don't know what will happen with jurisdiction—we're technically still in Idaho, but we're very close to the Montana border—but I haven't got time for anyone or anything. Parr is somewhere around here, and I won't let him breathe as a free man for a second longer.

I charge ahead, following a trail that leads into the Kootenay Forest, about half a mile from the trooper's car.

Parr has been on this trail. The signs he left behind are like an animal in heat. This is unlike what happened in Ball Creek, where he kept the trail of his movements clean. I think the monster somehow wants to get caught this time.

Guilt?

I doubt he has any.

Excitement?

More likely.

Mark catches me up in no time. No surprise there. He's the fastest land human I've known outside of the Olympics and the running world championships. We share the honor of three New York Iron Man titles each. While I thrived in the water, I'd never beaten his running time.

My partner watches the rear as we trudge further into the forest, keeping our eyes peeled for potential traps.

A branch snaps in the distance.

"Two o'clock!" I call out, leaving the main trail to dive into the thick landscape. We stay away from clearings this time, opting for undisturbed bushes in case Parr has concealed more makeshift weapons. I keep charging, tramping the sage grass and bulldozing the berry bushes.

Parr is firing shots, but the forest has become our ally. I know he won't get a clear line of sight.

As stillness returns, we split, with Mark taking the further route. We know where Parr is and we'll surround him until he's got nowhere to go.

A few hundred yards later, the monster comes into view—pivoting, anticipating us but having no idea where to look.

I stand still behind a conifer tree, only a couple of feet behind him. He steps right in front of me and still doesn't realize he's in the presence of a man who's ready to eliminate him.

Finally, his shoulder blades touch my chest. I snake my arm around his neck and snatch the gun off his grip. Then I push him down.

But the prick isn't the type who kneels.

I keep assaulting him, not caring if my fresh stitches are splitting. I'm not going to let him out of my sight, let alone touch another girl!

I kick the back of his knee, and he finally yields.

"Where's the other girl?" I bark, my gun to his head.

"There is no other girl. You spoiled my party," he replies. His excited face validates my assumption that this filthy prick yearned to be caught. "But it doesn't mean I can't still have fun." His eyes turn even filthier. "Your partner—well, I don't do boys. But, gee, he's the most delicious man meat I've ever seen."

It might be his fantasy, but that's just sick!

I press the barrel of my MK25 against his temple. Meanwhile, Mark is closing in.

"Actually, he reminded me of who I could've been," Parr whispers. "I would've loved to indulge in the sight of his open, bleeding chest and listen to his dying lungs."

My finger on the trigger budges. I'm gonna end his life right here.

"Sam! Don't!" Mark yells.

Neil Parr puts his hands up, leering at my partner, breathing like a bull. I block his view—nuh-uh, he's not going to take any pleasure out of Mark.

His excitement gradually fades. He now looks one-dimensional, even blank. However many dimensions Neil Parr has under his skin, they're just made of pure evil. Right now, though, that man can stay like a bad case of human taxidermy, but his reign of terror is over.

I press the gun harder as if I could drill his skull with it.

Elsa.

Vera.

Chloe.

And he wants to kill Mark because of his sick fantasy?

Rustles and footsteps tell me Brand and his men are approaching, but I don't move an inch. I won't hide behind the self-defense bullshit. I will tell everyone exactly why I kill Parr. The world would be a better place without him!

"Sam, let go. I've got him." Mark points his gun square at Parr.

My hand trembles.

"Samuel...." my partner grits.

With a big sigh to heaven, I lower my gun.

Shortly after, Brand and his Idaho counterpart arrive. The Idaho sheriff spits at the monster's face.

"Get him out of my sight!" he orders his men.

Suddenly Parr bursts out laughing as he's resisting arrest. His one-dimensional mask tears off, and I can see the son of a bitch's true demeanor.

Instinctively I cover Mark.

Right then, Parr snatches the arresting trooper's gun and turns to me, using one of the troopers as a shield.

But I stand firm. If he wants to kill my partner, he's got to go through me.

Desperate shouts from the police for Parr to give up continue. Knowing it's over, Parr points the gun right under his own chin, then fires.

That prick can't die like that! He can't!

But it's too late.

His body lays limp on the ground. His messed-up head rests in his own blood and brain matter.

It should be over—it shouldn't matter how he died. But I swear to God, I'd rather be the one who took that monster's life.

MY THROAT IS CLOGGED UP. I can't say a single word as Mark drives us home. But I've been observing my partner. There's anger mounting behind those steady eyes, weighing his gaze down, and I'm dying to fish it out so I can see him as crossed as me.

But he keeps everything to himself, including, I'm sure, his disgust for Parr's vulgar stare at him. He hasn't said anything about it, and I don't think he heard what that prick whispered to me—but he knew.

"Jesus, Sam," Mark breaks the silence as he sees blood starting to seep out of my shirt. "I'll drop by the hospital."

"Don't you dare!"

"You need stitches again, or you'll be just as dead as Parr."

"Well, I wouldn't mind that."

"Sam, when we get to Helena, I don't want to see your ass anywhere near Red Mark for the next two weeks," he says. "Is that clear?"

"The fuck?"

"Is that clear?"

"What are you trying to do, man?"

"I'm trying to put sanity back into you!"

"Well, take me to Dr. McShrink, feed me sleeping pills, I'll take it! But don't ever—ever—tell me to take a holiday."

"I mean it, Sam. I'm not gonna see you again until you sort your shit out."

"Tell me you wanted to do it too, Mark. To blow that filthy prick's brain off?"

"Yes, I did! But I didn't give myself a chance to do it."

"Chance... God, you love that word, don't you? You've always got it right. Heck, I should've pulled the trigger! And guess what, I bet you, I bet you, you would've been relieved that it was my hands that turned red. Because you always play by the rules, right, Mark?"

"Just think, Sam. Think for a moment," he says calmly. I don't know how he hasn't lost his shit already. What is he made of? Or perhaps his heart has hardened to the point of no return that he can't feel. "Had you killed that prick, you'd go to jail!"

"So what?"

"So what? Other kids who might need you could die! Because you won't be there for them."

I shake my head.

"Think about that!" Mark adds. "For fuck sake, just lose that ego!"

"Let me out!"

Mark has the central lock, and he keeps driving.

Killing him isn't an option. But I really, really hate him right now.

I remove myself from the heat and go to the only place of comfort I know. I look at Cass's picture, the only photo I tag as 'favorite' on my phone. My fallen angel is sleeping, her hand on mine. And her gorgeous hair—when she wants me, its scent gives it out before anything else in her body.

Cass would give me a hard time if she knew I hadn't deleted the photo as she asked. But I've gotta have her with me. She looks vulnerable there, though she's anything but. The woman doesn't need my protection.

I don't know if I'll ever tell her about what happened in this rescue. I guess the details don't matter to her. She will always comfort me the way she only can.

I take a deep, agonizing breath trying to find her scent in my mind.

God, I would give up anything to be back in her arms.

Right now. Right at this second.

9

CASSIDY

Something smells foul, and it's right in front of my nostrils.

Whatever it is, it makes me cough, and I almost cry from the burn. Inhaling is worse. The air feels like thorns scraping against the wall of my throat.

At least they've stopped pouring water on me.

My lids part a little, enough to catch a glimpse of two faces hovering over me. They may be assessing whether I'm alive or dead.

I'm sure I'm alive. Because if I was dead, I could safely say that I'd go to heaven, and this is definitely not heaven—it stinks, and it has evil in it. Those brothers—the mole man and his twin might've dragged me to hell with their merciless waterboarding, but it's not my time yet.

Although my situation isn't getting any better. I'm still tied up, and each breath that I take is torture.

The mole man stands on my right as his brother turns around to put away a small bottle on the table behind him. I think that foul thing they put on my nose was smelling salts.

"I thought we'd lost you," the mole man sneers.

Oh, he looks worried, alright. That gives me hope that I

might just live another day because they don't want me dead —yet.

"Now that you're back, should I remind you why you're here?" He picks up a white towel, still dripping from the last round of pouring.

Just seeing it makes my lungs scream in terror.

"You want... Harvey's money," I labor, almost blabbering as I struggle to control the movement of my lips. I gulp. "He never told me anything."

"Remember what I said about my interrogations?" The mole man walks to the end of the board, feeling the binds around my ankles. Then he saunters back to check my wrists. "Do you want to go with the two out of ten people who didn't make it? Or the eight who changed their minds?"

"He hated me. Still does, I'm sure. I can't give you anything else."

The mole man nods, giving a quick glance at his brother. "I know Harvey better than you do. He still loves you," he goes on. "So here's what I think happened. He told you about the money, and as smart as you are, when you saw the amount, God! Why share? That would set you up for life. And little Grace's?"

I feel the muscles in my stomach clench. The fear within me leaps to new heights—this is more than just a nightmare.

"Don't you dare!" I pull at my bound wrists and ankles so hard the brothers swoop to subdue me.

"Well, unlike your husband, we won't care if little Grace lives or dies."

"Don't you touch her!"

Panic sets into me. I have to get out of here—somehow.

"She's out camping with her school, isn't she? Perhaps she has some accident; maybe she slips into a river? Like mother like daughter?"

Convinced that I won't be able to free myself, they release their grip on me and straighten themselves. Then the mole man presses at my biceps. Perhaps when he profiled me, he learned too that I'm known as the Sarah Connor of Helena.

They wait for me to catch my breath as if giving me time to visualize what sort of torture they might impose on my daughter. I shake hard.

"I've seen you work at your bar—lifting things that should be a man's job. And you weren't too bad trying to fight us at your home earlier. But look at you. You've pissed your panties already."

His smile spears my chest. I'd been careful; I'd played by the book—but instead, all I did was roll a pair of dice in a game of chance. After running away for years, the safety I thought I'd given my daughter turned out to be an illusion. All of this is messed up! *I've* messed up!

"Leave my daughter out of this!" I throw my last-ditch effort to stop my captors from gunning for Grace. "I'll find Harvey and get him to talk and show you where the money is."

The two brothers stare at me, not giving anything away, only instilling fear in me.

The wounded one then says, "Look, Cassidy, we want the same thing. To get out of here and have our merry ways. I know you won't be able to pay us, and somehow I doubt your husband—sorry, your *ex-husband* is willing to give up his treasure for you. But you can help us."

"Harvey has numerous off-shore accounts," I pant. My whole face feels numb, and my water-clogged sinus is about to make my head explode, but I have to feed them something. "I may know people who can lead me to those accounts. I bet he would've distributed the amount across them if it's as much as you've made me believe."

"Now we're talking. The kid card is always a trump card,"

the mole man sneers, motioning for his brother to show me a sheet of paper. "What do these mean?"

I try to read them despite my hindered vision, thanks to trickles of water over my eyes.

"I'm going to ask again, Cassidy. What do these mean? We found a trace of these numbers on a motel's notepad. Of course, he had the written page, but boy, he presses down hard when he's writing, huh?"

He does. Harvey was always tense; he'd said his business made him so, and it looks like he hasn't changed.

"Think of little Grace before you say *I don't know*."

Lingering water laps against my throat as I try to gulp. My airway has been filled and emptied at a rate that resembles erosion. But I have to come up with something, or they will take Grace.

"It looks like his birthday, backward. Probably a password," I rasp, almost inaudibly. "The second number might be an account number."

"You don't look so sure."

"I'm just trying to think on his behalf," I say. "Wait... they could be coordinates. Harvey often contradicted himself. He often said that he didn't trust banks despite his many accounts. 'If you want your money safe, bury it,' he once said." I pant, unsure how much longer I can talk, but I persist. "Yes, that was what he said, I swear."

The brothers confer, punching numbers into their phones. They stare at each other, seemingly satisfied that one of my arguments is at least plausible because they soon free me from the board.

I waver on my feet and collapse. Like a body without muscles, I let the two men drag me out of the room with no resistance. They carry me outside and toss me into another building that looks like an old log cabin or shack.

Oh, the stench!

One of my captors then kicks my face. "That's for shooting me, bitch!"

They then leave me.

Metal clanks and keys rustle just outside the door.

My head falls, and my lips kiss the ground. The tiny breaths I manage to let out seem to disturb some dust, only for the debris to go straight into my lungs as I inhale.

And amongst my desperation, my thoughts circle back to one name.

Sam.

I've learned to live without the protection or love of a man. But how desperate I am now for him.

He might terrify me with what he does for a living, or rather, that he might die because of what he does. So terrified, I told myself I wouldn't be his widow—literally or not. Our future together may be up in the air, but when it comes to a life-and-death situation, there's no one I trust more than Sam.

But he doesn't know I'm here—and it's not his fault. He's out there somewhere rescuing a missing girl. The police wouldn't have called on him and his partner Mark unless they were desperate. So, however bad my situation is, I'm sure it's not as dire as what Sam is facing.

I can only hope that my captors are distracted enough with whatever information they think they have uncovered, giving Grace a chance to be back safely from her summer camp. Someone will surely report it if I don't turn up and pick her up tomorrow.

For now, I have to survive this dark room, the stench, and the bugs that start to take an interest in me—perhaps they haven't seen living flesh in a long time.

10

———

SAM

I drop off my gear at Red Mark headquarters and then walk away, not giving Mark a chance to lecture me again about taking a leave of absence. Or perhaps he's given up on it. After all, he knows not to provoke me when I'm like this.

Most worryingly, though, Cass hasn't answered any of my calls.

I skip the trip to the kennel and head downtown. Maximus is going to kill me, but I'll bear the consequences.

I need to see Cass.

Now.

"Here we go," Lisa, Cass's friend who also works at the Thirsty Fox, serves me a glass of Fallen Angel, the best ale in the world, brewed by my own fallen angel.

I hope she's still mine. It's unlike her not to answer her phone.

"She'll be here," Lisa says.

I look around. Almost all tables are taken—it's the Fox's famous Buy-One-Get-One-Free afternoon. Cass should've been here; she's always in during peak times.

Lisa explains, "She had to stay at the brewery for a big order that got derailed." She's soon called to the counter, and she leaves me be.

My side still hurts like hell, and the beer I'm sipping hasn't helped in the least.

I may or may not talk about Idaho with her, but just the thought that she'll be there if I do is immensely reassuring. She may not want to go steady with me, but one thing will never change—she's willing to listen. I know she has the strength to take in my troubles, no matter how gruesome and distressing. And with that, she'll be the gentle hand that will comfort me.

Cass has been my rock right from the first assignment I had after I met her. Upon my return, she gave me more than just her care. She didn't judge. She didn't advise. She simply lent a pair of ears and understanding, which I never thought existed. Perhaps coming from a military family, having lost her dad in a war, she knows me better than anyone I've ever been with.

Sharing doesn't make troubles disappear, but she helps me carry the burden.

I play with the beer coaster, spinning it, peeling it.

Elsa Jones.

Vera Clark.

Chloe O'Rourke.

If something ever happened to Cass's daughter, it would be the most terrifying thing in my life—more terrifying than losing my own brother to kidnapping. And Jack's kidnapping was devastating beyond comprehension. It tore our family apart, and being a young teenager then, I only had limited knowledge of what could've happened. Now, having seen what I've seen, the thought of Grace being one of the victims disturbs me to my core.

Yet I haven't met the little girl.

Cass has shown me her photos. She's as beautiful as her mother. The more I know Cass, the more I feel connected to Grace—as strange as it may sound.

"Is Grace with her grandma?" I asked Lisa as she passes by.

"Oh, it's Grace's summer camp today. It's an overnight thing with her school."

"I see."

I wince as I shift my seating position.

"You okay?"

"Yeah," I reply, discreetly glancing at where my stitched wound is, making sure no blood specks have seeped through my new shirt.

Trying to quash my impatience, I think back to Mark. I still hate him for stopping me from killing that monster, but my partner was right. If I had gone to jail, it would've prevented me from stopping guys like Neil Parr in the future, and that would hurt.

"Another one?" Lisa offers a Fallen Angel refill.

"Um… no thanks."

"Are you two official yet?"

I scoff. "Let me ask Cass how she wants to answer that."

"Well, it's not as straightforward, huh? It's like you're there, but then you're not."

"Is that what Cass told you?"

"No. Just an observation. She's happy when you're home. When you're away, she becomes this tight rubber band."

When I almost lost consciousness as Mark hauled me out of Ball Creek—what if Cass had been there to witness it all?

What if that spearhead had killed me?

Body armor isn't death-proof. The weapon Parr devised could've hit my neck, or it could've snuck into my armpit and pierced my heart.

Had I died, I would've broken Cass's heart.

This is exactly why Cass had said 'no.'

She wanted to keep our distance so that when the worst happened to me, Grace would be protected from grief—or what she cryptically told me as a 'disruption.'

When I first met Cass, I had resolved to walk away—not wanting to deal with any possible heartbreak, which was like a one-in-two chance in my life. Despite my resolve, I couldn't walk away from her. No man could!

Cass might've rejected my proposal to live together, but she hasn't rejected *me*. And hell, I won't give up. She's far too precious to let go just because she's terrified of what I do. We're all mortals—she's got to see that. If not, I have to tell her.

But where the hell is she?

Lisa takes away my empty glass and wipes beer off my table. "Are you sure I can't get you anything else? I'm sure she won't be far away."

"Well, alright. A club soda and a cheeseburger, then."

"It's your lucky day, because you'll get two of those burgers." They'll certainly make up for the hospital breakfast I wisely missed this morning. "Won't be long," she says and heads to the kitchen.

With nothing else occupying my mind, my thoughts go back to Idaho. Perhaps I should call Mark and clear things up.

I rest my chin on my steepled hands, watching cars passing by, hoping one of them would be Cass's so I can talk to her first before I say anything else to Mark.

A bus pulls over right opposite the bar—it looks like an empty school bus. Perhaps a school has organized a trip for their students to visit the Capitol, and the driver couldn't find a spot closer to the venue. But why here?

There's something odd about it all.

It could just be my hyperactive mind, but what the hell is a lone little girl doing in there?

11

CASSIDY

I must've passed out again. Somehow I hoped I'd wake up in my bed and find that I had been in yet another nightmare. But as I do a long blink, the blackness around me affirms that there is nothing to wake up from.

I'm lying on my belly, with my cheek pressed against the ground. It feels like a locomotive has pounded my face repeatedly—my whole head is throbbing.

While my brain is still processing where I am and how the hell I got here, I push myself up. The stench in this place sends me gagging, and it's not the smelling salts. Something is rotting here. I might as well be lying on a carcass.

One thing is slightly reassuring—there's no sign of my torturers. And I can speculate that there's no water around here either, not in a bucket or on a towel.

Unable to see my own hands, I assess myself in the dark. At least my four limbs seem to be intact and functioning. The skin on my legs scrape the rough surface they're resting on—and the tickling sensation? It's not from dust or sand. I haven't got my jeans on, and bugs are crawling all over me!

"Shit!"

That gets me alert, but even sitting up proves too much. Every muscle in my body urges me to lie back down.

Yes, I'm going to. I need to sleep off this throbbing pain in my head, which, now I remember, was the result of someone kicking me in the face. And before that—

The brothers showed me a piece of paper with numbers on it.

I'm soon reminded of what's at stake.

Grace.

Those brothers wanted my daughter, and I had bullshitted my way through to distract them. But it's only a matter of time before they're gunning for her, if not already. I'm sure there won't be any accounts relating to those numbers in the Caymans. And there won't be any secret holes in those coordinates I made up—hiding millions of dollars, or however much my dickhead husband is trying to hide.

Just like Harvey to fuck me up again. I hope one day I'll get to tell him to his face—with a bone-cracking punch, preferably—what he has put Grace and me through.

I don't know how long I've been in this shack, but I can't let them take my baby!

There's a tiny flow of breeze coming in from my right. Following the wall behind me, I walk toward the source.

It's a door. I shake it and then charge my shoulder against it. I do it repeatedly, but the damn thing won't even budge. I'm sure the brothers have put a heavy-duty lock or even secured it with a bar.

Crushed, I slink to the ground. Pain racks my body.

What a fucked-up mother am I? Thinking I could protect my daughter? If only I hadn't let my blissful life slip into complacency.

Life in Helena had been bliss. It had its challenges—as every single mother on the run would face—but this year had passed without an incident, without me scrambling for a safe place.

I've got to hand it to Harvey, though. I didn't think my ex would find me this quickly. As a gambler, he was a loner. But as a businessman, he was known to employ people haphazardly. This time, sadly, it seems he had hired the right men—they found me, to a devastating effect.

If only I hadn't let my fear rule me, I would've let Sam into our lives—mine and Grace's—and today might've turned out differently.

If Sam had been home, if he'd known about Harvey, if he'd known Grace or I could be in danger, he would've stood fierce like an alpha lion defending his pride.

But home isn't where his heart is. Danger is.

Whether we're casual lovers or a serious couple, separation will always be a part of us.

It's his job—his duty that I have no right to interfere. I appreciate the lives he saves and the family he serves. But every assignment leaves a tiny prick in my heart, and the hole gets bigger each time he kisses me goodbye while the bed is still warm from our lovemaking the night before.

No matter how things are between us, Sam isn't here.

My persistent heart keeps telling me that there is still hope that he'll find me—somehow. But this is about Grace's life. The situation calls for more than a glimmer of hope.

I force myself to get up.

The stench stings my already sensitive nose, but I swear there are two distinct odors in this shack. The persistent rotten smell is probably of a dead animal somewhere. Still, the other odor resembles a different kind of rot—it smells like the basement wall of a bar that termites had eaten. I remember that old dump in North Dakota, one of my first jobs after I ran away from Harvey.

I stoop to pat the ground, following the path of the insects that have been trying to make friends with me. This shack is made of logs, and it feels as damp and old as a water dinosaur. If these insects around me are really termites, there's gotta be a part of the wood that they've been feasting on.

On all fours, I let the swarm lead me. I pass what feels like a pile of metal, and then a stack of tins, probably paint. A few feet in, the texture of the ground changes. I feel crumbs.

"Come on," I pant, trying to find a weak patch that might just give me a chance to break through however I can.

I keep groping, and a log shifts. It's knee-high, probably the fourth or the fifth in the stack. I quickly lie on my back, my legs raised in an L-shape like a baby about to kick a ball. Only, I'm up against a wall—literally.

"Come on!"

I launch relentless kicks at the loose log. The one underneath it now moves, too, this time revealing a crack, letting the light come in.

Thank you, termites!

Fueled by the discovery, my energy soars. I keep at it. If only I was wearing appropriate footwear. With only a pair of house slippers, which might not be slippers anymore at this stage, my foot arches throb. If I have any hope of getting to Grace, I'll have to stop wrecking my feet.

I sit down low, continuing the assault on the wall with my elbows and fists. Morning coffee can only take me so far, but there's no time to quit. I've carried and lifted loads that few average women can. But what good would it do? If I can't even free myself from this shithole to get to my daughter?

No bruises will stop me now. I won't give up even if I have to lose my limbs. I have to get to Grace!

I keep charging. As the two logs crumble inch by inch, my last strike breaks the top one. The thrust disturbs the log underneath. With a push, the rotten trunk gives way without resistance.

Now, even more light is rushing in.

I retch as I learn where the rotten stench comes from. It's not a dead animal. All this time, a corpse has been a silent witness to everything I've done here—lying behind the stack of scrap metal in the far corner, swarmed by different kinds of insects.

Turning away from the gruesome scene, I climb through the hole, making myself as skinny as possible. The jagged edges of the wood scraped my bare legs, but I am out.

I appreciate the fresh air, taking in as much as I can with short breaths. But I can't linger.

I round the shack slowly, keeping myself close to the wall just in case there is someone on the other side.

There's movement.

I peek slowly.

It turns out to be a squirrel that happens to be passing the shack.

After waiting a few moments, once I'm sure that I'm alone, I step behind a nearby tree, scanning my surrounding.

It's a valley with lines of birch trees and lodgepole pines. A typical Montana wilderness, it's hard to know where it is.

Everything is still, apart from that lone squirrel who's watching me from a distance, perhaps waiting for me to get away.

About ten yards from the shack is a small cabin that looks to be in better shape. It must be where the brothers imposed the torture on me. My instincts say *don't even go there.*

But this isn't about me. If somehow the brothers have gotten Grace, and she's there, I don't want to leave without her.

I look in through the only window. It's a one-room cabin with messy piles enough to fill a unit you'd see in *Storage Wars.*

But those piles have been put aside, making room for a flat wooden bed.

The pain in my throat returns. So that was where the two men tried to 'drown' me. The scene is enough to make me coil, but I'm a mother desperately seeking her daughter. I have to see what's behind the messes. I won't forgive myself if I miss her.

Despite my trepidation, I investigate inside. Bypassing the bucket and wet towel, I weave my way between boxes that are big enough to conceal a five-year-old child.

"Grace... are you here, honey?" I whisper.

I look under old chairs, and lastly, I shift the fold-out bed in the corner.

There's no one here.

Now I've got to get the hell out of this valley, and there's only one way to do it.

I follow the tire marks running parallel to the cabin. It leads me to a single-vehicle trail which I'm sure will eventually take me to the highway. Even though it's muddy, the track is reasonably flat, making it easier for my feet.

But how far will I have to hike before I can get help? At least to make a phone call to Grace's school or the police? There's a chance I might lose the race against the light and be trapped in this forest. By then, I'm sure there'll be more than termites that want to check me out.

I halt my steps.

What if the brothers are on their way back here? That means I will be right in their sights because we will cross paths with each other.

My head hurts trying to make a decision, but the sound of a vehicle approaching ends my dilly-dallying. I hurl myself behind a sage bush.

It's not the maroon GMC; it's a black Jeep. The driver parks between the cabin and the shack and then hops out. He lingers next to the passenger door, looking around as if expecting someone. Then he takes out his cellphone.

"Where the hell are you? Call me!"

That man is one of the brothers, and since his arms aren't injured, it's got to be the mole man.

He paces around his car, making a few more calls that seem to go unanswered. As he curses to God, he walks toward the shack, his back on me. I dart forward. He's only a few feet away from me now, and there's only the car separating us.

While the man is standing by the shack door, checking the lock, I peer into the car windows seeking any sign that my daughter is there—and hoping the key is still in the ignition.

But the mole man isn't the sloppy type—he's got the keys in his hand, and he's about to open the padlock.

I bite my lip. I have to think fast because he'll find out that I'm not in there anymore.

12

———

SAM

I halt my investigation of the out-of-place school bus outside The Thirsty Fox and stay in my seat.

The bus driver is a middle-aged man wearing a yellow 'Sunshine Transport' polo shirt. He guides the little girl out of the vehicle, holding her hand while crossing the street. The scene is a little unusual, but that's not the body language of a kidnapper or a criminal. The way he lets himself out in the open, showing his face with no sunglasses or hat, and the way the girl acts around him tells me they know each other.

But—

What the hell?

They're going straight into The Thirsty Fox!

Judging by the urgency of his move, I don't think he intends to dine here—especially with that brooding kid in tow.

One of The Thirsty Fox servers stops him. "Sorry, kids aren't allowed here."

"I know. But this is an emergency," the man says.

Lisa soon comes out of the back, and her jaw drops.

"Grace! How? I thought you were supposed to be at school camp?"

The name jolts me like an electric shock.

"I hated it," the girl complains.

"Did you run away again?" Lisa holds her.

Cass told me her daughter had tried to run away from her daycare once before after fighting with one of her friends.

It must be her...

Of course, it's her! With her uniform and cap on, it has taken me a while to recognize her.

Grace stays silent, and the man answers on her behalf, "She did. I'm the school driver. I found her wandering around alone, far from the camp. I took her home, but nobody was there. Are you her mom?"

"No," Lisa answers.

The man turns to the girl. "Do you know this woman?" It looks like he doesn't want to take any chances—he wants to hear it from Grace herself.

"Yes. She's my mom's friend, Lisa."

The man looks relieved. He then says, "The girl said her mom worked here. Where is she?"

"She's supposed to be here, but—" Lisa's expression changes. "She hasn't answered my calls. I think she's just swamped."

"Too busy for her own daughter?" the driver raises his voice.

I leave my table, and right then, Grace turns to me. She tugs at Lisa's hand, pointing at me.

"What is it, munchkin?" Lisa asks.

Grace keeps pointing at me as I approach her. Then I kneel in front of her.

"Hey, Grace, I'm Sam. I'm a friend of your mom's."

"You're the guy in the news?"

"Maybe, yeah," I say.

"Sam… Sam… Kalahari?"

I suppress my laugh. "Yeah, I'm that Sam."

Lisa signals for the 'Sunshine Transport' man to let Grace stay with me.

"I'm Doug, the school driver," he introduces himself. "I found her."

"Does her school know?"

"Yeah. She has a history, apparently."

Grace bows her head.

The driver adds, half-whispering, "But I told the teachers Grace isn't feeling well. I didn't want her to get in trouble. So they let me drive her home."

"Thank you. I've got this," I assure the man.

Lisa gives Grace a glass of water and a donut, then takes her to the Fox office.

"What happened, sweetheart?" I ask.

"I can't find Mom."

Usually, the parents come to me looking for their missing child. This is the first time a child has come to me looking for their mother.

"I hated the camp, so I… I know Mom told me to be good, but I just hated it."

"It's okay," I reassure her.

"Doug drove me home, but Mom's not there. The house was messy. Mom would never leave the house like that."

"Has your mom told you about anyone? Her friends, neighbors, or anyone at all?"

"I think it's Dad."

My neck heats up in perturbation. Cass never said much about her ex. She always said they separated, and they had never crossed paths since.

"What makes you think so, Grace?"

"Um... we ran away from Seattle because of Dad. I mean, I don't know. Grandma told me."

"Okay... Do you know where he might've taken her?"

"Maybe Seattle?"

"I'll find her, okay? You wait here with Lisa."

I get up and quickly swivel toward the door. But I feel Grace's hand catching mine. Tiny it might be, her squeeze is fierce. When I face her, she scowls and gives me a shake of her head. "Please, I want to look for Mom with you."

Perhaps I was too eager to leave and hadn't considered how she felt. I kneel in front of her again. "Who else can take care of you?"

"Grandma is away in Kalispell."

I wrack my brain. I could call Mark, but my Yoda is still learning the ropes when it comes to handling kids. I don't know how long I'll be gone for, and it won't be wise to leave Grace with a man who's a total stranger to her.

One name comes up. Ben Winter. Cass has warned me of him. A Taekwondo master who would do damage to whoever is breaking his sister's heart. I don't want to test it, but at least I know Grace will be safe with him.

"How about your uncle? Ben?"

"Uh uh." The little girl shakes her head once more. "Grandma is visiting him in Kalispell."

"Okay..." I mumble, thinking.

"There's no one else. I want to look for Mom with you," she insists as if making a case. "Please, Sam. Don't leave me here."

What does one do when a little girl begs you to stay with her?

If she stays with Lisa, she'll be left to her own devices in this office. This is no place for a kid. Besides, there's no guarantee that Lisa can give her enough attention; she's working.

"Okay. Here's what we're gonna do," I propose. "You come with me and see what's happening at home. And if I find something, you'll have to stay with my friend. Okay?"

"Your friend?"

"This guy. Mark." I show her my partner's photo, where he dons his friendliest smile. "He's a good guy, I promise."

Grace twists her lips.

The girl needs convincing, so I add, "I'll call your Grandma and Uncle Ben once I know what's going on, so they can come and join you. That's the only way. Otherwise, you'll have to stay with Lisa."

She peruses my face, then agrees to my suggestion.

I return a stern look. "Promise me you're gonna stay close to me at all times, okay? And do as I say?"

"Okay."

I get up so quickly that I pull my side.

"What's the matter?" Grace asks.

I didn't think anyone would notice. "Nothing," I dismiss her concern.

"It's okay to admit your weakness."

I cock my head, studying her face. There's seriousness layered on top of her sweet countenance.

"Who told you that?"

"Mom."

What could Cass have discussed with her that admitting a weakness came up? I'm sure Grace's idea of weakness is unlike what I associate with my father.

And now, any show of weakness has no place in my body or mind.

"Come on, let's go," I urge Grace. "We'll find her, I promise."

No wound or broken bones will stop me from getting to Cass. I will walk through hell if it means she's safe.

I haven't been to Cass's house, and although I know the area she lives in, I don't know her exact address. I respect that she doesn't want me to be in her life like that yet. "Grace, sweetheart, what's your address?"

I dial Mark's phone while Grace replies to me with the details.

Mark answers, "Look, Sam, about what I said in Idaho—"

"Mark, that isn't why I called. Cass is missing. It might have something to do with her ex. Meet me at her house."

GRACE WRIGGLES in her seat as if trying to make the car go faster. I don't have a child seat, but I have secured Grace as best I could. And I would've driven faster had she not been riding with me.

"So, why did you hate the camp?" I try to break her apparent boredom.

"Well, the swimming was boring. They said it's a lake, but it's small. They promised horse riding, but we were riding ponies! When I'm with mom, we ride on real horses."

"You go horse riding with your mom?"

"Uh-huh. Since I was little. Mom is really good. When she was at school, she won trophies. I watched videos that Grandma made. Mom was fast! Real fast!"

"I bet." Cass has told me about her barrel racing days.

"Oh.. you know, at camp today, Mr. Riley showed us frogs and birds. But they were in cages."

I smirk. "That's no fun."

"I know!" Grace says, perhaps happy that finally, someone agrees with her. "Don't tell anyone, but I let one of the frogs go."

I laugh at the wildlife warrior-to-be.

"Do you know what your dad does for a living?" I ask.

"No."

"What do you remember about him?"

"Not much. I remember him taking me swimming. I was really little. Mom never takes me. She's weird. She's afraid of wat—" Then Grace slams her hand onto her mouth. "No. I'm not supposed to tell."

I smile at her. "I know your mom is afraid of water."

"You do? How?"

"She told me."

"See! She loves you."

I want to explore why the little girl thinks so, but there's no time. "Well, she and I are friends. Now, back to your dad. What else do you remember?"

She ponders. "Nothing else."

"What's his name?"

"Um... Harvey, I think."

As we approach Cass's house, I feel the need to remind Grace about Mark. I can't afford to have her freaking out. I might need her to come with my best friend at a moment's notice, and she'll have to be okay with it. "Now, I told you about my friend?"

"Mark?"

"Yes, you remember."

"It's an easy name."

"He's waiting at your mom's house, okay? I want you to be friends with him too. He's a nice guy."

"Does he know Mom?"

"Yes, he does."

"Does Mom love him?"

I raise my eyes. "Um... well, he and your mom are just friends. Just like your mom and me."

"Well, she loves you," Grace repeats, with confidence this time, like it was the truth.

I feel a tickle in my gut, the kind when you hear a pleasing secret. Then I brace myself to ask, "Did she say that?"

Grace ponders for a while. "Um... no. But she likes to look at you on her laptop."

Of course, Cass wouldn't confess the 'L' word to Grace. But I take delight in the revelation, wishing I'd heard it in a better circumstance.

"There he is." I almost warn Grace about my partner.

"Sam!" Mark runs to me.

Grace stares at Mark while I let her out. She stands behind me for a few seconds.

"Grace, this is Mark, my friend. The one I told you about."
Mark kneels. "Hey."

Grace reaches out her hand. "I'm Grace. Nice to meet you."

"I'm Mark. Nice to meet you too."

"Come on, I'll show you the mess." Grace tugs at my arm.

"Grace, stay close to me." I pull her back and shield her as Mark surveys the house first.

Following Mark's signal to come in, I scan the downstairs space. A chair toppled over in the living room, and coffee spilled in the kitchen. Someone has been here, although I can't figure out what exactly happened.

We make our way upstairs after Mark gives the all-clear.

"This is my room," Grace announces.

It looks to be untouched.

"And this is Grandma's room."

It's untouched too.

"And this is your mom's?" I ask, and Grace affirms.

"Wait here with Mark," I tell her before I enter.

It looks like Cass had just gone out of the bathroom. The towel is lying on the bed, still damp, and her jeans are beside it. In the bathroom, there's her shirt, stained with coffee. So she spilled her morning coffee and then had a shower—but it was interrupted. She didn't manage to put on her jeans.

There's a laptop on her bedside table.

"That's the laptop. You know, where Mom likes to look at you," Grace reminds me of her earlier confession as she's standing outside the room. That sends Mark giggling.

We make our way back downstairs.

"You're on the news a lot," Grace adds. "Mom says you're a hero."

Right now, I don't feel like a hero. I don't know where to look or where to start.

Then Mark nudges me, discreetly eyeballing a spot on the floor.

No, no, no!

I motion for Mark to take Grace outside.

"Grace, you stay with Mark, okay?"

"Okay."

Mark and Grace seem to be best friends already. He didn't even have to try to copy me—it's him being himself out there with the girl.

There's a cartridge case on the floor, the one Mark just discovered. There are tiny specks of blood too. I pray they're not hers. An attack on Cass is an attack on me. If her kidnapper ever touches her, I swear to God, I'll hunt and destroy him.

I study the casing. There's a dent near the living room chair. It looks like the shot came from the stairs. Did Cass fire the bullet?

I crouch, moving on all fours trying to find the gun under chairs, sofas, and tables.

It's not here.

I climb back up, trying to plot where she could've been.

After a quick scan, I return to the living room, studying the skirting around the staircase. There's a small scratch, and it's fresh.

Bingo.

A Smith & Wesson pistol is wedged between the back of a cupboard and the side of the staircase. It matches the caliber of the casing we found on the floor.

So, it was she who'd injured her attacker. But perhaps not well enough. He still managed to overpower her, forcing her to drop her gun.

My jaw clenches.

This shouldn't be her fight. I'm her man. This is *my* fight!

It's a long shot, but I call Cass's phone, hoping her kidnapper might be brave or arrogant enough to answer.

A "Diamonds Are Forever" ringtone blares upstairs. She left her phone under the bed.

I go outside and join Grace and Mark. I ask her, "Do you know your mom's password?"

"Yeah, but don't tell her, okay?" she says proudly. "It's 0815. I think it's Grandpa's birthday."

There are photos of a dark red GMC truck, which I show to Mark. A Washington plate.

"I'll find out who that car belongs to," he says.

"Grace thinks this has something to do with her dad. He's from Seattle."

Suddenly I see a truck nudging itself toward us. It's that fucking GMC!

"Hey!" I yell, but it drives off as soon as the driver realizes he has company.

"Take Grace with you!" I instruct Mark.

"Sam..." Grace trembles, tugging my hand.

I kneel in front of her; the last thing I want is to impose

fear on her just because I'm rushing like a mad man. "You'll be okay with Mark, sweetheart. I swear I'll find your mom."

"But Sam…"

"We had a deal, remember?"

"Okay."

"Mark has kept me safe many times. So he'll keep you safe too. You've gotta trust him."

Grace nods. And before she crushes my heart with her brooding face, I jump into my car like I'm about to chase a sworn enemy.

I'm gaining on the damn truck. I yell Cass's name as I pull alongside, but there's only the driver there. I nudge his truck sideways, forcing it to halt on a steep slope. The momentum sends both our cars running downhill at speed. Before the GMC rolls over at the bottom of the hill, the driver jumps out.

I stop my car in time to avoid the same fate. But the man is gone.

Barely catching my breath, an ambush pushes me off balance. A hand slaps my side. There's blood on my shirt, and this man knows I'm injured. He gouges at my wound without mercy.

I inhale deeply in an attempt to counter the pain.

But hell has to wait. The agony won't stop me. No one can break me when I need to be with Cass.

As the man throws me to the ground, I turn around to trip him, stopping him from stealing my car. But the man rolls up swiftly, sending a bullet my way.

13

CASSIDY

Using his car to conceal myself, I watch the mole man as he stands rigidly at the shack door. I wonder about his intention —is it just to check on me? Take me somewhere else? Or hurt me some more?

Whatever it is, I'm not seeing a man who's sure about what he's doing. He keeps checking his cellphone. I've seen him trying to call someone before, and it seems to have frustrated him that his calls have remained unanswered.

My options are either to try to attack him from behind or retreat and hide somewhere. Because soon he'll know there's only one body in there—the dead one.

The hole that I created will instantly draw his attention, so I may not have time to attack him. There's no way I could shop around for weapons before he notices me coming.

The mole man is carrying a set of keys. One is clearly his car key and remote, and the one that he's picking out is, I'm sure, for the shack padlock.

I go with my second option and retreat, crawling back into the bushes as a breeze sweeps through the field—masking the rustling sound I'm creating as I crouch down.

He inserts the key into the padlock, but a slamming noise halts him.

It's coming from the cabin where the twins had water-boarded me. The breeze has disturbed the front door. *Fuck!* I obviously didn't close it properly.

The mole man takes his keys back and abandons the shack, walking with a gun in his hand toward the source of the noise.

The bushes I'm hiding in are only feet away from the door.

My shoulders heave up and down, but I swallow my own panting. My back hunches, and I freeze so I can be as still as a rock.

Suddenly he bellows.

When I glance up, I see a furry red creature leaping at him, leaving scratches on his face. I think the man has inadvertently surprised the creature.

He curses, trying to capture the animal as if it had stolen his nuts. I think it's the squirrel that I saw earlier right after I freed myself.

That critter has saved me. I could name him Sam.

If I keep still long enough, the mole man might just miss me because his attention doesn't seem to be on his surroundings. He wipes blood off his scratched cheek as he assesses the door. Then he sticks his head in.

Will he notice that some objects have shifted? That I have been snooping around in there?

But he quickly steps back, shuts the door, and then stares at the squirrel, which is now perching under a juniper tree.

He aims his gun at it. "How do you like this, you hairy bitch!"

When you can't vent your frustration to anyone else, I guess a squirrel is your next best target. Or perhaps the critter has simply hurt his ego.

Run, Sam!

As if hearing my silent plea, Sam the squirrel hops away. Impossible to see where to exactly, but he's somewhere higher up in the branches.

The mole man grumbles at the critter, but soon he breathes a sigh of relief because a phone call comes through.

"Jesus, Denzel!" The mole man whips around. "You're cutting out. What?... Have you got the girl?"

Grace is with his brother?

So he won't find out that I've escaped, at least for now, but the possibility that his brother may have got Grace is worse than the mole man recapturing me.

"What? Company?"

What did he mean by 'company'?

The mole man dives into his car, cursing—perhaps the call has ended prematurely. Soon the door slams shut, and the engine roars.

What if I distract him now?

Wherever he's going, I want to be there because that's where my daughter will be!

I push myself up, but my muscles seem to have given up on me. I can't get on my feet fast enough, and my throat fails to let out a scream to let that man know I'm here. His car is gone.

As I rue the fact that I'm left behind, I ponder if that would have been a wise move.

Time is against me. I can't dwell on what could've been. There's only one thing I can do now. However long the trail is, whatever danger awaits, I'll have to get to the other end.

I swing my legs one after the other, pounding the muddy trail and following the tire tracks of the mole man's car.

I hobble my way along with only one thing propelling me.

Grace.

14

SAM

The bullet the GMC driver just fired passes right next to my ear. It would've punctured my head had I not kicked the son of a bitch off balance.

His phone flies out of his pocket. It's been ringing, but I've kept him so busy that he can't answer. But seeing his phone on the ground seems to give him an idea.

While he's releasing shots at me, he yells into his phone: "Call Am."

Calling Am...

The barrage of bullets forces me to roll down, and I take cover behind his wrecked GMC. His arm seems to be bandaged—that must've been Cass's doing.

My opponent follows me downhill with yet another gunfire assault. His injured arm hasn't slowed him down the least bit. He then desperately says to whoever is at the other end of the call, "Get her out of there! Shit... Am, we've got company. Got that? We've got company! Get her out of there!"

I want to keep the prick alive—I need to know where he has taken Cass—but I have no intention of being his target today. This man is a trained assassin, and he's closing in on me fast. His gun is aimed squarely at me. But I'm faster.

He's dead.

The call disconnects as soon as I snatch the phone off him. The recipient is simply called 'Am'—it must be a nickname.

There's a wallet in his pocket with credit cards under various names. I don't even trust his Montana driver's license. It could be fake, too, considering the fact that the truck has a Washington plate.

I run back up to my car. Only now do I realize how close it was to rolling over just like that prick's GMC. My phone is ringing continuously—it's Mark.

"What happened?" Mark's restrained voice and the lack of swear words tell me Grace is nearby.

"I sorted him out, but I need information. Grace still with you?"

"Yes. We're at the HQ."

"Good."

"The GMC is registered under the name Denzel Seth. He and his twin brother Ambrose run a security company. They claim to be personal bodyguards, but in reality, they're debt collectors, mainly serving the underworld."

So the name of the dead man is Denzel Seth, and he was on a call with his brother. 'Am' must be Ambrose.

Mark adds, "So far, they're known to have killed at least eighteen people—men and women."

The chilling statement clenches like a fist around my chest. On past missions, anger and brashness lurked in the back of my mind at times, but this is the first time I feel a sense of panic. The possibility of them having hurt Cass is real.

But a lifetime of being in danger has taught me self-control like nothing else. I shut down my speculating mind.

Only logic should rule my action right now. The only way to come through for Cass is by numbing myself of her.

"I need more, Mark."

"I managed to get hold of Cass's brother, Ben. He's heard the names before. The Seth brothers had dealings with her ex."

I know Cass and her husband didn't part amicably, but apart from that, she has never told me anything about him.

"Where's her ex?"

"I'm still working on it. He used to live in Seattle, but he's been moving around since his divorce from Cass."

Probably trying to find her.

Mark continues filling me in. "The brothers were in the Army. Denzel did two tours in Iraq, and Ambrose did three, and one in Somalia."

The brothers are no amateurs. Even though Denzel was a bit erratic with his distance shooting, the man could move. Something tells me his brother might just be slightly better than him.

I stare at the GMC wreckage, and something springs to me. I trudge back there, crawling into the driver's window to reach the satellite navigation. It's still on, and I go straight into the system's history. The bastard was at Lyndall Park—a popular spot for kids' excursions—which I'm sure is where Grace's camp is.

"Do you know if he has any connection to—" I scroll further to see where Denzel was before the camp. "Missouri Plains?"

"Hang on. I'll call Ben back. He might be on the way here already."

I keep trawling the navigation history as I wait for Mark to respond. When he rings back, Ben joins in on the three-way call. I can hear the guy cursing and swearing about Cass's ex.

"Does Missouri Plains ring a bell to you?" Mark asks Ben.

"No," Ben answers.

"How about Ralph Valley?" I throw in the next location from the satellite navigation history.

But once again, his answer is no.

"I want you to check this call, Mark." I text him the recent call log from the dead man's phone. "See where it's originated from."

"I'll call you back."

I take pictures of the satellite navigation history. It looks like those locations are east of here. So I take my SUV to climb up the slope, and I'm back on the road. As long as I'm heading east, I'm sure I'll be closer to Cass.

Mark soon rings back. "The call was made from around Ralph Valley."

"Fuck." I'm hoping it's not there. "It's a big area."

"I know. But here's a clue. A local man was reported missing a couple of days ago, a known drug dealer. He hunted in the Selway Bitterroot Wilderness regularly and reportedly had a cabin in the valley."

"She must be there!" I floor the pedal, ignoring the skidding tires.

"And Sam, the Seth brothers were guards in Guantanamo. Ambrose was dishonorably discharged for his involvement in the torture debacle there."

I huff out the stinging sensation on my side. If not for that Denzel guy grazing it, the wound wouldn't have hurt this much. Idaho seems so far behind me now, but the pain is trailing me fast.

"Sam, you okay? Are you hurt?" Mark checks in on me.

"No. No," I dismiss him. "Is Ben coming to you?"

"Yeah."

"Try not to piss him off."

I hang up and focus on the road.

Despite traveling well above the safe speed, it's still taking me a goddamned age to get to the valley.

There's a bridge ahead. If Cass is held around here, the river might deter her from escaping. Wherever she is, I'm hoping Ambrose isn't with her, or he will hurt her, if not already, knowing that his brother has stopped responding to him.

After driving for a few miles further into the valley, I arrive at the spot where the drug dealer's cabin is located.

I run a quick scan of the area with my MK25 handgun firmly in my hands. I venture inside a small cabin. Someone has turned this place inside out, but the space is dominated by one piece of fixture—a waterboard, angled so that the foot is raised. Next to it is a bucket of water and a drenched towel.

"Cass..." It hurts like I'd been on it. My fists tighten. Truly, I'm going to destroy Ambrose Seth! His brother would've been glad his death was relatively painless.

The Seths have been programmed to hurt people—men and women—I can't imagine what she had endured. Waterboarding is horrible for anyone, but for someone who's afraid of water, the drowning experience must've been doubly distressing.

I kick the bed. Knowing the brothers' history, I'm not surprised that they had prepared this for her—an innocent woman, a mother. It was a different kind of low. Either they're just evil, or what they're after is big. If her ex is behind all this, surely it's more than just the case of a man desperate to have his family back.

Returning outside, I head straight to a shack nearby. It's heavily locked, which only means one thing: there is someone inside.

"Cass?"

No response, not even a sign of movement.

I shoot the padlock and kick the door open.

"Crap!" The stench assaults my senses.

I shine a torch toward the source and find a dead body lying in a corner. If it wasn't for its round figure, I would've been screaming mad. But it still takes me a moment to calm myself the hell down. It's not Cass—it must be the missing drug dealer.

As I look around further, another surprise greets me, and this one gives me hope.

There's a hole in one of the walls—it's small, but if I was Cass, I would be able to squeeze myself in there. Near the wall, I find pieces of fabric that must've come from her clothing.

I run out through the door and round the shack, looking for a spot where Cass might be hiding. I examine the wall with the hole from the outside. The wood is rotten, but it doesn't mean it crumbles like bread. It must've taken Cass a hell lot of pounding to create this hole.

"Cass!" I call out.

She could be anywhere. The only sign that I can't dispute is the narrow footprints that run along the side of the main trail, where I drove from.

I know she's not far, but the question is: is she alone? Or is there someone on her tail?

For now, I have to follow the clue on-hand. Ambrose Seth may be hunting her, or he may have recaptured her.

For all scenarios, my option is the same: I must find her!

15

CASSIDY

The setting sun is blinding me, but I keep going. I'm hitting an incline after struggling to keep my balance on a downhill path behind me. This time the ground is no longer muddy, and the dry grass underneath my feet somewhat acts as a cushion to my mangled slippers.

There's a river somewhere around here, I can hear it—and I'll avoid it at all costs. With my system plummeting dangerously close to a total shutdown, I can't afford to witness anymore horror—albeit only my hallucination. If I saw the vision of that ghastly figure now, it'd no doubt send me over the brink.

Depriving myself of all sounds, while the sun is depriving me of clear sight, the only thing that keeps me moving is Grace. I've been hiking for at least three hours. Surely, civilization can't be far away.

I instruct my legs not to give up on me. After the stress on the waterboard, the kick on my face, and then my effort to create that hole in the wall, I know I haven't got much left in me.

The bush is getting thicker now—and as I tramp another up-and-down path, I stop.

Something isn't right. The sound of streaming water almost completely fades, and I swear I've seen this rock formation before. It looks like three faces laughing at me.

It could be my mind playing tricks.

My lungs and throat burn like hell, and blisters are eating up my feet. I'm desperate for water—ironic, considering I had been choking on it before.

As I leave the rock formation behind, I run up an incline. And this time, I know this isn't my imagination. I have passed this corner before. The distinct bend in front of me bears my erratic footprints.

"Fuck!"

I've been going around in circles.

Anger and cries will only sap my energy, so I decide to turn in the other direction. Somehow, I'll need to find that trail again.

I start hearing water now, an encouraging sign. On top of that, there's something purring. It's a vehicle running somewhere down below, over the slope on my right. Clinging from one tree to another, I haul myself up.

The urge to get to where that vehicle is going trumps my pain. Why or how, I don't know.

With my two swollen hands and legs that are barely functioning, I crawl up and finally reach the crest.

My legs shake as I realize where I am. There's a river about fifty feet below. Even if I tried, I wouldn't make it there. I quickly take two steps back, as my dizziness is about to cause me to tumble down.

I peer to my left and see a bridge.

My spirits rise. Now I know why I felt the urge to come up here.

A vehicle is approaching the bridge slowly, as if the driver is searching for something. It's not the GMC truck, and it's not the Jeep the mole man was driving. It's a familiar blue SUV—at least, that's what I make out from this distance.

It's Sam.

So all this time, he's been looking for me.

Can I call this a miracle?

No. This is the bond between us. It's proof of how far that man would go to get to me. I might've stopped him from entering my life the way he wanted to, but the man never quits loving me.

If I call out his name, the valley will carry my voice. But I can't even speak, let alone shout. The more I try, the more I croak—to the point that I struggle to breathe. Even though I wave my arms hard, I know he won't be able to see me. I'm higher up, and I'm behind him—and he's driving straight ahead.

In the despairing moment, my legs give up. I collapse behind a row of tall grass.

The sun keeps punishing me as I lie on my back. My vision fades, and my body feels numb and hollow. There's nothing I can do but leave everything to fate.

As pathetic as it sounds, I'm not losing hope. Hell, no! I'll fight 'til my last breath. Because when Sam is in the picture, the odds can turn.

Just like fortune, fate favors the brave.

16

———

SAM

I've driven too far. The trail is behind me, and I'm back at the bridge.

How could I have missed her? Perhaps Ambrose Seth has beaten me to her.

We always say the first forty-eight hours are crucial when it comes to a missing person. But with Cass—against opponents like the Seth brothers—every second counts, and I can't help but think the critical window of time has passed.

This makes me wonder if my dealing with Neil Parr in Idaho was worth losing Cass.

"Fucking hell!" I punch the steering wheel.

The fact that I contemplate such a conundrum makes me mad. I shouldn't have had to choose. I can't regret saving Chloe O'Rourke, no. *I don't.* I'm damn proud of it, and I still haven't lost Cass.

I take a moment to reset.

The easy way is to drive across the river and hit the highway—and then try to track Ambrose from Red Mark headquarters with Mark's help.

There are risks no matter what I do, and my instincts tell

me Cass is still here. I promised myself to use logic when I embarked on this rescue—trying to shut my raging emotions —but I can't rule out my instincts.

I make a U-turn to revisit the trail. I must have missed something! I stop my car—I have to go on foot just like she did.

"Cass!" I yell as I jog along the trail.

There's no sign of her footprints until—

There's something different about this section of the trail. Not only because it narrows, but there also seems to be activity around here. Call it experience, instinct, or even sixth sense—I *know* she was here. There's an inexplicable connection that ties me to her, and it's telling me so.

I turn into a small clearing. There I see wayward footprints veering off to the right of the trail. Somehow Cass must've thought the clearing was leading to another track—or she could simply be distracted, and she wasn't meant to leave the main trail.

The distance between footprints gets shorter as I trawl along. My heart sinks. These are signs of a person struggling to keep moving.

"Cass!" I call out.

The canopy obscures the sun as I deviate further from the trail. The prints in front of me fade as mud is replaced by grass and rocks.

As I negotiate an uphill path, I finally discover a sign. I pick up a rubbery object—it's likely a part of her shoe outsole.

Then I find another piece about ten feet away.

Jesus, is she walking almost barefooted now?

The low sun hits my eye as I come out into a clearing. Three big rocks side-by-side reflect the light. They have distinct textures and dents as if someone had carved smiling faces on them.

The path then bends around the rocks, and her footprints reappear—in two directions as if she had gotten lost and circled back. Turning right would've taken her to where she came from, but turning left would've led her to the river.

"Cass!" I keep calling her.

The set of footprints to my left seems to be fresher. So I follow the direction, despite the fact that it's leading to a spot that would terrify her to death.

The trampled tall grass and broken twigs ahead give me signs that she might've just been here. Her presence is becoming even more apparent on the uphill slope beside me —I see another piece of fabric that matches one that I found near the shack.

A sudden surge of energy propels me to the top.

And I see Cass lying face up, one hand on her chest. Her mouth gapes stiffly, and her lips have turned a shade of blue.

I kneel, sheltering her from the battering sun. Bruises mar her cheeks and arms, and her bare legs rest limply on the ground.

"Cass!"

But she doesn't respond. She's not even breathing. I try to find her pulse.

None.

Five or ten minutes ago, I felt her—that connection. Was that just a made-up thing? A result of wishful thinking?

No!

My connection with her is more real than anything I've ever possessed. She can't be dead. If she is, I'll bring her back.

I will!

"Come on, Cass."

I arrange my hands on her breastbone and start a series of chest compressions.

One, two...

... twenty-eight, twenty-nine, thirty.

I lean into her, placing my lips over her mouth, blowing air. A dry crust plasters her lips, but they don't stop me from feeling her. She's still my Cassidy—the woman I'll give everything to.

"God dammit. Breathe, Cass! Breathe!"

Cass' face falls limply to its side as I continue the compressions. Her closed eyes appear soft, and her lips remain parted like she's asleep. But her colors don't lie—I'm losing her.

My hands tremble with fright as seconds turn to minutes. Her heart has to wake up *now*.

After another count of thirty, I go down and blow air into her once more. I'm giving all the life I have within me—for her, for little Grace.

Her chest rises slightly, then falls.

"Cass..."

Her chest moves again, and as I place my ear on top of her mouth, I hear a soft breath.

"Cass, sweetheart... it's me."

"Sam..." she croaks.

I cradle her on my lap. Her lips shiver under my light kiss —in fact, I think it's me who trembles.

"Sam, where—"

She coughs.

"Shh... don't talk."

I give her water, but she moans in agony.

"I'm sorry. I'm sorry." I help her sit up.

Drowning or choking on water can damage your throat. And with the exertion from her trek, her throat must be burning. Seeing her so close to death has made me momentarily forget about her earlier ordeal.

I'm sure we're alone, so I let her settle.

The river is just below us, and I'm certain she hadn't meant to go this far. The sun is harsh around here. She must've been severely dehydrated, perhaps causing her to get disoriented.

"Sam..." She lifts her hand feebly, but she's able to reach my chest.

I hang on to that hand, keeping it close to my heart. "Sweetheart, don't talk."

But she insists. "Grace..."

A mother will always have it in her—the urge to protect her child. This is why she fought. This is why she came all the way here despite her injuries. Clearly, she had reasons to believe that Grace was in danger. The brothers might've tried to use her daughter to get what they wanted.

"She's safe. She sent me to go looking for you."

"Those brothers..."

"I know about them. They're nowhere near Grace."

This time she's unable to utter anything.

Behind me, the sun is setting, and so is her alertness.

"Cass... Cass, stay with me!" I nudge her shoulder.

Slowly her lids bat open again as she squeezes my hand.

I've got to get her out of here. She has fought, and now it's my turn to fight for her.

"Promise me you'll stay awake?"

She blinks in two quick successions—I'm sure it means yes.

I secure one arm around her back and slip the other under her knees. With her head resting on my chest, I lift her up.

My side stings like hell.

Only now am I reminded of my wound—the one that was gouged by that prick Denzel Seth. I push air out through my mouth, letting go of the pain. It should've been easier on me to take her on a fireman's carry, especially with the distance that I have to trek to get to my car. But the method might hinder her breathing. Besides, I have to see her at all times.

Most of all, though, carrying her in my arms means Cass will be more comfortable.

A burst of energy fills me with will and confidence as she reaches out to my shoulder, helping me to shift her up. With her so close to me, pain doesn't mean a thing.

"Cass, you with me?"

"Sam..." She nuzzles into my chest.

Her voice comforts me, but seeing her exposed legs, I feel a surge in my heart. She didn't have a chance to put on her pants before the brothers took her. Did they—

It's no time to process such thoughts. But deep in my heart, I'm certain the brothers hadn't touched her. Also, seeing no bruises around her thighs and the fact that she didn't react with discomfort when my arms got close to her delicate area, I trust that I'm right.

I keep pushing through. But adrenaline only lasts for so long.

Cass starts to sag as I start running, her legs hitting my waist like a drum. I know I'm bleeding, but my job is only half done. I've found her—nothing can break me now and stop me from getting her to safety.

She fidgets, murmuring, "I can walk, Sam. Let me down."

"No way."

"I'm hurting you."

"Nonsense!" I keep my grip tight while increasing my pace.

"Sam..."

I gulp the lump of agony that's been wrecking my midriff. "Well, if you want to do something, nudge yourself up and hold on to me."

A smile breaks through her lips. She flings her arms up and around my neck, pulling herself up and away from my injured waist.

"Good job." I kiss her crown.

I've carried men to safety, in battles and in training. Never have I thought I'd be doing it for Cass. Ambrose Seth is a coward who doesn't deserve to live!

I let my anger work to my advantage as I slog the last mile. Despite my side feeling as if it has been slit open, I press on.

As soon as I make it to my car, I call Mark.

"Sam!" Mark yells as if he's been waiting forever.

"I'm okay, buddy," I huff as I lower Cass onto the passenger seat. She's barely conscious, but she takes the time to squeeze my hand, letting me know she's still with me.

Mark doesn't respond straight away. I know he picks up my pain.

Then I hear Ben in the background, "God dammit! Is she okay? Sam! Is Cass okay?"

"Yeah. I've got her."

"Let me talk to her!" Ben insists.

"Not a good time, Ben!" I gripe as I round the car to the driver-side door.

"I need to hear she's okay."

"Take my word for it!"

Ben curses some more—I know the guy is venting out his nervousness and hatred toward Cass's ex. Soon his voice fades, though. I think Mark has just imposed his no-bullshit get-out-of-here stare.

"How's Grace?" I ask my partner.

"She's asleep. The troopers are hunting Ambrose Seth. He was spotted by one of Grace's teachers near their summer camp. But he's disappeared since." Mark pauses as if something has just dawned on him. "Jesus. That little girl—luckily, she ran away."

I wonder who she's gotten her stubbornness from.

Cass starts to writhe.

"Hey, I'll catch you later," I tell Mark and end the call.

"Sam..." she moans.

"I'm here."

Her chapped lips quiver. "Water..."

I reach for my water bottle, but I'm not about to repeat what I did earlier. I wet a couple of tissues and help her sip water from them. "Easy."

She seems to be swallowing better. After a few sips, she falls back asleep. I resist the urge to hold her hand—her knuckles are scraped and bruised, her palms swelling.

"I'm taking you to the hospital. We'll be there soon."

I drive even faster than I did getting here. Cass needs medical help, or she might lose her limbs.

Suddenly she wakes up again. "I lied to the brothers."

"Cass, you can tell me all about it later."

Somehow she notices the stain on my shirt. There's no hiding it. The stitches on my wound have come undone. I might as well have been shot five minutes ago.

"Sam... you're bleeding!" I don't know where she's got her strength from, but she turns to me in an instant.

"I'm fine, Cass." I reposition myself so she can't see my wound.

It's like her brain has been short-circuited. Her attention is now all on me.

"Sam, stop and dress that wound. It's fucking bleeding like..."

I think she's about to say like a river.

She's right—I'm losing blood fast. I can't let her down because of my own stubbornness, so I pull over and take off my shirt.

"Jesus, Sam..." she grumbles as she helps me wrap my wound with it.

Her lips clamp together—this time not because of her own

pain. She loosens the seatbelt and shifts herself even closer to me, hissing out her fear.

"I'm okay, Cass. It's just a flesh wound. Come on. We've gotta go," I say, gently nudging her back to her seat. "I'm okay, trust me. Please. Trust me."

She lets me reposition her seatbelt. Another thought seems to have taken over her.

"I lied to the brothers about some numbers...." she pants. She winces as she shifts in her seat but carries on. "They would've realized by now that I fooled them. They'll be gunning for Grace. We've got to get to her."

"She's with Mark, and Ben is too, at Red Mark headquarters with them."

"After the hospital, please take me to her."

"Sweetheart, I don't think you want her to see you like this."

She touches her face.

"Let your injuries settle first, and then I'll take you to Grace."

Her chest heaves in and out as she ponders. She casts a glance at me and gives me a small nod.

Cass finally leans back, her breath steady. I'm expecting her to close her eyes and fall back asleep, but she turns to me with a narrowed gaze. She appraises my bare arms with a flicker of lust now that I'm only wearing a singlet.

There, I know my fallen angel has survived the worst.

"You're welcome," I quip.

Soon she dozes off.

I want her to stay awake, so I can admire those cornflower-blue eyes and know she's okay, but she looks peaceful like that.

As we arrive at the hospital, the noise and movements in

the emergency room stir her. Horror radiates from her once peaceful countenance. She tries to sit up, shivering. "Sam!"

"I'm here, Cass." I walk alongside her as the nurses wheel her bed.

"Sam... don't let me drown." She gulps again and again, her hands desperate to release the IV tube.

It's the bed and her position. It must be reminding her of that waterboard. "Nurse, raise her head. Please."

"We've got this, Mr. Kelleher," the head nurse replies as her team tries to calm Cass down. Then her attention shifts to me. "You need help too. I'll get someone to look at that wound."

"I'm fine!" I huff. "Please, raise her head. Trust me. She needs it."

Cass's agitation hasn't subsided despite the medical team's efforts. The head nurse knows they've got to do something. She stops for a moment to adjust the bed.

"Don't leave me, Sam," Cass begs as the bed head tilts up slowly.

"No, I won't leave you." I kiss her crown and let her lean on me for a few seconds, my palm carefully wrapped over her cheek, wishing I could absorb all of her pain.

"You swear that Grace is safe?" she labors.

It might be the drugs that make her forget she's asked the question, it might be the hospital environment that plays with her mind, or maybe she just needs to hear it again.

"Yes, sweetheart. Grace is safe." I respond.

She exhales deeply and closes her eyes. I kiss her just before the medical team takes her away, and a nurse pulls me toward another room.

I stand my ground. "I'm right here, Cass. I'm not going anywhere."

"I'll need to look at that wound, Mr. Kelleher," the nurse insists.

Cass has stopped fighting now—at least on the outside. I know she will keep at it. She won't let Grace down, that's for sure.

When I first met her, my life got made. And for every day that she's with me, it keeps getting made—renewed, with love that doesn't exist anywhere else but in her.

I look at her face for as long as I can before the doors slam shut. Despite her bruises, she's still the breathtaking Cass that I know.

She's still my fallen angel.

17

CASSIDY

Flashes of white awaken me.

Was that a towel I saw?

Am I back in the Seth brothers' hands?

I can't be. I'm sure Sam has found me.

Either way, coming out of my sleep doesn't appeal right now. I know pain is waiting, whatever the form. So I shut my eyes tight, and gradually everything turns black.

But nightmare still finds me whether it's light or dark. I'm back in it, crawling on a muddy path. It's endless, but I eventually reach the top. I peer over—there's a river below, and the water is raging.

As if the earth had turned upside down, a mighty pull takes me over the edge. I'm falling...

Now I'm desperate to wake up.

"Sam! Please don't let me drown," I plead.

Sam is wading through the water and taking forever to get to me.

The current pushes us apart, propelling me toward the river bend. There, the ghastly figure lies face down, draping over a rock. It doesn't have a head, and it shouldn't make a sound, nor should it be recognizable. But I hear it moan, and I know it's the same man I saw in the video on my mom's laptop —the video I shouldn't have watched.

Now it's calling my name, warning me about something.

"No!" I scream as a gunshot blares right behind me.

"He can join your father now." It's the mole man, staring down at me from the bank as the water around me turns red. The headless man is in grief—I can feel it in his slowing heartbeats and the smell of rock jasmine in the air. The mole man was right—that ghastly figure *is* my father.

Then a hand brushes my side.

"Saaam!" I scream at the top of my lungs, hopelessly watching his lifeless body floating toward the rock.

"Cass?"

"Sam! No!" I flail my arms, desperate to get to him. He can't be dead. He can't be!

"Cass, sweetheart."

I sit up, crying and shaking as if I'm on the verge of insanity.

"I'm here. Calm down."

I try to stop my cough because it goddamned hurts.

"Sam..." I open my eyes and find myself caged in his embrace. Do I dare look up? What will I find? If Sam has turned into yet another ghastly figure, no one will ever wake me up from such a nightmare.

But his arms comfort me like a Christmas blanket. The jasmine smell is taken over by the scent of safety, like I'm sheltered while a storm is raging outside. My face presses against his massive chest, heaving in the rhythm of his breathing.

And unmistakably, I can hear the beating of his heart.

I slowly tip my chin up. His gray diamond eyes greet me, speaking to me softly, telling me I'm okay. But how about him?

"Sam... you were shot..." I mumble, patting his torso.

"Cass, calm down."

The more he tries to stop me from rolling up his t-shirt, the more I persist. In the end, he lets me have my way—before I can rip that garment.

A heavy bandage runs around his abdomen. "You were shot!"

"I'm fine, Cass. It's no big deal."

"Did one of the brothers shoot you?"

"No. It was… it happened in Idaho."

I huff, blaming my foggy memory. Of course, he had an assignment in Idaho. And his wound—I remember now. He sustained it while he was saving me.

"Did you find the girl?"

"Yes. We saved her."

Emotions swirl on his face, telling me it was the kind of assignment that has left a scar on him, and he's battling with himself whether to keep that scar hidden or to show it.

I put my arms around Sam loosely, and then I let my head fall onto his uninjured side. I'll give him time and let him decide—the worst thing I can do is to force him.

"How did you find me?" I murmur. "You said Grace sent you. How?"

"She ran away from camp."

"She what?" My eyes widen.

"Well, a school driver found her and took her home. But you weren't there, so they went to Fox. By then, I was done with Idaho, so I was waiting for you at the bar. I knew it wasn't going to be an ordinary day when your Grace turned up."

"Huh…" I guess, in this case, it pays to have a kid with a stubborn streak.

"She was actually looking for a Sam Kalahari."

I burst out laughing, punishing my swollen cheeks in the

process. But my heart is jumping for joy. Grace has saved herself, in a way, and me.

"I figured," he adds. "There shouldn't be another Sam in your life, so it's gotta be me."

I shoot a stare at him, affirming he's the only Sam in my life, the only man, the only hero.

He plants a small kiss on my cheek with pride painting his face.

"You know, one of the brothers. He came back and almost found me." I recall the events when I was sure the mole man was going to recapture me. "But a squirrel saved me. He was so pissed at the critter, and he completely missed me."

"Are you saying I wasn't the first one to rescue you?"

"No, I'm not. Because I named the squirrel Sam."

He smiles. "So there *is* another Sam?"

I hold his hand, letting him know that he's still the only one—Sam the SEAL.

Suddenly I feel as if my brain has leaped out of my head. "Jeez..." I press my temple. The room is spinning.

"Lie down." Sam inserts a second pillow under my head.

Everything looks white here. Of course, it's a friggin' hospital. No wonder I saw flashes of white when I opened my eyes earlier.

"Who are they from?" I frown at the bouquets of flowers. I can't remember the last time I had flowers on my bedside table—or even in my house.

"From Grace's school, and from your boss."

I stare at my lap. I don't want to be a diva, getting rid of people's gifts, but they're not helping.

He seems to notice. "I'll take them away."

"Sam, leave that one." I point at the rose and ranunculus bouquet.

"You don't like white?" Sam asks as he hides the others behind the chair in the corner.

"Not here," I murmur.

"I'm glad you like these ones." He winks.

I just realized there are three bouquets, and Sam only mentioned the school and my boss.

"Who are they from?"

"Yours truly." He gives me a side gaze.

"They're pretty." I reach out, my fingertips hovering over the pink rose petals. I do miss having flowers around. I'd forgotten the joy they can bring to a flattened soul. As long as they're not jasmine, or anything white, at this stage.

Seeing Sam watching, I clear my throat and say, "So what happened before you found me?"

"The GMC truck you took a photo of came back to your place. The brothers must've thought Grace had returned home when they couldn't find her at camp. Perhaps they also thought it would be an easy capture, so only one of them turned up. Well, they were right. Grace was there, but with two men who would do anything to keep her safe."

"Mark was with you?"

"Yes. I pursued the truck and then searched for you while Mark stayed behind with Grace." Sam frees my face from strands of hair. "God, when I saw the waterboard, I felt sick to my stomach. I can't imagine what you went through."

As if he was going to lose me again, Sam gathers my hands as softly as he can as not to hurt me. A kiss lands on my lips.

Then something seems to rush through him as if he's running out of time. He blurts, "I love you, Cass."

I should say I love him too, but tongue-tied, with my daughter firmly on my mind, I say, "Sam...You and I need to talk about that, but right now, I need to see Grace. I need to be with her."

"Sweetheart, not now. You're in no state to see her. Give it another day."

I move my jaw, and it fucking hurts. I touch it, and it's like I've been stung by a nest of hornets.

I know Grace is safe; I remember Sam told me she was at Red Mark headquarters. But I'm her mom. It's been more than a day since I last saw her. Who's making sure she eats her dinner and brushes her teeth? Where is she sleeping? Who's going to comfort her?

"Grace is with Mark," Sam says slowly, perhaps suspecting that I might've forgotten.

"Are they still at your headquarters?"

"No. They're at Mark's house. He's got a state-of-the-art security system, so you've got nothing to worry about. If anything, Ben and Max are with them too. If that's not more secure than Fort Knox, I don't know what is."

Ben is there? I feel better already. And, I would imagine Staff Sergeant 'Tri-pawed' Maximus would be following Grace everywhere she goes.

I don't care if I'm going to faint, but I sit up and hurriedly kiss Sam. He has to know he's appreciated.

"Wow," he remarks. "I didn't expect that. I thought you were put off by the 'L' word I brought up."

I'm desperate to say I love him too, but what if I'm wrong?

My love life isn't important right now. Soon I give in to my lack of energy and lie back down.

"How about the brothers? Have the police got them?"

Sam gulps. "One of them is dead."

Looking at his expression, I'm sure he's got something to do with it. "How about the other one?"

"Still on the loose."

"Shit..."

Sam rummages into his pocket to fish for his phone. "Why don't you speak to Grace now?"

"What time is it?"

"Eight."

"She might still be awake."

Sam fiddles with his phone. "Hey, buddy," Mark's voice comes out of the speaker.

"Grace still awake?" Sam asks.

"Yeah. She's just playing with Ben."

In the background, a ruckus is unfolding. 'No! That's cheating!' I hear Ben's voice, followed by Grace protesting whatever they're playing.

"Cass okay?" asks Mark.

"Yeah."

As Maximus seems to join in the fun and game, I hear my brother approaching fast. "Cass! God dammit. Is that you?"

"Hey, Ben."

"Fucking Harv! I'm gonna break his throat!" Ben curses softly; I'm sure to avoid Grace listening.

"Shh! Ben, please," I say. "Where's Grace?"

"Is that Mommy? Is that Mommy?" Grace blurts.

"Here she is," Mark says.

"Grace, honey?"

"Mom!"

Hearing her voice forces me to sit up. I'd have left the bed if Sam hadn't stopped me. It's as if my muscles have gained their strength back, and the pain has been erased.

"Mom... please don't be mad at me."

"No. No."

"I hated the camp, so I ran away. I'm sorry."

"It's okay, honey. You found Sam. That was the main thing. Are you okay?"

"I'm fine. Uncle Ben and Mark have been taking care of

me. And Max, too—Sam's dog. You've gotta come here and see him. He's a German shepherd, he's big, and he has three legs."

What does my little Grace know about Maximus? I look at Sam, who's smiling back at me—recalling our encounter behind The Thirsty Fox, I'm sure.

"Apparently, he was injured when he was a soldier dog," Grace carries on. "And, oh, Sam was right. Mark is a good guy. But I don't think he loves you."

They talked about love? In response, Sam shrugs, not wanting to admit what was exchanged between him and Grace.

"You had dinner?" I ask.

"Yes. Mark made chicken wings." Then she quickly adds, "But I had vegetables too. Ask Uncle Ben if you don't believe me."

"Good girl."

"Mark has lots of books here. They're all thick, and they don't have pictures," she describes. "But he downloaded some books for me, so he has them on his iPad. Are you coming, Mom? I want you to read this story about three bears having an adventure."

My heart shrinks, yearning to be with her. "Maybe tomorrow, okay?"

"Come on, pumpkin. Mommy needs rest," Ben chimes in.

"Okay," Grace says. I can imagine her nodding her head.

"It's almost time for bed," I tell her.

"Can I have ice cream?"

"Just one small scoop, okay?"

"Okay."

"Good night, honey."

"Night, Mom. I love you."

"I love you too," I purr. "Now, put Mark back on the phone, please."

"Mom wants you," I hear Grace handing over the phone. In the background, I hear her say to Ben. "Mom says I can have ice cream, one scoop."

"She said one *small* scoop," Ben badgers.

"Don't remember that!" Grace quips.

Sam and I both laugh at the interaction.

I relax into him as if my spine has turned into a sweetgrass stem.

After it goes quiet in the background, Sam asks Mark, "Any update on Ambrose Seth?"

"No. Zander and his men have lost track."

"Damn..."

"The brothers want Harvey's money," I explain. "I don't know if the money's real or not. But it sounds like a lot. I don't know exactly how much. They discovered some numbers. I had no idea what they were—I just told some random stuff."

"What random stuff, Cass?"

"Like a password and account numbers. And I even suggested they might've been coordinates."

"Do you remember the numbers?" Mark asks.

"No. There were a few sets. I think there were ten or twelve digits per line." I wish I remembered. But my water-clogged brain was more than just hazy then, and it still is.

"Hey, it's okay," Sam comforts me.

"Thanks for taking care of Grace," I tell Mark.

"It's not a problem at all. Don't worry about her," Mark assures me. While Sam tends to have grit in his voice when he tries to reassure me, his partner's tone stays constant—reassuring in a different way, like everything is under control. "Her grandma is on her way. So she'll feel at home here."

"Thank you. I hope she isn't giving you too much trouble."

"Well, that's Ben's job," Mark quips. "Get some rest, you two."

Suddenly a new email message pops up on Sam's phone. The sender is 'Bing Photo Restoration Experts.'

The subject: *Sam, your order.*

Sam quickly dismisses the notification.

"What is it?" I ask after he hangs up.

"Never mind." He switches off his phone.

Wrinkles of tiredness, worries, and agitation form on his face. I think it's got something to do with Jack, and I decide not to probe further.

I lie flat on the bed. "Stay with me, Sam." My lids slowly shut.

"Of course." He coats my lips with his.

As I drift off to sleep, I think about my own brother. I can't imagine life without Ben. For Sam to have survived such an ordeal when he was a twelve-year-old, and persisting in finding Jack to this day, just shows how thick his courage is.

Then there's him and me. Earlier, he said he loved me—that was courage of a different kind. It's true that we have to talk about it sooner rather than later because we're more than just 'Hey-I'm-in-town' lovers. But it isn't the right time to have such a conversation.

Love is one thing. To talk about it is another. Love doesn't just exist simply because we're together—it comes with commitment, promise, and expectations.

I've sworn not to fall in love again or to introduce another man into my life. Yet the yearning for a new start with Sam screams louder than my inhibitions. And contrary to my initial will to protect my daughter from him, deep down, I admit Grace needs him too. The question is, do I have the courage to take the next step?

18

SAM

As soon as the doctor gives Cass the all-clear, I take her to Mark's house. I know she has tried hard to stay calm, but every now and then, she breaks her silence and asks about Grace. Not that she doesn't trust Mark or me, I think it's just her motherly instinct in overdrive. She can't wait a second longer to see her daughter.

Mark's house is about ten miles out of Helena, a classic Montana stone home set in a ten-acre land. Apart from a couple of cameras placed near the gate, he has hidden the security features around the estate. You wouldn't guess this is the home of one of the best security experts in the country.

I hear Maximus' bark when we arrive at the front door—zest and impatience roll into it.

Mark greets me while the furry one lurks behind him. Without hesitation, Max lunges at me. His only front leg flails aimlessly as he loses his balance.

"Down, Maximus, down," I command as I hug the shepherd.

"That ain't the way to control a dog, buddy," Mark advises. "You said 'down,' yet you invited him to climb all over you."

"Did I?" I deadpan. But Mark is right. I'm such a softie, I don't have the heart to discipline that mini-bear. "Well, look at him!" I gesture at Maximus' droopy eyes. "He's gone through a lot, you know."

"The dog needs leadership, not pity," Mark counters.

Having somewhat settled the mutt, I get to Cass and help her out of my car.

"Cass, you okay?" Mark gives Cass a peck on her cheek.

"Yeah. I've got bruises everywhere, but they'll go away in a few days," Cass responds.

"And you?" Mark glares at my wound.

I glance at Cass. "Don't remind her."

"Come on in," Mark opens the door wide, only to reveal the formidable figure of Ben Winter. When Cass first warned me about him, I never thought I'd be up against a mountain.

"Ben," Cass hobbles to reach her brother.

"God, Cass. You don't look okay!" Ben studies her face and then eyeballs me as if he's about to eat me.

"They're just bruises. I'm okay," Cass maintains. "This is Sam."

"Hey," Ben says in his deep voice, shaking my hand. "Thanks for bringing her back in one piece." A good sign that the mountain is warming up to me, but he keeps my hand in his hold. He then pulls me and whispers, "Now, don't break her heart."

"Mom!" Grace runs toward her, seemingly from out of nowhere. Her excitement prompts Maximus to join them. That dog surely knows where to be, to get maximum attention —and in return, he knows how to love his humans ten times over.

"Grace!" Cass, apparently having forgotten about her injuries, meets her daughter just as fast as the little girl got here. She takes her daughter into her arms. "You're okay, honey?"

Whether I've saved a mother or a child, the reunion will never grow old. I remind myself again that I've done something right.

I know Mark is watching behind me. I owe that guy for many reasons—but the one that plays on my mind right now is his decision to stop me from shooting that sick Neil Parr in Idaho. Had I done that, I wouldn't have been here—and I wouldn't have been there for Cass.

My gaze is fixed on the mother and child—hugging, kissing, and sharing stories. If I turned around to face Mark, I'd surely lose my shit and become a melancholic mess—I'm that fragile right now.

While I'm busy trying to stay composed, a woman steps into the room. She hugs Cass, exchanging a few words, then she approaches me.

"Bless you, Sam Kelleher." She wraps her arms around me. When she lets go, she raises her tear-stained eyes to mine.

"Nice to meet you, Mrs. Winter."

"Alice," she says.

"Nice to meet you, Alice."

She smiles as she retreats, letting Grace have me.

"Sam!" The girl stretches herself as if wanting to climb onto my shoulder in one leap. I have forgotten that I'm still nursing a wound. But no pain can stop me from welcoming that little munchkin. I carry her up on my hip.

"I'm proud of you," I start. "You kept your promise to come with Mark, and you've been a good girl."

Her tiny mouth puckers, then she gives me a peck on the cheek. "That's for saving Mom."

"That's nice." I would have her with me for longer, perhaps taking her to the park or going out swimming if this was an ordinary day. "Why don't you come with your mom and grandma? I'm sure you and your mom have a lot to talk about."

"Come on, honey," Alice reaches out to Grace.

I wave at Cass to give me five. She follows the rest of the Winters and moves on to the dining room.

Mark pats my shoulder. "You good?"

"Yeah." I give him a brotherly hug, which seems to surprise him. "Thanks, man."

"For what?"

"For everything." Confronting his stoic face, my need to shed tears disappears in an instant. After all, I know how not to embarrass myself in front of him.

I then fish my phone out of my pocket. "Hey, I've got the photo back—the sidewalk boy. Now I know why this was found in a Georgia cold case. Look at the reflection in the window."

"Spring Hill Butchers."

"There is a Spring Hill in Georgia, Mark," I say. "This boy must've been ten or so, which matches Jack's age at the time the photo was taken."

"I'll be damned..."

"Look!" This time I grab my wallet and take out a photo that I've kept since I embarked on a mission to find my brother. "This was Jack, aged seven, just before he disappeared." I place it side by side with the photo of the sidewalk boy. "If this boy wasn't him, then I must've had another twin brother!"

"What are you going to do?"

I peek into Mark's dining room. Cass, her mom Alice, Ben, and Grace all sit around the table. It looks like Cass is trying to convince everybody that she's alright.

Had I still abided by my oath to be married to the job and

stay off women, I would've gone to Georgia right at this minute.

"I can't leave Cass and Grace."

Mark looks me in the eye. "I can go if you want."

"No. It's gotta be me. I'll sort it out when we get Ambrose behind bars."

I observe the happy family once again. Ben gets up and disappears into the kitchen, only to come out with a tray in his hands.

"He bakes. Can you believe it?" Mark says.

It is surprising, considering neither Alice nor Cass is a baking or cooking type. In saying that, I wonder if Alice had smuggled in a few bottles of ale. The mother-daughter team knows crafted beer like it's their bread and butter. Their brew is hands down the best I've ever had.

"Who wants cake?" Ben says cheerfully. I guess a Taekwondo master's hands can be useful for kneading dough.

Dare I imagine being part of that family one day? It's a gratifying thought but, at the same time, daunting. With the lifelong baggage I'm carrying, the last thing I want is to disappoint Cass—believing that I'm her perfect man, and in the end, I'm not cut out for it.

Mark nudges me. "Look, I took the liberty of securing your house while you were at the hospital. It's basically a clone of my system here," he explains. "While I'm hoping we can get Ambrose sooner rather than later, we're not sure how smart the guy is. I figure you would want some privacy with Cass and Grace."

"Thanks, man. I appreciate it."

In the dining room, Alice hands over two plates to Grace. "Go on, give these to Sam and Mark." I barely hear her voice.

"Sam, this is for you," Grace offers.

I take the plate. "Thank you, sweetheart."

"And this is for you, Mark."

Mark chews his first bite of the carrot cake quickly. "Jesus, I can have a whole tray of this."

I agree, finishing mine even before my partner does. My palate is dancing!

Before Grace returns to the dining room, I ask, "Can I talk to your mom?"

She spins around, yelling, "Mom! Sam wants to talk to you."

"I'll leave you to it," Mark says and joins the Winter family, asking for more of the cake.

Cass arrives at my side, her eyes still on Grace, who is now carried by Ben.

She then turns to me. "What is it, Sam?"

"Here's the plan. You and Grace come with me and stay at my house."

"Sam, I don't want to go back to the creek!"

I take her hand. "Come on, I'm not that cruel. I bought a new place."

She cocks her head. "Sam... did you... when you asked me if I would move in with you—"

"Yeah. I was serious."

"Oh, Sam..." She ducks helplessly.

"Listen, right now, that house will be your refuge. I'm not asking you to move in with me. It's just a safe house for you and Grace until we get Ambrose behind bars."

"Okay. Thanks." She leans into me, looking down at first, then she raises her gaze to mine. "Sam, I'm sorry I didn't realize you were serious."

"No need to be sorry," I say. "I told you it was a hypothetical question, and you answered truthfully. I know you'll never bullshit me."

She smiles, nodding.

I add, "Hey, Mark has installed cameras, alarms, and the whole shebang there. We'll be safe."

"He's done a lot in three days!"

"Yeah, he's the kind of guy who'd get married in the morning and catch a bad guy in the evening in time for his wedding night." Although that's an absurd way to describe Mark, he is actually *that* efficient.

Cass gives me a lukewarm look.

"Never mind," I sigh. With Mark's doomed wedding, I hope someday that description won't be a bad joke anymore. I then ask her, "How long is your brother gonna stay here? He lives in Kalispell, right?"

"He's thinking of moving here. But for now, he'll stay for as long as he's needed."

"Good. When I'm out and about, Ben should be with you. But—" I tug her close. "—when I'm in the house, it's just you, me, and Grace."

A smile plays on her lips. "Understood. But where's he gonna go?"

"Good point." Ben will have to be able to come to us at a drop of a hat if this is to work. And really, my house can't accommodate two alphas, not counting Maximus.

"My agent has another listing in the area. About ten or fifteen minutes away from my place. I think it's still empty. Ben can take that one."

"Alright. Can we go now?"

My girl is back—her impatience tells me so.

"Okay, sweetheart." I give her a peck on the lips, and for the first time in a long time, I see her blush.

19

———

SAM

Cass seems to be playing it cool as I drive to my new home. Sitting quietly in the passenger seat, she periodically glances back to check on Grace. The girl is sleeping in her child seat, which Mark had bought (more proof of the guy's efficiency), with Max sitting next to her.

Cass then wrings her hands. Perhaps because we've passed by a few creeks—not that we're traveling close to them—I think she might suspect that I've been hiding something.

"Relax. I swear this place is nowhere near any river or creek."

"Good. It's not the time to encourage me to face my fear, okay?"

"Will I ever do that?"

"You tried."

I nod in amusement, although perhaps it wasn't so amusing for her then. I once took her to a riverside restaurant in Big Sky and told her it was a surprise. Honestly, my intention was to walk her phobia with me, showing her that she didn't have to face it alone. But, as I found out, her fear was more than just a phobia. It was like a force that took over her. It was in and around her.

"I'll miss the creek house, though," I maintain.

After Maximus tried to matchmake us at the back alley of The Thirsty Fox, we parted ways without introducing ourselves. But as fate had it, Cass crashed back into my life when she recovered my dwindling alcohol supply at my home party.

She turns to me. "As a matter of fact, I will too—sans the creek. A lot happened in that house, I mean, you and me."

That afternoon, she had a panic attack driving her delivery van along the causeway.

I give Cass a side smile, saying, "I thought you were going to kill us both when you sped along with your eyes closed."

"Don't remind me," she complains.

I put my hand on hers, just like I did when she clutched the steering wheel white-knuckled. We would've ended up in the creek or straight inside my living room had I not taken control of the van.

Cass stacks her other hand on top of mine. "I can't believe you bought a new house just—"

"Just for you?" I wink. "Yes, mainly for you. But seriously, I'm not asking you to move in with me."

"You understand that I need time, right?"

"I do, Cass."

Soon her attention switches to the scenery spread in front of her. "Sam... is that?"

"Yeah. Welcome to my new abode. See, no water." I follow her gaze as she explores the land. "Although we might need to put in a drinking pool near the stable if we decide to keep horses down the track," I tease her.

"Sam—horses, really?"

"I'm not trying to lure you in, so don't kill me just yet." I know how much she loves horses, so the stable is really for her. "I just wanted to be... well, accommodating. That's all."

"Well..." Her voice trails off as she's seemingly lost for words.

I let her take in the moment.

While Ben is following our car, Mark arrived before us. 'Always double-check,' he told me this morning before he left to make sure the house was safe and ready.

Ben joins us as Mark helps unload Cass's and Grace's bags.

The Mountain pulls me aside. He doesn't seem to care about the house that I'm providing for his sister. His close proximity reminds me that I'm not out of the woods yet. He says, "You find Seth, and let me deal with that prick Harvey Whitlock! I was the one who found out about his piling debt—when he suddenly disappeared on Cass. I will find him again!"

"Ben!" Cass interrupts. From the look on her face, I'm sure she has been following what he says.

"Remember when my first Taekwondo school closed down?" Ben turns to his sister. "I stooped so low as to ask Harvey for a job. Sure, I did it out of desperation because I was in debt myself. I was treated like a slave, but boy, in return, I got to know him and his business acquaintances—especially those he owed money to. I can expose his whereabouts, Cass."

"Let's plan this carefully," I tell Ben. "He might not be the same man. He might be smarter now."

"There're only two ways Harvey Whitlock could've changed—either his ass has gotten bigger, or his balls have shrunk. Smarter? Pffft!" Ben gripes.

"Right now, Ambrose Seth is our priority. I killed his brother. He will want revenge. I'll find that son of a bitch, and when I do, you will be here with Cass and Grace."

Ben huffs. "Fine. But I want Harvey!"

"Not your call!" My voice thickens.

"She's my sister!" Ben doesn't give up.

I step closer to the big man. "Yeah. And she's—"

Cass bows down, knowing I'm looking at her.

The woman that I love.

"—she's under my protection. I make the call, Ben."

"He's right," Mark supports me.

Ben The Mountain fusses.

"Ben, please," Cass begs him to relent.

"Fine." He narrows his eyes, questioning me. "Look, if you were Ambrose Seth, would you pursue the money? Or would you pursue your revenge first?"

That gets me thinking. "Whichever he has a chance to do first."

"I think Harvey really has that money," Ben says, his rational face returns. "He's a lousy businessman, but his love of gambling is another thing. When he's on a lucky streak, he wins big, and I mean, million big." He slants his head in thought. "But what are those numbers that the Seth brothers got hold of? Offshore accounts? It's kinda 'been there, done that' for Harvey, and he had been screwed by banks before."

"So you think he really buried his money?" Cass says.

Ben shakes his head tentatively. "I don't think he's quite that caveman-like."

"Ambrose and Denzel Seth obviously split up after they left you in that shack," Mark recaps, facing Cass. "Denzel was tasked to find Grace. When he couldn't find her at camp, he went to your house."

"Ambrose is the boss, the one with connections—especially with underground financiers," Ben clarifies. "I think he could've been the one pursuing the possibility that those numbers were bank accounts and passwords."

"Leaving Denzel to do the dirty work—checking up potential sites, in case those numbers were really coordinates." Mark follows Ben's logic.

"Wait..." I say. "Mark, before you found that dead drug dealer's property where Cass was held, I scoured the history on Denzel's navigation system. Do the police still have his car?"

"As far as I know, yes," Mark replies.

"What if one of the locations on Denzel's satellite navigation is a place where Ambrose could be hiding?" I suggest.

"I'm calling Zander now," Mark says with urgency, walking away from us to make the phone call.

My hand is in my pocket. Car keys rattle in my grip.

"Wherever you're going, I'm going with you!" Ben insists.

"No." Much as I see his potential, the guy is too brash and tends to take things far too personally.

Besides, I decide not to go after Seth this time. I want to destroy him—hell yes, I do—but taking him into custody is more important than my ego. Also, I just got here with Cass at my dream house, which I'm hoping is hers too. I feel like a loser leaving her so soon, even though I know Ben will do a good job of keeping her and Grace safe.

I stop fiddling with my car keys. "Leave this one to the police," I instruct.

"Good idea," Mark affirms. "I'll keep a close eye on the operation."

"Listen to Mark and Sam," Cass tells her brother. "For now, stay with Mom, okay?"

"I've arranged for your lodging," I tell The Mountain. "It's only a few miles from here. Mark will lead you there. You're welcome to join too, Alice." I turn to Cass's mother, who rode here along with Ben and has been quiet since.

"Thanks, Sam," Alice says in her usual calm voice.

"Pass me the keys then," Ben groans. I toss the house keys

right into his open palm. He then hugs his sister and whispers something to her. Before he jumps into his car, he turns to me and says, "I'm watching you, Kelleher!"

Cass smirks—perhaps life isn't that bad when you have so many men protecting you.

GRACE WAKES up as Cass takes her inside the house. "Wow… this is cool," she murmurs, stopping a yawn. "Where are we?"

"It's Sam's house, honey," Cass mutters as she roams the living room, paying attention to the huge fireplace with rugs, blankets, and pillows scattered in front of it.

I've always dreamed of a country winter, with my own Lady Winter—relaxing on the floor, reading a book or two with wine in our hands while Grace is rolling around with Maximus. We'll be warm while the snow is falling outside.

I stay by the front door, letting the girls roam by themselves while Maximus sniffs every nook he can find. It's the first time the mutt sets paw in this house too. I hope he hasn't forgotten about his training and doesn't start marking his territory.

"Those fences are wired now," warns Mark as we walk around the front yard. "The control is inside—and in these." He hands over a couple of remotes. "You'll show Cass how it works, won't you?"

"Of course."

"I'm gonna head back to town. I'll keep you in the loop." Mark pats my shoulder.

I look at him. "What would I do without you?"

"Take it easy, buddy," he says, then leaves.

When I step into the house, I find Grace playing tug-a-war

with Max, using some rags either of them has found. They're rolling around on the rug in the living room.

Perfect—just perfect.

"She has never owned a pet." Cass giggles when Grace tumbles backward after losing out to Max. In return, with all the doggie love he has, Max nuzzles at Grace and gives her face a good licking.

"Have you been upstairs?" I ask.

"No."

"Come, I'll show you the bedrooms."

Cass and Grace follow me keenly. The custom-built log staircase seems to intrigue the little one. She taps her feet as if trying to gauge the strength of the treads.

"Be careful around stairs, okay?" Cass warns.

I take them to the rooms closest to the landing. "These are the guest beds. I guess Grace can take one of them."

"Wow... this is amazing, Sam." Cass admires the view of the hills. That window is facing west, revealing the golden hour before the sunset. Then she studies the painting in the first room. "This is beautiful."

"The Grand Teton. A friend of mine painted it."

She steps into the bedroom next door. "Oh my! Grace, look at this."

Grace joins us after exploring the other guest room. "Three bears!"

"You want to sleep here tonight?"

"With that photo above my bed? Of course!"

"You like that, huh?" I really want her to say it.

"I do, I do! Do you have Three Bears on An Adventure on your iPad? Like Mark has?"

"Well, I can certainly download it for you." How can I say no?

"Thanks, Sam!" Grace hugs me. "Can Max sleep with me?"

"Sure."

"Come on, Max," invites Grace.

We leave her be as Cass and I move on to the other side.

"This is another spare room," I point out. "In case we need a bodyguard." I wink at her as we move on to the most important room in the house.

She nods, approving the largest bedroom with windows facing the evergreen forest on the eastern side of the property.

"I thought we could take this one. Don't think of it as a honeymoon suite, okay? If you don't—"

"It's fine, Sam. We can sleep in there."

"Good. I didn't particularly want to sleep in that bodyguard room."

She leans into me, and I hug her waist, hinting she needs to get closer.

"You've done so much," she murmurs.

"I did it with pleasure," I reply, rubbing the curve of her hips. I slant my face toward her head, kissing her crown and absorbing the divine smell coming from her hair.

Suddenly Grace darts into the room. "Mom, I'm hungry."

"Um... we might need to settle with pizza tonight," I admit my unpreparedness.

"Why?" Cass responds. "There's plenty of food in the fridge."

I stare at her. "What do you mean?"

"It's a huge fridge. Got to see what's in it," she quips, reminding me of the state of my fridge when she came to my party at the creek house, rescuing my beer supply.

We all head downstairs to the kitchen. I stand in front of the fridge, pondering as if I'll see an alien jumping out if I open it.

"You don't believe me?" Cass says.

I open the door. Damn! It is well-stocked, and it's not with booze.

Hands on hips, she watches me as I check the shelves. "Did you have amnesia or something?"

"Um... well, this wasn't me."

"Mark?"

I shake my head even though my answer is yes. I'm just not believing how far my best friend would go. Among the fresh fruits and vegetables, juices, sodas, and milk bottles, there's a pack of pre-marinated chicken wings. With a note.

Grace loves these. Put in oven for 40-45 mins at 400 degrees.

"Grace, we've got your favorite chicken wings," Cass says.

"Really?"

"Yeah, Mark bought them for us," I tell her, not wanting to claim any credit.

"Yesss!"

Cass unties Grace's messy ponytail, then runs her fingers through her hair. "Well, you go and have a shower while we make dinner."

"Okay, Mom." The girl heads upstairs, followed by Maximus.

"Let me put them on the tray." Cass takes over the pack of wings from me.

"You know what you're doing?" I tease her. The first (and last) time she tried to cook for me, when I rented a cabin one weekend, she almost burned the whole kitchen down.

"Hey, I learned my lesson, you know," she replies, obviously remembering the same thing.

I watch her spreading the well-coated wings on the baking tray. "He's so good. Mark. Why is he still single?" she quizzes me.

"I don't know, Cass," I reply while chopping carrots and celery.

"Is it true about him and Ivy Cavanagh?"

"Sort of, but he's just being Mark."

We have wine while waiting for the chicken to cook. I managed to download the book that Grace was after, and she's now reading it by the fireplace, using Max as her pillow.

The oven dings, and I challenge Cass with my eyes, telling her I'm going to judge what's going to come out.

The wings come out beautifully.

"Well done, sweetheart." I snake my arm around her neck and give her a peck on the cheek.

"Well, it's all Mark, really," she concedes, serving the juicy poultry. It smells damn amazing. "Don't forget to eat the carrots and the celery," she tells Grace.

"Hmm... okay," the girl pouts.

"Does this house have a name?" Cass asks.

"The previous owner named it the Tree Cottage."

"This is more than a cottage," Cass counters. "This place is huge."

"Alright, what should we name it then?"

"The Tree House?" Grace suggests.

"Well... maybe." I show her my pondering eyes.

"How about The Woodhouse? One word," Cass chimes in.

"I like it."

"What's the difference?" Grace challenges my verdict. "Tree House, Wood House?"

"It just sounds nicer, honey," Cass teases her daughter.

"I don't understand." Grace shakes her head, taking another piece of chicken.

For a moment, I forget about the world as we sit at the table, eating with our hands. There's nothing more I could wish for.

"Mom, I need napkins." Grace shows her sticky hands.

"Um..." Cass looks around.

"No, you don't," I determine.

While Cass cocks her head at my remark, I attack her with my hands, smearing buffalo sauce all over her cheeks. Seeing that, Grace laughs until her belly shakes.

"Sam! No!" Cass squeals.

While I'm still busy saucing up my lovely companion, I feel tiny hands reaching out to me. When I turn around, Grace immediately rubs her palms on my jeans, over and over.

"Hey! That's not on!" I holler and touch her nose with the remaining goo I have on my fingers.

Soon Max abandons his dinner and joins in the fun, pouncing at Cass, licking her face with zeal.

Laughter and bark fill the room as we roll around on the floor trying to get at each other. Not a bad night—not a bad night at all for our first time together.

CASS PADS SLOWLY TOWARD GRACE, who has fallen asleep on the rug in front of the fireplace—well, on Maximus, to be exact.

"Let me take that." I grab the iPad, which Grace tries to hold on to even in her sleep.

"I hope she sleeps through to morning," Cass sighs.

After a satisfying dinner, followed by ice cream (we let Grace have a bowlful this time), and being showered with so much attention from us, she surely will.

Cass picks the little girl up, and she doesn't even stir.

I watch Grace's sleeping face resting on Cass's shoulder as we make our way upstairs.

We enter the 'three bears room,' and I quickly turn down the comforter to allow Cass to tuck Grace in. Then I step away, lingering by the door. Not that I don't want to stay close, I simply want to absorb the whole scene of my two precious girls having a peaceful night—with me, inside the house that I provided for them.

How far would I go to protect them?

Beyond what I'm capable of.

I can't fathom what would happen to me if Grace were hurt or taken. I would kill, that's for sure.

The silence makes my heart go heavy. The night has gone well, but I can't help thinking about reality. I know Grace is safe, but I haven't forgotten about what happened to Chloe O'Rourke and the other girls. Every good father believes he can protect his family. Yet, the worst can still happen.

Cass joins me.

"Ready for bed?" I ask her.

"Absolutely," she replies. "I'm spent."

I put my arm around her waist, guiding her to our bedroom.

Our Woodhouse bedroom.

I take off my top.

"Does it still hurt?" She nods at my wound.

"A bit. Don't worry about it."

She looks at me. For once, she doesn't insist on seeing my wound to believe what I told her. She seeks something else from my eyes, and she seems to find it because that comforting gaze shoots at me.

"Samuel," she murmurs, a call to let me know that she's ready to listen. I don't even have to ask.

"It's late."

"No, it's not. I know you've wanted to tell me something about Idaho since we were in the hospital."

I sigh, kissing her forehead, thanking her for giving me a chance.

"Her name is Chloe. We saved her, but I almost killed the son of a bitch that took her," I confess.

She simply squeezes my hand.

"Executed him," I clarify. My finger tingles as if I'm about to pull the trigger of my MK25. "God, I was close. But Mark stopped me. I was mad at him, and I was mad at myself for not doing it because in the end, that monster killed himself. I'd lost my chance to eliminate evil with my own hands.

"In the military, we have rules of engagement. I had always abided by them—there was never impulse or out-of-control emotions. We followed orders, and we delivered. End of story. But that day in Idaho. Fuck! I was prepared to go to hell in exchange for taking his life. What he did to those girls—God, Cass..."

I lean into her, looking for her gentle support. She places her lips on my forehead, and from there she kisses me deeply, like I'm a hero. I know I am in her eyes, but there's nothing heroic about stopping one man, only for others to continue on in this never-ending circle of cruelty.

I whisper to her, "Three girls. We saved one of them. That means two still died—innocently."

"It's unfair, but you didn't fail. You've got Chloe safe."

I sigh—and she knows I mean it's not making me feel that much better.

"Sam, this world is bigger than any of us. It's more fucked up than any of us can handle. But one girl means the world to her father. Saving Chloe means saving her world—and her father's. That's got to make a difference."

If she puts it like that, I do feel better. Things might be fucked up, but right now, she's the one who's keeping my world stable and sane. I tell her slowly, "You know, Cass. That prick fantasized about killing Mark."

"Fantasized?" She frowns.

"He told me Mark reminded him of what he could've been. I think deep down, he hated his sickness. And you know Mark has a boyish appearance. Perhaps that just triggered him. I mean, that prick was fifty years old. But the way he described Mark, the way he leered at him—it was absolutely vile."

"That's sick, Sam. Did Mark hear all that?"

"No. He was close, but the prick whispered it to my ear. But Mark knew. He didn't have to hear it to figure it out." I remember Mark's steady but heavy eyes when we got back into the car before we argued about me taking a break. "Christ, I can still hear his voice and smell his filth."

She nudges herself closer to me, but not before checking my wound.

"It's okay. You're not hurting me," I say.

Her gentle fingers trail my jawline, and her head falls onto my shoulder—her crown so close to my nose as if inviting me to smell her. Of course I will. I have to erase Parr's sick odor, and only Cass's divine scent can do that.

"Sometimes I wish I could take a pill to forget," I confide.

She takes my hand and kisses the top of my palm. "If you forget, you'll have to do it all over again when the next time comes. Brutality and evil can do two things to good men. Either it breaks them or it makes them stronger. It's the latter for you, Sam."

I smile painfully—a good kind of pain, though. She's right, I don't want to forget. Because I have her.

"The same goes for good women, too," I quip.

Losing a parent when you're still young is tough, and it's even tougher when it's sudden and violent. Cass has experienced that, and now she has become my rock. If she had taken a pill to forget, she wouldn't be who she is today.

Cass stifles a yawn. Tears drop from the corner of her tired eyes.

"Let's go to sleep." I turn off the light.

"Thank you for everything, Sam."

"No, no. Thank *you*."

"Good night."

"Night, sweetheart." I give her a peck on the lips. "I've got a feeling you won't have your nightmare tonight."

Her nightmare at the hospital wasn't the first time I saw it. During some of our 'trysts,' she sometimes woke up in the middle of the night panting, but she always dismissed it as 'just a bad dream.'

"You will wake me up if I do, won't you?" she purrs.

"Of course."

She closes her eyes, breathing serenely as I caress her gorgeous hair.

I kiss her again, whispering, "I love you, Cass."

"Sam..." she mumbles softly.

I'm not sure if she hears me, but she ought to feel me. She sighs and then turns on her side. I follow the curves of her silhouette—she's like a shadow rising in front of a sunset. Quiet, mysterious.

Tonight has been magical, not just having Cass and Grace in my dream home and the fun we had at the dinner table. But a huge burden has been taken off my shoulders because she comforted me.

If I could, I would get down on my knees right now and ask her to marry me.

I told her this room wasn't a honeymoon suite. I told her I'd understand that she needed time before taking things to the next level. But no one knows what tomorrow will bring. I can't wait too much longer.

I'll talk to her in the morning.

20

SAM

I peel the bandage off my side after my shower. The wound is healing nicely, although there are still specks of blood left on the bandage.

I wrap a towel around my hips loosely and step out of the bathroom.

"Good morning," I greet Cass as I open the door. She's still in bed, wearing my t-shirt. God, I love her messy hair—with that look, she'll be all over me sooner than later.

But something else seems to be drawing her attention.

The bandage I left on the vanity.

"Is it still bleeding?" she asks.

"No. That's just buffalo sauce." I smirk as I turn around and toss the bandage into the trash.

Cass purses her lips sideway—unimpressed. "Do you want me to dress that?" She points at my stitches.

"Don't worry, sweetheart. I'll do it."

"You do that. I'm going to check on Grace."

"Yes, ma'am." I watch her long legs swinging out of the comforter. She's got a damn fine pair, that woman.

I apply a thin layer of petroleum jelly on the stitches and apply a fresh dressing.

If I want her in bed, I should stay naked or put on something thin. One side of me wishes I didn't have to talk about anything, and everything will stay as splendid as it is. I could stick to my original plan and wait until she tells me she's ready.

But hell, I can't wait any longer.

It has to happen today or I'll be forever fighting with myself. I almost lost her in that valley—she wasn't breathing for goodness sake! Now that she's with me, I can't afford to lose her again. Period.

But I have to discuss our relationship with her—that is, me becoming part of Grace's and her lives permanently. As their man who loves them, not a disruption. May I say, it's much more important than asking her to marry me. Because what I have in mind is bigger than just saying 'I do.'

Cass comes back, seemingly unsure why I'm in my sweater and casual shorts.

"Grace okay?" I ask.

"Yeah. She had a big day yesterday," she replies. "I'm glad she's still asleep. She's not very good at sleeping at new places."

I agree with her. Even at Mark's house, I heard her sleeping pattern went out of whack. Luckily, Cass's mother was there to bring in some kind of normalcy into her days.

"Hey." I hug her waist.

"Sam?"

I don't have a poker face like Detective Brand from Helena PD. I know Cass is sensing I'm going to say something that she might oppose.

"Please sit down." I offer her the unmade bed, and she takes a seat at the bed's foot. "I've been thinking." I plonk myself next to her. "I know I said I wouldn't ask you to move in—"

"Sam, I thought I told you."

"Hear me out, please, hear me out. After last night. In fact, after all of the nights we've spent together—granted, they were few and far between—we're still here, Cass. Stronger than ever. Don't you think it's time for us to talk about it?"

For a while, she simply stares at her own feet.

"You know, Sam," she slowly says. "When you first introduced yourself to me, I was relieved that you weren't in the Navy anymore."

I nod.

"And when you found out about what I do as a Red Mark?" I ask.

"I was horrified. I didn't want to have anything to do with you."

"But you kept seeing me anyway."

She bows her head. "It was an easy decision, yet the hardest I made. There's just something in you that I couldn't turn away from. At the same time, what you do has stopped me from moving forward. That was why I said no about moving in."

"I know you asked for more time. If it is going to take a long time, then why don't we start now?"

"The second, third time that we were together, I thought... I didn't even know if I'd ever be ready. And now, even after all this." She points at our bedroom and the open windows. "I'm still not sure, Sam."

"We need to try. Then we'll know."

"I can't muck it up again—not with Grace. I can't just try and see what happens."

"Then how do we move on, Cass? I want you. I want us to work."

She moans as if her heart hurts. "I married Harvey, thinking it'd be forever. I was never under the illusion that everything would be rosy, but I never thought I would've messed up that bad."

"How is it you who messed up? He was the asshole, Cass. Not you."

"I chose him, Sam," she argues. "Grace was only two when we got divorced, but she took in a lot. I lied to Harvey, convincing him that the distance between us would make me miss him, that I'd come back to him and start again. But I ran away."

It's the best goddamn decision she made.

"Grace is a sweet girl," she continues. "But she has buried a lot of things inside. Moving from place to place, never having any long-term friendships, it took a toll on her. She picked fights, she retaliated against her teachers, and she ran away from daycare. Well, she saved herself by running away from that summer camp." Cass chuckles. "But, you see what I'm trying to say, Sam?"

I cup her chin and draw her face to me. "I'm ready to fill that void, Cass. Grace and I get along well. You've got to see that. I'm ready to be her father if that's what you want me to be."

"Sam!" She grimaces. "In the six months that we've been together, how many days were you actually here? I'm the one left behind without knowing anything. If you were Grace's father, what should I tell her?"

Words escape me. My thought goes back to Idaho. I could've died then, and if I was Grace's father, it would've been Cass who was left to do the explaining and carry on without me.

Cass adds, "I won't want to spend my days thinking if you'd come back alive tonight, tomorrow, next week—or if I'd find you in a body bag, or even worse, missing in action, presumed killed, or... or...."

"Stop there, Cass," I ask her gently.

"Don't say that it'll never happen."

"Look—"

"You're not unbreakable, Sam."

"Maybe not me—my body—but my heart and my love for you are."

"What good is love when you're not around?" She holds back her tears. "My dad loved me. But without him, I don't feel it, Sam. I don't feel loved."

"Cass... come on."

"Tell me. Tell me how I'm supposed to feel loved by you if you're not around?" she argues. "I might've come across as cold and not needing anyone. But I have fears."

Her voice trembles and her eyes look at me in horror as if those fears have manifested themselves.

She carries on, "I'm proud of my military family, and I'm proud of you as a former SEAL and a Red Mark. But I don't want to present a possibility to my life—and Grace's life— where my fears might be realized. I can't handle my own fears. How can I expect Grace to? How will I teach her to overcome them?"

"You're stronger than you think, Cass."

"I don't think so." She shakes her head. "Remember your assignment that followed our first night together? Your neck was bruised and—I might not have shown it, but I went crazy inside, Sam. And that was just a bruise."

I remember that assignment. When I got home, complete with a neck brace and a pitiful attitude to get her attention, she treated me as if I had broken all the bones in my body. It was comforting to have her playing nurse with me, but I remember the fright on her face every time she looked at my injury. I guess I hadn't thought much of it since.

"I'm still that woman who dreads you going away, and gets terrified of what might or could happen," she emphasizes.

"Mark and I will recruit more men," I assure her. "So the chance of me not coming back will be slashed at least in half."

"But the possibility is still there."

My phone buzzes against the bedside table—a call from my dad.

"Answer it," Cass says.

"No, it can wait." I put my phone on silent. "We can work this out, Cass. Being apart will be part of our lives. There's no denying it."

"I'm not denying it. I'm telling you, I'm struggling with it."

"Cass, you have the right to worry about me, but fear is another thing. You can't fear the future just because of what I do."

"Possibility..." she murmurs. "That's what I fear, Sam."

"Cass, you can't cheat death. If it's your time, it's your time. It could be me, it could be you. I know it sounds harsh, but you've got to understand that."

She holds her chest, and her eyes shut tight.

"Cass... I'm sorry. I didn't mean to upset you." I thought she'd appreciate me being straight to the point. But I should've known even the strongest soul has a fragile spot. The word 'death' seems to bring it home even more to her.

She acknowledges me with a nod, although remaining somber.

"Hey, I've been injured many times," I say. "So far, I've always come home with my head screwed to my shoulders, haven't I?" I rub her arm, trying to fish out just a little smile from her.

Her features sag. The smile I'm desperately seeking turns

impossible. I see a horrified face, like when she woke up in the hospital the first morning, screaming, 'Don't let me drown.'

She backs away when I try to touch her.

"Cass, what's wrong?"

"Please, leave me alone, Sam."

"Cass..."

"Please." Her eyes flare, her frame goes rigid. Her wall is up.

I've never seen her like that.

Slowly I step away, leaving her be. To my surprise, Maximus is waiting outside the door. He releases a soft bark, and I let him in. The mutt knows something, and I'm hoping he can be a cheerleader for her while I'm unable to.

I pass the 'three bears room' on my way downstairs. I can't imagine living without Grace now, without her mother. How have I messed this up already? I acted too soon, going against my instinct to wait. And I had forgotten to put myself in Cass's shoes.

Cass shuts the door, leaving me cursing to myself.

21

CASSIDY

"Mom, come and play with us." Grace stands by the bedroom door, donning a Major League Baseball cap that keeps drooping down her forehead. No doubt it's Sam's.

I sit up, although I wish I could keep my heavy eyes shut, just like Maximus, who's lying on the floor next to the bed. My unfinished conversation with Sam loops in my head like a bad record.

"You had your breakfast?" I ask Grace with a guilty tone. A bout of migraine just now had forced me to enlist Sam's help to feed my daughter.

Grace taps a ball against her gloved hand. "Of course. Sam makes good pancakes." Her crooked smile tells me his were better than mine. I make no protest and smile back.

I run a hand over my hair as I glance out the window. The morning sun shines through the fir trees that line the backyard. In the spotlight is Sam, doing his warmups—whatever they're for, he's just going to play ball with a five-year-old.

He faces away, but I bet he knows I'm watching.

His shorts ride up and down following his movement. They keep him decent, but there's no hiding his Herculean legs. Meanwhile, his tank top exposes his buff arms. Against the light, its thin white material gives me a glimpse of the silhouette of his torso—and the bandage around his midriff. No matter how hard he tries to mask his injury, my mind is conditioned to sense his pain.

I enjoy the view, nonetheless.

"Are you coming?" Grace cuts short my indulgence. She taps the ball even harder against the leather glove as if preparing herself for Sam's throws.

"I'm still feeling a bit tired. Go on, you play with Sam," I encourage her. "But be gentle, okay? His side is still sore."

"Okay," Grace says. "Come, Max." She tries to lure him with the ball, but the mutt isn't budging. "Alright. Don't say I don't let you play!" she complains and walks away.

"You okay, Max?" I nudge him with my foot and then brush him with my toes.

The mutt rolls over, belly up. He soon throws me a doggy grin when I rub him vigorously.

"Why did you choose me?"

He simply writhes left and right; I know I'm hitting his ticklish spots.

"You pounced at me, remember?"

It would have been almost an ordinary afternoon if not for the fact that I debuted Fallen Angel at The Thirsty Fox—a pale ale crafted in my own brewery using my mother's recipe. I'll never forget Max's ferocious lick. Up to that point, I don't think anyone had ever been so excited to see me.

"What did you see in me, huh?" I play with his ears. "Or smell in me?"

Max whistles a soft woof.

"I'm no good for him, you know."

I couldn't even handle his joke. I can tolerate him being a clown. First thing this morning in the shower, although it annoyed me, I could take the 'buffalo sauce' comment when I caught a glimpse at his blood-stained bandage. But his remark about his head being screwed to his body?

I let out a loud sigh, prompting Maximus to watch me closely.

The remark was innocent. It upset me then, but it wasn't his bad joke that brought me down. The man doesn't seem to realize how much I fear his demise. He's the type who keeps others safe but doesn't do a good job of doing it for himself. He might've been lucky all this time, but any winning streak will end at some stage—what will happen when his luck runs out?

"What do you think?"

This time Max nuzzles at me, perhaps saying I should know the answer. His piteous face begs me to allow him to jump up to bed. I let him, and he drops his head on my lap.

"Can I throw now?" I hear Grace yelling at Sam. She ditches the glove.

Sam hands over the ball. "I think you're just tired," he teases her.

"No. I can throw!" Right then, she releases the ball wayward, prompting Sam to bend down low.

I wince as if the wound was mine. But the man doesn't even flinch. Perhaps he's having too much fun playing coach with Grace. The pair goes on to challenge each other as if they'd been pros in their fifth or sixth season. They get serious one minute, showing off their best moves, and the next minute they laugh at each other. The interactions tickle me deep in my core—Sam is probably the best thing that has happened to Grace since I left my ex.

How far can I take this relationship? My heart certainly tells me *all the way* as sudden happiness from watching the sporty duo inundates me. But what about my head?

A throw goes wide to Sam's left, and this time he glances my way. I duck and close the curtains, unable to make eye contact with him.

I have nightmares when I'm with him, but he may never know why. Nobody knows—I never talk about it. I don't want to test how far my courage goes. Once I've fallen apart, I may not come back whole again.

I've broken so many rules I posed on myself. But Grace's future isn't one of them. At the end of the day, Sam is still going to be an absent dad who may not come home at all—and that's the one thing that I don't want to break yet.

What the hell should I do?

My attention lands on Maximus, who's now taking almost half of the bed. I lie next to my furry companion, still listening in to the cheers outside, which slowly turn into soft, comforting noise as I'm overcome by drowsiness.

But after a few breaths, I perk up.

Jasmine.

It takes me a few moments to shirk off the smell. Whatever I'm going to do today, the Black Crow Bridge won't be my destination.

Max wakes up too, but obviously for a different reason. He bypasses me, jumps out of bed, and then runs out of the room.

I nudge the curtain open. Ben is here. That means Sam is leaving.

I rush out, too, joining the men and my daughter. "What's going on?" I ask.

"They spotted Seth," Sam replies, striding to his car.

The name weighs me down. My brain tells me to catch Sam—I don't want him to leave, let alone confront danger on my behalf. But my legs never get the message.

"I'm going there." He climbs behind the wheel, glancing at me with determination. In his black shirt and pants now, the smell of his cologne travels to me as the breeze sweeps through.

I cringe as I feel my heart crumpling.

Ben appraises me and then plods toward Sam, who's ready to shift to drive. "What have you done, Kelleher?"

"Ben, drop it! He hasn't done anything." I tug my brother away.

Ben retreats. Sam winds the window down and reaches out to take my hand. "Did you hear what I whispered to you last night?"

I shake my head. I really didn't.

"I told you I love you. And I meant it," his voice is barely audible over the breeze.

I hold back words that are flying in my brain—*don't go, I love you too.*

Sam soon drives off, leaving my legs weak and numb.

"You okay, Cass?" Ben asks.

"Yeah, I'm fine."

"She's been cranky all day!" Grace retorts.

I cock my head but then admit it with my eyes.

"Come on, Uncle Ben. Let's play catch."

With a smile on his face, my brother hauls Grace up and carries her on his shoulders. As the two take their positions as pitcher and catcher, I return to my den, followed by Maximus.

I gaze out as I did when Sam was there 'coaching' Grace. Ben has always been my man, the dynamic between him and my daughter is one that I've admired since she was little. But it's not the same watching him with Grace—even though I'm looking out the same window. When Sam was with her, my heart bloomed—full of colors and magical sounds that I'd never experienced before.

The magic of Sam and Grace.

Like a garden in spring, I feel tiny sprouts of hope.

He said he would be a father to Grace. Hell, he would be a great father to her.

All I need to do is to say 'I love you' back to him.

Why is it so hard?

Now that the threat of the Seth brother may be over soon, I have to make a decision. My ex may still be lurking—but that's something that I will face head-on. I won't let him ruin my life. I can't let Sam wait any longer.

I will tell him everything.

I'm ready.

Grace's and Ben's laughs fill the air as if cheering my decision. I move sideways, trying to get a better angle at them as they run to the other end of the backyard. Close to the corner, my foot kicks something under a pile of Sam's clothes. I shuffle away the folded shirts and pants to take a peek.

It's a box. The lid has been placed sloppily, as if it has been recently opened. I peer inside.

A face stares back at me.

A sketch of a young man—and underneath it is written: *Jack Kelleher – age: 24.*

22

SAM

When I get to the location where Ambrose Seth was discovered, he's already in cuffs.

As Captain Zander is distracted by a call, I zero in on the son of a bitch. "Where's Harvey Whitlock?" I gripe.

"Sam Kelleher," Ambrose spits out his words. "I guess we're looking for the same man. But I haven't forgotten what you've done."

"Back off, Sam!" Zander yanks me aside.

"Don't ever lose him," I whisper-shout to the captain. "Or the next thing you'll see is his dead body."

"I said, back off!"

Leaving the police to deal with the bastard, I watch Seth being shoved into the sheriff's car—with a gallant smile on his face. "This ain't over, Kelleher! Do you hear me? I always get my revenge. Blood for blood!"

Following Zander's departure, one by one, the troopers also leave the scene. I linger, following the police tape hung around the house where Ambrose Seth had been hiding.

Blood for blood.

Having faced off many like him before, it's not the first

time I've had a target on my back. I guess it's one of the reasons why Mark decided to stay single. It would've been wise for me to do the same, but I've arrived at a point of no return with Cass. Whether she sees our relationship the same way, I don't know. So far, she has stopped short of declaring she loves me, and I know it's more than just the burden of her ex.

Leaving the crime scene, I drive off to Red Mark headquarters, where my partner is keeping tabs on the development. I can hear him having a call to Zander while the muted TV shows the news in the background.

Most of Red Mark's assignments have become public knowledge, as our subjects are usually everyday people. We're not against publicity—just for our work, though. Everything else—either I'll protect it or make little to no comments on it.

So far, I've maintained the line between business and personal—well, ninety percent of the time—but the killing of Denzel Seth and the arrest of his brother have changed that.

I plonk myself on the chair in front of Mark as he ends the call with Zander. "Let me guess, Zander was pissed with what I said."

He scoffs. "What did you say to him?"

I shake my head. "Never mind."

"He's agreed to keep you and Cass out of this, as far as the press is concerned," Mark says.

If it ever comes out, I will take the brunt. I'll shield Cass from any kind of hounding.

"Ambrose Seth seems to be alone in this now. Not even his lawyer answered his call," says Mark. "He's staying silent, which means we still have nothing on Harvey Whitlock. But Whitlock will come up for air sooner or later. If he's far, it means he has no interest in Cass—at least for now."

"Yeah." I stretch my arms—whatever I've done to make

them stiff. Surely, it's not just from playing baseball with a five-year-old.

"How's Cass?"

"I don't know."

My partner cocks an eyebrow.

I lean back with a grunt. "God! Even my dog has spent more time with her."

"She may just need some space."

"I get it that she's having a hard time dealing with me being away."

"I don't blame her. We've been saying we'll recruit more men, so it's not just us, but I admit we've been slow in actioning it. This is our wake-up call. What do you think of Ben Winter?"

I frown. "Cass's brother?"

"Who else?"

"Well... that won't help, will it? She'll have two people to worry about then."

"True." He taps the armrests of his chair. "But there's just something about the guy. He's like a papa gorilla when he's with Grace. And when I talked to him, it reminded me of you when you were still a SEAL."

I shoot a glare, challenging his point. I didn't think I was that brash then. But I let it slide.

"Well, let's see what happens after all this is over." I grab the TV remote and get rid of the news. "Cass may not be with me anymore, and that means Red Mark will be the last company on earth Ben would ever consider."

Mark shakes his head. "*Not with you anymore*? You've screwed it up that bad? I thought you two were good. She was all smiles when she arrived at your house!"

"She was. Then—"

"You asked her again?"

"Well... sort of..."

"Come on, buddy. She has been through a lot."

"I couldn't help it. I just couldn't lose her."

Mark looks at me with understanding.

I say, "I get it that having a partner who's constantly away isn't the dream of any woman. But—why can't we see that she and I are more than just what I do? I mean, she's *terrified* of me being killed, beyond just worries. Terrified like an obsession. Maybe paranoid is the right word."

"Well, to love a woman is to know her like no other man."

I treat him with a cynical stare. The guy doesn't even know how to deal with a woman who's head over heels in love with him—and whom he's in love with, too (he never admits it, but I know it with a strong degree of certainty). What does he know about women?

But my partner passes me a look, telling me he has the authority to give me such advice. "I have something for you." He swipes a folder across the table.

Inside the folder is a classified document from thirteen years ago, produced by the US Army.

"No way!"

Gunnery Sergeant Phillip Winter, an Army sniper with a hundred and fifty confirmed kills, was beheaded near Basra. Even more cruelly, his head was apparently tossed into a creek.

"Jesus, Mark." I sink into my chair. I knew her dad died in Iraq, but not this way. "God... fuck!"

"Now you know why she's afraid of losing you."

My spine might as well shrink as my head falls in shame. For the first time since I got injured in Idaho, I feel real pain.

"This morning," I sigh, "when she told me about her worries—you know, about the possibility of me being killed in action—I joked around, saying that so far, I'd managed to come back with my head still screwed on my body."

Mark huffs as if now he's in pain too. "Well, it was a bad joke, but surely, she knew you didn't mean any harm."

"She's still not talking to me. I think I've broken her heart."

I'm used to my own heart being broken. Breaking someone else's heart would be ten times worse—and if I've done it to Cass, it'll be something that I won't forgive myself for.

"Come on, she's stronger than that," Mark says.

Maybe I haven't broken her heart. I may never will. But it's my death that will, someday. And I can't even prevent that from happening.

"What have you tried?" asks Mark.

"Nothing. I'm too scared to try anything. Even my dog knows better. He hasn't left her side. That's how special she is."

"Hmm. I guess her fear of losing you is all too real. She has lived it, Sam. And you should be the one who takes her out of that fear. Don't settle for my-dog-is-better-than-me bullshit."

"I won't stop doing what I do as a Red Mark. And I won't stop looking for Jack. But I can't let her go."

"No one says you should let her go."

People say you can't have it all. Maybe this reality is catching up with me.

"I don't want to have to choose, Mark."

"You may be underestimating her, Sam. What if she loves you as much as you do her?"

Cass has endured inscrutable adversity since she was young—she was only fourteen when her dad died. She's still in pain now, but it doesn't mean she's turning away from life and its challenges. It doesn't mean she's about to turn away from me, either.

Mark is right. I am underestimating her.

My mission to find Jack has been dominating my life for

more than two decades, but what I have with Cass is a once-in-a-lifetime event that I can't ignore. She's got to be my priority now.

BEN WINTER OPENS THE DOOR. He towers before me as if I'm facing even a sturdier barricade.

"How's Cass?" I ask.

"Fine."

"Grace?"

"Fine. She's with her mom." He steps away from the door, letting me in, and then shouts toward the bedroom. "Grace! Come here for a minute."

Grace comes down. "What is it, Uncle Ben?"

As I pass him by, Ben whispers, "Go and talk to my sister." He then takes Grace's hand and says to her, "I want to show you something. Come on."

The door to my bedroom is ajar. My heart runs like a jet engine; I can't even trace its beats.

"Cass." I knock. "Can I come in?"

She scoots herself to sit at the edge of the bed. Her 'yeah' is barely audible.

I settle myself next to her as she tidies her hair.

"Leave it like that," I murmur, catching her hand. "I like it messy."

She tosses me a shy smile, then places her hands on her lap. "Did they really catch him? Seth?"

"Yeah. He's in custody."

"Good. Good." Her head wags back and forth. "How about my dickhead ex? Anything on him? Ben has been itching to go all out to find him, like an agitated hound dog." Her attention switches to Maximus, who's sleeping soundly at her feet.

But the mutt was in bed earlier, I know—his fur is everywhere!

"No chance of that dog tracking Harvey."

She chuckles. "I guess not."

"We'll find your ex. At least we'll make sure he won't bother you again, whatever he's up to with those numbers."

"I'll deal with him later," she murmurs.

Our breathing reverberates through the four walls as we let the silence linger. At the same time, I can feel nervousness crawling—hers and mine.

"Sam, I saw what's in there," Cass confesses, pointing at the box where I put some of my research on Jack.

"It's okay." I sense her guilt. "Whatever happened or happens in my life, you have the right to know."

"I saw the sketch."

"A forensic artist drew it about five years ago. Jack looks so much like Mom in that sketch. He's twenty-nine now. If he did look like that when he was twenty-four, I'm sure he hasn't changed that much today."

"You've scoured almost half of the country."

"That's just one of many piles of stuff." I stare at the box. "The rest is inside the Red Mark office."

Cass nods her head. "I'm sorry, Sam." Then she tips her head in the direction of my phone. "I saw that message the other night at the hospital. I know that look on your face. Did you hear anything about Jack?"

"It's not important."

"Well, it is."

"You're right, it is, but that's for another day." I turn to face her. "I'm not here to talk about Jack or any kind of assignments. I'm here to talk about us."

I nudge my palm closer to hers, touching her little finger.

She shifts her hand toward me, wrapping it around my four fingers.

"And firstly, to apologize," I add.

"It's o—"

"No, it's not okay. I'm so sorry about what I said this morning. I know it wasn't a joke to you. I know about your father, Cass."

Her lids close, letting out a few tear drops. "You didn't know, and I overreacted."

I shift my hand so it rests on top of hers. "No, you didn't."

She gulps, straightening herself.

"I don't want you to die, Sam," she confesses. "I know it's stupid because, as you said, everybody dies. But you… I can't…"

Lines form on her face as she suppresses whatever she's feeling inside. Then she sighs deeply as if letting her guilt and regret out into the open.

"Look, Cass. I'm capable, I'm highly trained, and I'm careful. You've got to have faith in me. I'll do everything in my power to come home to you safe."

She nods. "I don't want you to die like my father."

"Come here," I murmur, offering my shoulder while keeping my hand steady—no force—I want her to come to me on her own accord.

She slants her face, smiling tentatively. Her fingers shake under my palm.

"Let it out, Cass."

"Ah…" She chokes back a sobbing cough as her shoulders heave up and down.

Her lips tremble as she keeps fending off whatever is attacking her from within.

Then she collapses onto my shoulder, howling and weeping.

Like she's letting go of a mighty weight, she helplessly slinks down onto my lap. I've never seen her so fragile. That's how strong she is.

"Let it all out, sweetheart." I stroke her back, kissing her nape while she's holding my hand so tight I almost shake with her.

It breaks my heart to see her like this, but I'm glad she's falling apart—with me.

"I watched the whole thing, Sam," she says shakily. "There was a video..."

From the heaviness in her voice, I sense that she watched it shortly after the news about her father's death came to light. She was only a kid. God. Fourteen—she was only fourteen.

But how? Philip Winter's death was classified. No mainstream media broadcasted it, and back then, it was impossible for such a clip to make its way through social media. She must've obtained it from a secret source.

"I'm so sorry, Cass."

"He looked so calm, somehow. I thought the video would show that he escaped. He had escaped before, you know. He was a wanted sniper. The insurgent group had put a high price on his head." She draws a sharp breath. Then, perhaps realizing she might've been lying on my wound, she lifts her head.

"Keep lying there." I soak in her words as much as her tears.

Her head is soon back on my lap. "You probably don't want to hear it anyway. Aren't you here to talk about the 'L' word?"

"We are talking about it."

Cass pulls herself up, inhaling. "I wasn't supposed to see it." She gulps as she shakes her head. "I was in eighth-grade then, borrowing Mom's laptop to complete my biology assignment. At the time family friends were visiting, I remember the flowers they brought—they had a distinct smell."

Cass holds her breath and wipes her tears. "We buried Dad the week before, and Mother had shielded Ben and me from the whole thing. We just knew that Dad died in an ambush in Basra."

Her head flings back, squeezing her eyes shut, perhaps wishing something from up above—or maybe wishing she hadn't done what she did next.

Slowly she leans back, seeking my shoulder. I encircle my hand around her waist, guiding her to find me.

She continues, "I found a video on that laptop like it was calling for me. It was titled 'Philip.' I opened it and played it."

So it was Alice who first discovered the clip.

"I watched it until the end. I waited and waited, believing there would be something else—a miracle that somehow it was just a stunt. But there was nothing. And I could only smell the jasmine scent coming from the living room that our family friends had left that night. That's why I hate flowers, Sam. White flowers, especially jasmine."

Cass stares into the air, but her hold on me doesn't relent, as if she's clinging so she doesn't get sucked into the past.

In my thirty-four years of existence, I've seen evil and other appalling acts that no one else should see in their life-time. Yet, hearing her harrowing account, I can't fathom how she could ever go through it. Nothing that I do will ever heal her. For now, I try to comfort her the best I can—telling her that she's not alone.

"The next day, I overheard my mother telling my grandma that those murderers had tossed Dad's head into a stream. They hated him that much."

My God! They found out about that too?

"I hadn't slept in days, and sleeping pills had started to turn me into a zombie. One night, while the storm was raging, I went to the river—the Black Crow River, not far from our house. When he was home, Dad and I went there almost every week. But instead of solace, I saw this figure draped over a rock. Not alive, and not dead either. The head is missing, but I can hear his voice. It was my dad taking his last breath."

She exhales—deep, really deep, as if she hadn't been breathing all this time.

"Sam..." she sighs, completely letting herself fall on me.

"Yes, Cass?"

"I've never told anyone else about my nightmare," she reveals. "Something I'd wanted to do for a long time but never felt okay."

I place my chin on her shoulder, cheek to cheek, telling her silently that I'm here for her no matter what.

"You know, Sam. It's killing me that my way of remembering my dad is that friggin' nightmare. I even called that figure 'it' to separate the horror from my memory of him. But it hasn't worked. It, he, him, Philip, Dad—they always end up merging into that headless figure."

"It might take time, but it doesn't have to be that way."

"He was a good man. He was my best friend. It's a terrible way to remember him." Her tears return, and she doesn't even try to hold them back this time.

Cass knows full well that my relationship with my father is coated with hatred and blame. I hold him responsible for Jack's disappearance, and I haven't made peace with it. Cass had a great dad, and I don't want her to lose it.

"We have our way of grieving. And because you've been alone in this, that's why it's doubly hard. I'm here for you, Cass. We can share the load, just like what you've done for me."

"Sam..."

It's a different call, albeit familiar. It's her fear talking.

"What is it, sweetheart?"

"I've been having nightmares about you too. There, I receive news that you died on duty. And at the hospital, I dreamed that you were shot dead by Ambrose Seth. It felt so real, Sam."

She looks me in the eyes as if I was in her dream at the moment. But I'm awake and ready for her.

"The possibility of me getting hurt or being killed—it's real, Cass. I won't shy away from that. If you want to be with me, that will be the reality."

"I don't want you to stop doing what you're doing because of me. Yet, every time you go, it terrifies me. Now you know why I dread it so much." She tenses up once again. "We never saw Dad's body. It was probably no more than stitched-up limbs and torso. I don't want you to end up like him."

"Oh, Cass," I pull her into a hug. "We will leave each other eventually, well, physically anyway, as everyone does. But do you know what love is?"

Her eyes glisten. She gazes down low, avoiding me. I tip her chin up. She gulps as if daring herself to look into my eyes.

"Love is to know that your partner is always there with you, no matter where, on this earth or in heaven. Love is beyond life itself, I believe."

"That hurts, Sam."

It's not the response I was anticipating, but I have to accept it.

"Sam, my mother loved my dad. So much. His death devastated her even though she knew he was still with her. And she's as sturdy as a woman can be. We're humans. We're not cut out for coping with that kind of grief."

"Okay, that may hurt. But I can also say that your mother had her own way of grieving. And you know what? You're stronger than her, Cass. Because aren't children supposed to be stronger than their parents? And in time, Grace will be stronger than you if she hasn't gotten there already."

As if the sun has just risen, I see the joy on her face. "You've just given me the answer to why I fell for you. I've sworn not to fall in love with a military man or anyone who has the possibility of dying in battle. But you're not just another man."

"No, I'm not. And you're not just another woman," I remind her. "Remember the pill to forget?"

She nods.

"I'm glad you never took it. Call me selfish, but what you've done for me, Cass, the way you handle *my* hurt—with what I've seen out there, the monsters that I'm up against—with such care, consideration, and love that can only come from the deepest place." I press my hand on her heart. "Because you've lived the terror, you love in a way that is impossible for others to do."

"I never thought about my nightmares that way."

She sniffles her last remaining tears. I point at my shoulder, giving her permission to use my shirt as her handkerchief.

"You've been amazing to me, Cassidy Winter. If it's not you, I don't want anybody else."

"It goes both ways, Sam."

"I promise I'll be honest with you during my assignments."

Articulating it makes me realize that I never call her when I'm away and sometimes keep her waiting even after I come home with no contact at all. Not that I don't want to talk to her or be with her—hell, I need her, period—but at times, I keep things to myself, not wanting to make her my emotional dumping ground.

"I'll tell you whatever I can share, Cass. You know I have to keep certain things to myself, though. But I promise I won't keep you in the dark."

"That's all I ask. The dark is the worst place to be."

Her lips part, and I kiss her before she can say anything else. I don't care if she never says she loves me—because I *know* she does.

A smile forms on her face as we break the kiss. "Samuel Kelleher... even your lips feel amazing despite the darkness."

"My lips feel the most amazing *when* the worst of times come," I quip.

Her face shines. "Being philosophical, are we?"

"Let's just focus on me being a great kisser."

With that, we kiss again. But this time, I withdraw shortly after because I long to see her face. Her cheeks look rosier, complimenting her sharp blue eyes that are just starting to soften—Cass at her best, when she opens herself up unconditionally.

"I'll never keep you in the dark again," I affirm my promise.

"That means a lot, Sam."

"We can make it work. The two of us."

Her gaze bolts to me—her no-sitting-on-the-fence gaze. "Yes, we can."

I admire her belief. The long road that I've traveled to get to this point convinces me that I've earned her love.

"I can't imagine living without you, Sam. The way you hold me—like this, like now—it's like nothing else, even better than a Christmas blanket." She rubs the top of my palm, drawing little circles with her finger. "We'll make us happen. I love this house."

"You do?"

"Yes. You've picked a great one."

"I'm glad."

"I want you, me, and Grace in it."

"You serious?"

"Yes." She smiles sweetly. Sweet isn't my type, but that smile is a treat I need right now—not that I'll ever get over her impatience and stubbornness.

"Max, too, by the way," she adds.

Oh yeah. That dog has proven that his love goes beyond his antics. He seems to be calmer when the girls are around him. Like man, like dog... I guess.

"The Woodhouse is yours, Cass. Ours."

She nods, beaming from ear to ear. "But please give me time," she says. "With what happened between Harvey and me, I've been moving Grace from city to city. Our current house is the only stable place she knows right now."

"I understand."

"Grace loves her books. They're her happy place. You should see the shelves in her bedroom." Cass chuckles. "And there are more in the storage."

"I've got plenty of space for her." If the girl needs a library, I'll put one in my house. "So, while you're getting ready—take your time, no pressure, okay—I'll start thinking about putting in that drinking pool for our future horses," I banter.

"You don't ride, though?"

"In time, I'll give it a shot. As long as you can guarantee that I won't kill the horse." I wink.

She suppresses a chuckle. She knows I'm not a small man. Riding clumsily may mean something more than being thrown off the horse.

By now, Cass is completely leaning on me. She turns her head, and our lips find each other again. I swear I feel her strength, the strength that she doesn't even know she possesses.

As we run out of air after the long kiss, we close our eyes, serenely listening to our heartbeats.

"So this is what it feels like to be loved?" she murmurs.

"Only you can answer that."

"I believe so," she sighs, tilting her head to look at me. She reaches out her hand to caress my cheek. "So this is what it feels like to be comforted?"

"Maybe."

"To be protected, to be unbroken?"

"I just love you, that's all."

"I love you too, Sam."

She doesn't have to tell me, but I admit hearing it out loud takes me to a place where I'm contented, believing that I can do anything. My hands move up to cup her breasts while I keep kissing the back of her neck.

How the hell we manage to stay clothed, I don't know.

Well, because this *is* love. The holy grail that I never thought would be mine in this lifetime. After so many failed attempts, after all, I am one of the lucky ones who found it.

23

———

CASSIDY

To feel safe with a man is one thing. Letting myself fall apart and still feeling safe shows that Mr. Gray Diamond isn't just about physical protection and a male presence.

Sam is a man forged in fire whom nothing can bend. He's like a scaffolding that keeps me standing when I start to crumble. And when I'm strong, he lets me shine, retreating like a foundation underground—out of view but mighty.

I might've failed with Harvey. I denied love because of what he did. I thought I'd played it by the book, insisting on surviving alone. Now, I owe it to Grace. I'll make sure I do everything in my power to keep love alive between me and my man.

Actually, I owe him. And myself, for that matter.

My aversion to military men was a blind oath, born out of fear and grown off my naiveness. But you live to learn.

The terror that stemmed from my father's gruesome death has shaped me to be who I am. Dare I say, life made me go through it because I was made for Sam.

The manifestation of that terror is ghastly, but to have come out on the other side like this, I know I've made my dad proud. My strength and tenacity weren't just handed over to me, my parents taught me, and circumstances tested me.

Nightmares are what you make them. They're the worst and the best I've experienced—because they have equipped me to be Sam's strength when reality becomes too much for him.

I still have a lot to learn. Many more of Sam's assignments will no doubt test my resolve. But with how much he's done for me, I know I'll come through for him. To falter is almost a betrayal.

With Ambrose Seth behind bars awaiting trial, Grace and I move back into our house despite Sam's reluctance. But true to his words, he never twisted my arm to make me stay.

My dickhead ex is still somewhere in the universe, but Grace has got to have some normalcy back into her life—school, chores, routine. The best lead that Ben has for Harvey is that he's escaped to Jamaica. With three men and a German shepherd circling around us, we feel more than safe.

"Sam..." I moan out my satedness.

What's better than sleeping in my own bed? Waking up in it with my man beside me. Technically, not beside me, but spooning me and rubbing his chest against my back. I'm still panting, trying to bring myself back to earth after he gave me one this morning—a big one.

Sam breathes behind me, spreading warm vapor on my neck. I push my back against him, not wanting any part of me not to touch him, not to be drenched by his sweat.

"Good morning, by the way," Sam growls in his sexy pillow voice.

The best morning with him so far.

"How did you sleep?" he asks, his crotch brushing against my ass.

He's still stone hard.

"Do I even have to answer that?"

He releases a breathy moan—coarse and masculine, tickling my senses. His shoulders shrug, while at the same time he moves to wrap my arm. "You didn't have your nightmare?"

"No. I haven't had it in a while."

Maybe because I've talked about it, maybe because of Sam's close presence. Whatever it is, it's because of *him*.

The floor creaks. I'm sure Grace is getting up.

"No, no, stay, please," Sam begs, tightening his grip around my chest when I wriggle out of the comforter. My still sensitive nipples are almost unable to handle the contact.

"Did you lock the door?" I ask.

"I think so."

"You think so?"

"I did, Cass," he hums as he kisses my spine, vertebrae by vertebrae.

"Jesus, Sam..."

He rolls on top of me, the sheet barely covering his ass cheeks. "You don't mind me on top now?" he asks, his rip trunk hovering over my belly.

This morning I was humping him like a cowgirl at a rodeo, so I had my share of being on top. "Whatever you need to please me."

Even if he eats me alive, I'll be up for it.

Sam lowers himself, awarding me with an abundant amount of kisses in the process. His broad torso engulfs me; his hard muscles castle me in. This is what mornings are made for.

"Mooom!"

Or... maybe not.

We both sighs and then laughs.

"I'll make breakfast," Sam murmurs, still kissing me.

I stretch happily. Yet another morning where we make love, and I don't hear that he has to go.

24

———

SAM

I'm making bacon and scrambled eggs for my two favorite people—my fallen angel and her mini-me. I might be getting ahead of myself, but this already feels like we're family. It helps that in the past week, we've had the house to ourselves. Alice and Ben are back in Kalispell, finalizing the sale of their family home as they plan to move to Helena permanently.

I can still feel Cass's curves lining my body—her smooth skin, her flesh, her heat. How did I ever wake up in the morning without her?

After serving everyone their breakfast, I drop my apron and join them at the table.

"The other day, we talked about eye colors at school," Grace says, munching her hashbrowns. "Sam, what's my eye color?"

She tries not to blink as I examine her gorgeous eyes.

"Blue," I reply.

"Correct," the girl grins.

"What's mine?" I ask, presenting my eyes to her.

Grace squints like a doctor checking on a patient. "Umm... it's not blue. It's not brown." She then turns to Cass, seeking help. But for some reason, her mother blushes, trying to hide her smile. "What's Sam's eye color, Mom?"

"Gray diamond," Cass answers confidently.

I hold my gaze while Grace knits her brows.

"That's fancy and—precise," I comment.

"I never heard of that eye color," Grace ponders. "Sam, what's Mom's eye color?"

I mimic the way Cass talked about mine, "Cornflower blue."

Cass raises her eyes. "That is very precise."

"You guys are weird," complains Grace as she continues her meal.

I look at my watch and excuse myself. "I'll be back!" I then head upstairs two steps at a time.

Cass didn't notice I'd hung out one of my best suits in her wardrobe. It's still inside a garment bag, and I haven't found a suitable occasion to wear it—until today.

Feeling like reliving my days as a bodyguard, I start my routine.

When I was on duty, I had to be ready in ten minutes or less, wherever I was. Plans, events, and situations changed, often without notice. And when your clients were billionaires, getting ready means *getting ready*, impeccability included— hair, face, suit, shoes, and gun.

Today though, it's all of those minus the gun.

Ten minutes fifty seconds.

Damn, I'm slow!

Whistling the tune of *I Will Always Love You*, I join the gang back downstairs. Both Cass and Grace drop their knives and forks, watching my every move.

"Who wants more bacon?" I offer the plate around.

"Whoa! Gimme that greasy thing," Cass takes over the

plate quickly, putting it in the middle of the table. "You're not going to ruin that suit."

I smirk, lapping up the attention. She's seen me in a suit before, but this is the first time I have opted for a structured style—complete with a crisp white shirt and a silver silk tie.

"Come on, Grace, finish your breakfast. We're leaving soon." Cass stops her from staring.

"Where are you going?" Grace asks.

"Driving you to school," I answer.

The little girl stops chewing her eggs, and pieces fall back onto her plate. That statement, too, freezes Cass as she hovers the hot water jug over the coffee plunger.

"Really?" Grace says.

"Yeah."

"How about Mom?"

"I'm taking her, too."

A grin parts Cass's lips as she studies me from head to toe, the jug still firmly in her hand. Just like the hot water pouring into the plunger, the stare from her cornflower blue eyes steams up the room.

"Don't spill it," I quip. She may be admiring my look, but I think I've just pushed her button—hard. She has a few weaknesses when it comes to me. Now I know another weakness of hers. God, look at her! The lady just can't wait to have me again.

As the clock dings at a quarter to eight, the suit effect wanes, taken over by the urgency of daily life. I help Grace with her school bag while Cass rushes back upstairs to get her laptop.

"Are you going to rescue someone?" Grace further questions my choice of clothes.

"No. I have a meeting."

"Oh, okay." She watches me zip up her backpack. "Is it hard to rescue people?"

"Yeah, it can be hard. But I've got Mark. He's my partner, and he's really good at taking the bad guys out. We watch each other's back."

"So you look at each other all the time?"

I chuckle. "It's an expression. When you and someone watch each other's back, it means you take care of each other, making sure you and the other person are safe."

"Oh. Like Mom and Uncle Ben? They watch each other's back?"

"Yeah. Like that," I say, handing over her school bag. I then stoop to help her tie her shoelaces.

"Sam, what should I tell my friends? They'll ask if you're my dad when they see you."

Saying that I'm Grace's friend is lame. I'm much more than that, and I want others to know. "Just say we're still working on it. Or if you want, tell them I'm your bodyguard."

"Okay."

"Ready?" Cass juggles two bags in her hands.

"We were ready ages ago," I jokingly jeer. "Come on, munchkin."

Grace hops into my car. I can see that she's thinking. "Lisa calls me munchkin. What does it mean?"

"It means 'child.' Why is that?" I observe her face. "You don't like it?"

She shrugs. "Hmm... maybe not."

"You're right. That nickname doesn't suit you," I acknowledge, searching for an alternative. "Hey, are you good in the water?'

"Yes!" She smiles proudly.

"How about a SEAL Pup?"

I don't know if Cass has told her about me being in the Navy. Either way, Grace probably wouldn't understand what I truly mean. But she welcomes her new nickname with enthusiasm.

If she ever becomes my daughter, I'll teach her all I know about being in the water, the SEAL way.

"Alright, SEAL Pup," I call. A different kind of protective instinct kicks in as I make sure Grace is secure in her child seat. The girl is under my care now—I'm truly part of the Winters family. "You're all strapped up?"

"Uh-huh. Let's go, Sam Kelleher!" she says my full name fluently.

Hearing that, Cass reaches out her hand. She places it on my cheek, nudging me to look at her as if I wouldn't. We simultaneously move toward each other, meeting in the middle, and our lips touch.

"Mom! That's gross!"

Cass's pucker stretches into a shy grin.

I'm no stranger to schools and playgrounds, but this is the first time I have visited a primary school as Sam, a man, and not a Red Mark.

There's no child to be rescued, no investigation to be had. Being ordinary has never been so appealing. The newly-found fatherly instincts overwhelm me to the point that I have to restrain myself from getting down on my knee and asking Cass when we're out of the car.

A lot of eyes are on me as if reminding me that I am still a stranger here—that I'm not quite a father yet.

"You're too handsome to be around those deprived single mothers." Cass seems to notice.

"You were one of them. Just remember that."

She pinches my arm.

Meanwhile, a boy comes to us and greets Grace.

"Hi, Oliver," Grace greets him back. I think they're good

friends with each other. "Meet Sam Kelleher." She introduces me as if I'm a superstar.

"Hi, sir." The boy named Oliver tips his head up to look at me. Then he quickly turns to Grace. "Your new dad?"

"Um... we're still working on it," Grace responds.

Cass gapes, looking at me and asking for accountability. I simply shrug.

"Well, he's actually my bodyguard," Grace adds.

This time Cass and I let out a silent laugh, unable to hide our amusement.

"Cool." Oliver looks up at me. He then disappears into the classroom.

"Hey, you know what?" I say. "While I'm looking dapper..." I pull Grace and Cass into my arms. Then, as awkward as my stretch is, thanks to the rigid suit, I take a photo of us.

The three of us.

A picture of happiness I'd never envisioned before they came into my life.

"Nice one, Sam!" Grace beams at seeing the photo. Her voice affirms that this isn't a dream. "Bye, Mom. Bye, Sam."

Cass waves at her.

"You okay?" I say, noticing her grimacing.

"Why do I feel that it's her first day at school?"

I wink at her, hinting that it's because of me. The corners of her lips quirk into a smile

If I can keep her smiling like that, I know I'm doing it right.

The Thirsty Fox is only ten minutes away. It's not opening time yet, but Cass usually arrives early.

"Have a good day." I kiss her.

She licks her lips while running her finger along my suit lapel, then the tie. "The silver suits you, Mr. Gray Diamond," she moans as if we were about to take our clothes off.

"Huh..."

She then plays with the knot of my tie.

"Don't tempt me, sweetheart. Our investors are waiting."

"Next time." She smooths my collars. "Get that money then."

"I will," I say as she pushes the car door open, swinging her impossibly sexy legs out. "They won't be able to resist me."

Cass rounds the car and then leans into the driver-side window. "What did you say?"

"They won't be able to resist me." I play with her indignation. She knows both my investors are women.

She yanks my tie right under the knot, tugging me to her. Without restraints, she smears her pink lipstick on my mouth as she kisses me as if marking her territory.

Then I hear someone clearing her throat—Lisa.

Slowly Cass's fingers unfurl, and she lets me go, but not before pinching my heart one more time with her sexed-up look. And that smell at the crown of her head—Jesus, I'm hard.

Lisa stares at us like we're a movie. "So, you two are official now?"

"If a kiss at a workplace is considered official, then yes," I quip.

I smirk as the ladies are letting themselves in. Lisa asks about my suit, thinking Cass has got something to do with my makeover. Since I moved to Montana, I've toned down my look. They have no idea how I dressed when I was in New York. Hugo Boss and Armani on Fifth Avenue knew me by name.

Here, though, as long as Cass and Grace keep me in their minds, I don't need anyone else to make me their VIP.

25

SAM

Plans to upgrade Red Mark headquarters and team expansion were approved the day following the investor meeting. We started by acquiring the current premises, which we used to lease, and adding two new floors, which will include a state-of-the-art command center.

Entering our third year of operation, Red Mark has come a long way since our first assignment. We started out by providing security services to diplomats and prominent figures, carrying on from what we did best in New York. Our first client was none other than Ivy Cavanagh (then Forbes, her married name). Mark and I became the attorney general's security when she traveled to Canada amid tension between mining workers and environmental activists.

Work trickled for most of our first year, then steady, and then—a change.

Not long before I met Cass, a desperate abduction case called on us. Ivy once again became a target, but this time it was her son who was in peril. Snatched in the middle of the night from his bedroom. Professionals don't take work personally, but with a case so close to home like that, drawing a line between head and heart was almost impossible. I was prepared to die for the safe return of the boy.

Seeing the boy back in his mother's arms, there was immense satisfaction and pride that I hadn't felt before.

And it wasn't just me. At that point, Mark and I knew it was our calling to reunite families torn apart by missing loved ones.

In a way, my job compensates for the loss that I haven't made up for—and that's how it's going to be until I find Jack. But knowing that the 'compensation' has led me to do others good, I'm okay with it. Actually, it's more than okay. Especially with Cass and Grace by my side, what's ahead will always be beautiful, even though the grim reality of life will no doubt take a swipe at me again sooner or later.

With the start of the headquarters upgrade, I've been dividing my time between Cass's and my own home.

The news of the funding had Cass beaming—particularly that we are starting to recruit more frontline personnel. Today, I'm back at her place. It's her day off, and she's not expecting me.

Grace opens the door. "Sam!" She leaps, and I catch her mid-jump.

"Hey, pup!" I greet my SEAL girl as I carry her on my hip. "What're you up to?"

"Building a zoo." She points at her animal toys scattered around the back porch.

"Where's your mom?"

"In the shed." Grace tips her head in the direction of the outbuilding Cass calls the 'Pour Me Up, Scotty.' She experiments with ale recipes there before taking the successful ones to her brewery.

"She's making drinks, is she?" I'm stating the obvious, but I'm looking for Grace's reaction, being left to her own devices.

"No. She's planting flowers."

Before I can take in the bizarre answer, I hear Cass.

"Grace!"

She looks very country in her floral summer dress. As soon as she realizes her daughter is with me, she runs to me like I was a prize she'd got to win.

"Sam!" Surprise, joy, and ambivalence emerge on her beautiful face. "Is everything okay? I thought you were supposed to be—"

I shut her up with a kiss.

"Not again!" Grace complains as she leaves us in the living room, going back to her toys.

I was supposed to go with Mark for a joined exercise with the police in Helena Forest, but Mark was more than willing to handle it by himself. Probably because Ivy Cavanagh has been rumored to come and check the proceedings. The last thing my partner wanted was for me to give him an earful about taking a plunge with her.

"This is a surprise..." She appraises my man-in-black ensemble suspiciously. "Did you have another investor meeting?"

"Maybe."

"Hmm..." She trails a finger around the knot of my tie. "You know, the approval for Red Mark funding has nothing to do with your persuasion."

"How's that so?"

"Your suit sealed the deal." While my tie is in her grip, she gives me a narrow gaze, reminding me that she hasn't forgotten about the women who agreed to invest in Red Mark.

"Jealous, are we?" I smile at the discovery—she's not the type who's willing to share.

Our investors are businesspeople who have ridden the ups and downs of the cut-throat shipping and oil industries since they were teenagers. With certainty, I can say none of them would let a man's look nor his clothes influence their decision-making. Besides, the ladies are both happily married.

I tip her chin up, look her in the eye and say, "You have nothing to worry about."

"So why the suit today?"

"I want you to invest in me."

"Damn you, Samuel Kelleher," she growls. Then she stretches to see what Grace is up to outside. The girl is in her own world, filling a plastic box with water and tossing a couple of seals in it. "I've invested in you since the day I found out about your existence," she huffs, grinding her pelvis on mine.

"Howdy!" the voice of Ben Winter suddenly blares through the open door. Then he gapes. "Oh, gee... am I interrupting something?"

Cass grunts loudly—not caring that Ben hears her. My day is getting better!

With a smile, I tell her I'm enjoying her frustration.

Not for long, though. She gathers herself, stands tall, and asks her brother calmly, "So, everything okay with the sale?"

"Yup. The money is in the bank," Ben says. I swear he shoots me a satisfied look, perhaps for catching me red-handed and stopping me from fucking his sister—or stopping his sister from fucking me.

I give him a cheerful look, convincing him he's not interrupting anything. I'll have Cass today, sooner or later.

"Where's Mom?" Cass asks.

"She decided to stay with Giordano for another week."

"I guess she needs an extra hug for losing that house."

With her father in the military, I know Cass's family moved a lot. But she told me that the Kalispell house was their last home as a family before Philip Winter was killed, and it was her mother's favorite.

"She's okay," assures Ben. "She knew it was time."

"Uncle Ben!" Grace zooms into the room.

"There she is!" Ben exclaims, hugging his niece.

"Come with me. I need trees for the monkeys!" Grace pulls Ben's arm.

"Okay, okay!" Ben follows her impatient strides.

Cass stares at me once we're alone. She grumbles to herself.

"The moment's gone?" I tease her.

She coos and lets herself fall onto me. Then she gazes out to the backyard. "Hey, let's go into the shed."

Noticing where Cass and I are heading, Ben says to his sister, "Hey, how's the new recipe going?"

"She's planting flowers," Grace answers on her mom's behalf.

Ben guffaws like I've never seen him before. "Planting flowers?"

"Shoosh!" Cass hauls me to walk faster.

Inside the shed, I see three small planters filled with soil.

"So Grace wasn't kidding," I say, inspecting an unopened box of rose seeds.

She blushes. "I was trying to find one that looks like the roses you gave me when I was at the hospital."

It surprises me that those flowers made an impression on her. "You have your backyard. Out of anywhere, you're trying to plant those flowers here?"

"Well, if I fail, I don't want anyone else to see. Besides, it's pretty sunny by the window, and they'll bloom. Right?"

I stand behind her as she opens the pack of seeds, snaking my arms forward to align with hers.

"Let me help you." I slip my hands under hers, moving

them like she's my puppet. I get her palms to scoop up a few seeds. "Put two or three inside each pot, sweetheart."

"Okay..." she sighs as I lightly control her moves.

"Now cover them with soil." I'm still holding on to her hands, guiding her to get the right thickness. We even out the surface on each pot while I reward her with small caresses on her fingers.

"It's so easy when you're here," she confides.

"Now, you need to moist the soil," I murmur in her ear. "I mean with water, not ale." She giggles as I watch her pour water from a can. "That's it. We're done."

After washing her hands, Cass inspects the cuffs of my shirt and flicks some soil.

"I'm free today," I hum. "You can have me however you want."

Before Cass can unleash her fervor, two faces emerge from behind the window. "Boo!" Ben and Grace say simultaneously.

"Guys!" Cass rolls her eyes. She opens the window as the two mischiefs giggles away.

"Hmm... I smell roses!" Ben banters.

"Go and play!" Cass exclaims.

"Come on, Grace! Mommy and Sam have got things to do," Ben says, dragging Grace away from the shed.

"They're gonna kiss again, aren't they?"

"Likely, yes."

When Mark suggested we recruit him for Red Mark, I didn't know what to make of it. I wonder if my partner would change his mind if he saw the Taekwondo master sitting among Grace's toys—like Tom Hanks in *Big*.

"Why are you looking at my brother like that?" Cass asks.

"Nothing." I appraise her expression. *Damn!* I think the moment's gone again. "He really loves Grace, huh?"

A smile creases her face. "He's a gem, my brother." She pauses, taking the time to watch them.

"He keeps me in check, that's for sure."

"That's what a brother's for," she says. Then another pause, and her eyes seem to gaze further than the porch this time. "He saved me from certain death."

"What do you mean?"

I feel her—her hands have turned cold. Her eyes widen as if she's trying to see in the dark. I spin her around so she's facing me.

"What happened, Cass?"

She takes a deep breath. "I told you, I went to the river in Kalispell and saw that headless figure."

I keep silent, handing the floor completely to her.

"It was a stormy night, and I stood at the wooden bridge, leaning onto the fencing. The figure kept gasping and calling me. The next thing I knew, I was in the water. I couldn't even move. It could be the sleeping pills sapping my strength, or it could be just the currents. But one thing was sure. I was ready to die.

"Ben saved me. I never know exactly how or why he went there. I asked him, and he said he just felt it—that he had to go to the river when he couldn't find me in the house."

Ben Winter may be impish around Grace and easily provoked when it comes to his sister's ex, but Mark's comment about him being a papa gorilla was spot-on. He would've only been thirteen when he saved Cass. Yet, not only his physique but, more importantly, his instincts were phenomenal.

I wish I had that with Jack—I would've found my little brother that night at the carnival. People kept telling me then that I was too young to understand and that there was nothing I could've done. But if Ben Winter could do that with his sister, I surely could've done more for Jack.

"So your brother was strong even as a teenager? It was a feat to drag you out of the water in the middle of the night in a storm."

"Well, I wasn't like this then." She shows off her biceps. "I was stick-thin. But you're right. Ben did miraculously well to have saved me."

She turns around to watch his brother and Grace, who seem to be expanding the zoo beyond the porch on to the grass area.

She pulls me into another corner of the shed. "Well, enough with my fret. We should make the most of your time. I've been experimenting with a couple of new recipes. Would you be my tester?"

"Gladly."

"Here, what do you think?" she pours me a sample into a cup.

I taste it, spreading the liquid across my tongue. "Okay..."

"Not impressed?"

I wrinkle my nose. "The Fallen Angel is still better. This one's too dry."

"Hmm... How about this one?"

I have a sip of the other sample. "Oh yeah. This one's good!"

I end up gulping the whole thing, but my mind isn't on the drink anymore. I'm not here to have a good time this way in the 'Pour Me Up, Scotty' shed. The moment might've been gone, but I know it'll only take a small flame to light up Cass. "Stay here."

I jump across the shed to close the window blinds and lock the door.

"Sam?"

I return to Cass, showing my true intention by taking off my jacket and loosening my tie.

"Where were we?" I take over her cup, filling it up. She's about to take it, but I swing my arm wide, bringing the cup out of her reach. "Let me."

I grab her by the waist, securing her like she's my prisoner. I slowly serve the drink to her. As her luscious lips touch the brim, I tip the cup, pouring ale all over her chest.

"Oops…" I murmur, my finger tailing the traveling amber liquid from her mouth down to her neck. I then seal her lips, making my way down, licking her ale-laden cleavage.

She sighs hopelessly.

I lift her up so she sits at the edge of the bench.

"The rose seeds will be okay, right?" She points with her chin at the shut blinds.

"A few minutes without the sun wouldn't kill them."

"Only a few minutes?" Her seductive eyes shoot at me as she unzips my pants.

I push myself in between her legs. Thank goodness for her dress, allowing me to slip her panties down with ease.

"How long would you like me, sweetheart?"

I bow down so I can kiss her thighs, then land my tongue on her slit, letting her answer my question with sighs and moans—no doubt saying, 'as long as you give me.'

She shudders, throwing her head back like she'd been tickled with a hundred feathers. I keep lapping her wetness and the scent of her blooming rose.

"Sam, I want you too! Fuck, I want you!" She gets up, panting like the sky is about to fall and she's running out of time.

After stripping herself naked, she charges at me, pushing me to the ground.

"Easy tiger," I warn her as her eagerness unfolds. Although I must say, I enjoy it, especially from this angle as I lie on my back. After all, I'll always give myself to her the way she wants me.

She yanks my boxer shorts down, and her lips pinch. Then she lies on top of me, facing my crotch, her knees on each side of my shoulder. Her open clit immediately flicks my switch—I waste no time in relishing that bud.

Meanwhile, my fallen angel leans down, moving her face to my cock. Her mouth is like a warm cave that shelters you after a long hike.

I let out a sigh.

Soon her mouth tightens around my shaft. Her nibbles become ferocious, perhaps a side effect of me pleasing her. Jesus... this is how I like to be blown—how every man would like to be—but I'm not going to last if she doesn't stop.

"Cass..." I groan as she sucks her way up to my tip.

My shuddering hips prompt her to ease her speed.

"Jesus..." I moan, relishing the steadiness of her action.

Now I can enjoy her while I'm pleasing her.

I part her pussy. Her clit has swollen even more, gleaming in her own juice. But against my overeager tongue, somehow, it feels tender. I've got to have more, so I bury my face in her.

She tastes sweet—very sweet. Yet she's intoxicating—just like the ales she brews.

"God... sweetheart!" I moan as Cass makes a sudden move. Her tongue slides under my length while the tip is squeezed relentlessly. Fuck, how can I be this sensitive?

Cass sits up.

Well timed, as I have to call it, or I'll spurt my cum all over her face.

"I want to come inside you. Please," I sigh.

Panting, she carefully lifts her leg and rolls herself to one side before climbing back on me, facing me this time. She grabs my shirt.

"Wait! Wait—not this one." I stop her and take it off myself. I love this shirt, and I don't want it to be a casualty of her impatience today.

She growls out her frustration, but soon it turns into a growl at my pecs.

"I don't keep condoms here," she huffs, which I chuckle at.

"Don't worry," I say. "I'm okay without. You?"

The tops of her cheeks crease as she smiles. "I'm okay too."

If she got pregnant because of today, I'd be the first to smile and kiss her. I'm ready for whatever life wants me to be. As long as she's with me.

"Damn, you're hard!" she growls, so wild. But I should know Cass—that woman has an appetite.

I'm so turned on, my erection begs for more friction and force. And Cass knows. She swathes my hungry manhood, taking me in deeper.

"I'm close," I say. It's not very often that I peak before her.

She flashes a smirk. "I'm ready for you."

Cass bends forward to kiss me with her breasts squashed between my chest and herself. She spreads fire on my already burning lips, and then she clenches her core.

I writhe in pleasure, and right then, I release.

She presses her slit right up to the base of my shaft, gasping. Finally she collapses in completion.

I hold her as we're both huffing. "Lie here," I say, laying my jacket on the concrete floor. "And put your head here." I tap the shoulder pads.

She takes my offer, and I lie sideways, facing her. I play with her curves, running my finger along her smooth skin.

Cass writhes, countering the tickling sensation.

"I wouldn't trade this for the world," I murmur.

"Me neither."

We lie in silence, looking into each other's eyes as if we'd just met.

Gray diamonds and cornflower blue—a perfect combination.

Suddenly we hear Grace's laughter in the distance, followed by Ben guffawing—whatever they're up to.

"Don't you think your brother is too old to be playing plastic zoos with Grace?"

"He is too old, Sam," she admits. "But before you know it, Grace will want to be on her own, doing grown-up stuff. I guess he's trying to make the most of it."

"I mean... how about giving Grace a brother or a sister?"

She nudges herself up, resting her head on her arm. "Sam? Do you mean it?"

"Of course."

She cups my chin and steadies it before giving me a kiss.

"When I married Harvey, I told him I wanted five kids."

"Whoa! Slow down, slow down."

She laughs. "But of course, I stopped dreaming about that when I left him."

"You don't have to stop with me. Well, maybe five is a long way to go... but hey... I won't rule it out."

"I'll talk to Grace about moving into the Woodhouse."

"Seriously?"

"Yeah. The sooner, the better."

I kiss her.

"Cass..."

"Sam?"

"When the time comes for my next assignment, please be honest with me. If you're worried or scared, say it. Don't sugar-coat it."

She takes a deep breath as if it would erase her trepidation. "I'll never stop worrying about you when you're away. That's a fact. But I'm behind you, Sam."

I caress her cheek, thanking her, yet encouraging her to say more because I need to hear it.

And she gets me. "You're good at what you do. You save lives; you reunite families." She puts her hand on her heart and the other on mine. "Being apart from you—is not a barrier. It's an anchor that will tie me to you. I'll keep myself together, I promise. Whatever you do, wherever you go. I'll be waiting for you, with Grace."

Her voice goes straight to my heart. *That* is the love of a woman.

Right from the moment I met her, I knew she had strength, more than mine could ever be. But I never thought that, in return, I would be capable of building genuine courage because of her strength. I can face anything as long as she's behind me.

If life had been ordinary, I wouldn't have met her. Well, I would've met her—being the manager of a downtown bar, I was bound to meet her sooner or later when we relocated Red Mark headquarters to Helena—but not in the manner we crossed paths.

Call it fate, chance, or God's will. I've always known she's the one for me.

I wrap her in my arms. "It means a lot, Cass."

She raises her eyes to mine, and I observe her beautiful face.

Her warmth will never dissipate. It's something I will crave no matter where I am. One day my heart will stop beating, but with her, I'll always be alive.

26

CASSIDY

I recognize that bark, although it sounds like it's coming from a far.

I step out, sauntering along my driveway, looking left and right. When a blue SUV comes into view, I smile. Of course I recognize that bark!

"Sam," I greet the driver, who's looking as sharp as a man on a mission.

"Hey." He slips out of the car, his gun hanging on his waist.

"Are you off? A new assignment?"

"Yes, but not the usual assignment. After all, I can't escape joint training. I've got to head to Helena Forest. It'll be too much for Mark to handle by himself this time—it's a bigger group."

Maximus barks again as he stands on the back seat.

Sam grimaces. "Can you take care of that rascal for a couple of days? He didn't do so well at the kennel."

"Of course." I let the mutt out. "Come, Max, inside."

"See, he listens to you." Sam watches Max calmy walking into my living room. "Grace at school?"

"Yeah."

I peek into Sam's car, noticing a bag where he usually puts his back-up gun and ammunition, and his bulletproof vest lies next to it. He said he'd got a new one as the one he wore in Idaho was damaged.

Sam notices. "They're just for show, well, for this time anyway. Don't look so worried."

Growing up in a military family, I've been around guns since I was a kid, although I only fired one for the first time when I turned eighteen. I'd seen Dad target shooting and sometimes cleaning his weapons. He always made sure firearms in the house were locked away. It was Mother who taught Ben and me how to shoot. Unlike my brother, who has kept it up, I never really took the time to improve my skills. Denzel Seth was proof of how rusty I was and still am. The best I could do was hit his arm, that son of a bitch!

Seeing a gun on Sam doesn't have an effect on me. I know it's training this time, but when he's up against evil, that gun will bring that evil down—if it comes to that. But seeing his bulletproof vest is another matter. It's heavy, and it's ominous.

That vest will be on him, close to his skin, his flesh. It's there to take bullets, bullets that might otherwise penetrate his body—in other words, bullets that might kill him.

Training or not, though, I stand by what I said.

My fear of losing Sam was from me, and for me—and it's no good for anyone.

I've moved past that turmoil when I just wanted to leave him every time he left.

Sam looks at his phone, muttering, "Where the hell is Mark?"

"Why don't you come in?"

"Alright."

As we sit down in the living room, his phone beeps. He

frowns at the screen. "What the..." he mumbles, looking distressed.

I approach him, and he lets me see what's on the screen.

About Jack. Pls open.

"I'm sorry, Sam. We haven't resumed our conversation about Jack. You said you found further lead."

He pauses as if contemplating whether to open the message or not.

"Well, I purposely didn't bring it up," he confesses. "I didn't want to spoil our time together."

He shows me what that message is. It's a photo of a couple of boys standing in front of a run-down house.

"Sorry, Cass. I have to make this call."

Sam presses the number the message is from and then gets up.

"Who's this?" he talks suspiciously. Then he shouts, "How dare you trick me!"

His face has turned crimson. He blinks furiously.

"Well, guess what? You're twenty-two years too late!" He then swiftly hangs up.

"Sam?"

"I'm sorry about that." He slumps into the couch as if the call has zapped all of his energy. "I can't believe my father changed his number just to trick me," he sighs, his head shaking. "He knew I'd blocked his old number."

I stroke his back.

"He kept giving me stupid information—like he was trying to make up for all those lost years. That photo was an old lead. My father thought this boy," he shows me the photo again and points to the boy standing on the left, "was Jack. But I investigated this. He wasn't Jack. He was a boy from Connecticut, and he was safely returned to his family."

"I'm sorry," I murmur, my hand on his shoulder. "I'm sure

he meant well. When I saw him at your party—of course, it was just that one time—I swear, I didn't see a bad streak in him."

He scoffs. "A bad streak is one thing, lack of strength is another. He was weak. He chose not to believe that Jack was alive. I don't know why he starts feeding me with this shit that he thinks is intel." He tosses his phone next to him. "Like I said, he was just trying to make up for lost time. But it's too late."

"It's not too late, Sam."

"I still think of him as my father, Cass. Don't get me wrong. I just haven't forgiven him. And he's not helping." He draws in a frustrated breath. "He dug a grave for Jack, for goodness sake!"

"What are you talking about?"

"Jack was 'supposedly' buried next to Mom. That's how much he wanted to memorialize him."

"Oh, Sam..."

"So every time I go to Mom's grave, it's always there to remind me—the symbol of his weakness." He purses his lips, staring at the coffee table. Then he turns to me. "You're a damn strong woman. I know who you got that from. Philip Winter—now, he was what you'd call *a man*."

His pained look tears me apart. His statement about me and my father may be right, but I don't think this has got anything to do with strength. This is about the love between a father and his family that is tangled in barbwire.

"The lead that I'm pursuing now," he continues. "It's an old photo from a cold case in Georgia."

I can see jumbles of emotions and thoughts shooting at his head from within.

He concedes, "But I'm not sure what to do with it."

"Sam, listen to me," I say. I can't let him leave like this. "For now, you need to put this aside. Focus on kicking those Helena troopers' asses. Show them how it's done."

He chuckles and then takes my hand, kissing the top of my palm.

His phone rings again. This time Mark's name is on the screen.

"Yeah? Okay, I'm on my way," he answers and then quickly ends the call.

He gets up, pulling me with him. "We should wrap things up in three days. I'll call you."

"Okay."

"Get your brother to annoy you while I'm away, won't you? Tell him the deal doesn't expire until I say so."

I'm sure he's reminding me to remind Ben that he should be keeping an eye on me while Sam is away.

"Alright. Now go."

"I love you, sweetheart." A gentle kiss lands on my lips.

Since I left Harvey, becoming the recipient of a man's love had never been on my agenda. Now, my dream man has reaffirmed his love for me. There's nothing else for me to say but, "I love you too, Sam."

I call my brother on my way to pick up Grace from daycare.

"Hey, how's my favorite sister?" Ben greets me.

"Living the good life," I reply, winding down the window to let air in.

"That Frogman still sweeping you off your feet?"

"Always," I gush. "He's my hero. Nothing and no one will change that."

"Huh. Just don't dream of a rose garden," he warns.

"You know I don't dream, Ben. Sam is a great guy—for real."

"Alright, just sayin'!" he drawls.

"It's time you got off his back."

"You're my sister. It's my job to give your boyfriend a hard time."

I chuckle. "Found a place yet?"

"Geez. I didn't think it'd be this hard finding an apartment in Helena."

"You should've stayed at that house Sam arranged for you."

"Now, that's too big even for me. It's like living with ghosts."

Ben is very particular about his living space, and he has way more stuff than me. I don't know how he became like that. I mean, he's not untidy, but he's just not very efficient—and he's dead set on how he keeps and lays things out. I'm sure no Marie Kondo in the world can ever switch his habit.

"I'll sort it out," Ben convinces me.

"Just don't be too picky."

He huffs. "You've seen my gear, right?" Ben says as if reminding me. "Besides, I need space to practice my Taekwondo."

"And irritate your downstair neighbors?" I poke at him as I brake to let a couple of pedestrians cross the street.

"Well, I'm a considerate person, you know. I'm sticking to ground floors, which makes it even harder for me to find somewhere."

"You know you can practice at the Helena martial arts school, right? The one near the Target store?"

"Yeah. But I still need to do it at home—with my own set-up."

"You need to find a house for yourself, brother, not an apartment."

"Maybe. I need to watch my spending, though," he says. Then I hear him pulling up a chair. "Hey, I've been looking into Harvey's whereabouts."

My gut tightens upon hearing the name. "And?"

"He's still in Jamaica. An old banker of his, one that he screwed up, contacted me and confirmed he's been busy setting up accounts there."

"Ben, be careful."

"You know I am. That's why I'm going to go there. No middleman. I've got to find out for myself."

"You're crazy!" My hair stands from another kind of fear.

"Look, this is between him and me, Cass. Ambrose Seth is behind bars. Harvey is running out of allies because he's pissed off too many people," he explains. "I'm not going to do anything to him. I just need to know what he's up to."

"I still don't think it's a good idea. We don't want to wake him up too soon."

"He won't know. No one will know! Right?"

"I'll need to tell Sam."

"Cass, this is between Harvey and me. You haven't forgotten how he treated me, have you?"

I still remember. Ben worked for Harvey for a few years, and he was really pushed to his limits. At the time, I thought it was exactly what my brother needed—a kick in the butt to get him going and fulfill his potential. Now, looking back, it was slavery. I remember Ben lost a lot of weight then.

Ben continues, "But I haven't told you this—" He draws a deep breath. "Because he was still your husband at the time, and I didn't want to ruin your relationship."

"What did he do, Ben?"

"He... um... he told me once that—when you were pregnant with Grace..."

"What did he tell you?" I grit.

"He... he didn't want her."

This time I slam on the brakes, earning a honking and cursing from the driver behind me.

"Hey, you okay?" Ben says.

"Yeah." I pull over and wave an apology to the driver.

"I'm sorry, Cass. I never meant to tell you that."

So Harvey isn't just a scumbag—he's a heartless bastard.

"Well, I'm glad you told me."

All this time—the guilt. I mean, I knew it was the right decision to take Grace away and keep her from knowing her father. But there's a nagging feeling like I had robbed my daughter of what could've been her happiness.

Now, knowing this, I can say with zero guilt—*fuck him!*

"He changed his mind when Grace was born."

"You don't have to soften the blow."

"Well, it's not your fault, Cass. We both know how charming Harv could be. We were both fooled. We didn't find out about his gambling until after Grace was born—he was that sneaky!"

Ben is right.

He adds, "And I wasn't being a good brother to you. I should've killed him the moment I realized who he was."

"Hey, it's not your fault either."

Ben sighs, perhaps not buying it. After seemingly calming himself down, he asks, "Is Sam home? Or is he on an assignment?"

"He's got a training job with the Helena PD. He'll be back in a few days."

"I'll leave after Sam has come home, then."

"Ben, are you sure?"

"Let me have this, sis."

I stay silent.

"Please, Cass. I'll be in and out in a couple of days."

"Alright." I give in.

"I'll swing by tomorrow."

"Okay." Then an idea comes to me. "Can you bake that carrot cake? Sam loved it."

"The one I made at Mark's place?"

"Yeah."

"Sure. Don't take it as a peace offering, though."

I let out a laugh. "Go and find that perfect house, then."

"I will. Don't you worry about that."

I drive on and turn into the daycare parking lot.

There she is—waiting on the front lawn with her friends and teachers, is the most precious miracle of my life. How could Harvey ever reject her?

I still want to punch that heartless bastard in the face someday, but I can smile now, knowing that Grace will have the father that she deserves.

"Hey, honey," I hug her.

"Hi, Mom."

And I keep her in my arms—silently apologizing and promising that I'll do everything to make her happy and safe.

"Mom... you're embarrassing me!"

I let her go and smile at her.

Oliver, Grace's bestie, catches us before we turn to the gate. "Hey, Grace, where's your bodyguard?"

"Saving a kid," Grace proudly tells her friend without even knowing where Sam is.

"Cool." Oliver nods to himself, seemingly mulling over what that could entail. He then looks up to greet me. "Hello, Miss Cass."

"Hey. Do you need a lift?"

"No, thanks, Miss Cass. My dad will be here soon."

I say goodbye to him as I hold Grace firmly in my hand.

"Mom, I can walk by myself."

"You know that I love you, right?"

"You're acting weird..."

Maybe. But I'm weird because I'm changing to be someone better.

I'll make it happen with Sam and the Woodhouse. And sooner rather than later, I want to hear Grace calling Sam 'Dad.'

He is her true father—not that scumbag Harvey Whitlock.

27

———

SAM

"The more you sweat in training, the less you bleed in combat." I close my debrief by quoting Richard Machinko, a legendary Vietnam vet and the first commanding officer of SEAL Team Six.

The participants clap—I'm sure because they're glad hell day is over. I know some of them were close to killing Mark and me.

"Well, our work here is done," I say to Captain Zander.

He shakes our hands. "Thanks, gents. We'll do it again sometime next month."

"You know our rates have gone up, don't you?" Mark quips.

"Get outta here!" Zander says.

Mark and I amble to our car, patting each other's back.

"Well, that was a mission and a half. Peaceful, nonetheless," he reflects. "Well, almost."

"Almost," I echo. "At least no sickos, no cartels, no Rambo wannabes."

There was no danger here. Only our patience was tested.

"Back to Helena, then?" Mark starts the car.

"Play some Taylor Swift, will you?"

My partner glares at me. "Is she still reminding you of Cass?"

When I first saw Cass, I thought her eyes somewhat resembled those of Taylor's.

"Nah, not really." Now that I've known Cass, I think her eyes are simply her eyes and nobody else's. "I'm just being nostalgic," I reason with Mark.

"I can do without your terrible taste in music." He tunes in to a local classic rock radio station. "Home sweet home!" he sings.

And to the woman that I love.

"When are we gonna test our new recruit?" I ask Mark about the new kid who has just joined Red Mark as a contractor, an ex-Army recon.

"I'll take him with me when we get our next case, and we can see from there."

"Okay. But if it's anything like Neil Parr's case, you take me, or I take him."

"We can decide when the time comes," he says. "By the way, did you hear the news?"

"About what?"

"Seth ordered a twenty-grand marble headstone for his brother. And apparently, his funeral cost almost as much as that of Frank Costello's."

Ambrose Seth—the man I helped put in jail and has a target on my back for killing his brother. Apparently, he's still loaded despite his incarceration, but I wonder how much influence he has these days in the underworld.

"Since when did you keep up with trash?" I tease him. "Was Denzel Seth buried in Seattle?"

"Yeah."

"The State didn't give Ambrose permission to attend, did they?" I ask.

"Of course not."

I wish I could bury the two brothers side by side. Ambrose Seth's trial is looming, and I'll make damn sure he gets the maximum. If I had to force my partner to marry the attorney general of Montana to get that—I would.

But sooner or later, I'll have to face the reality of Seth being a free man again. I'll deal with that son of a bitch, then. If he ever comes near Cass, Grace, or me, I'll give him more than a funeral and a marble headstone.

"There's still no news about Harvey Whitlock, though," I say.

I've been keeping in touch with my Caribbean intel, but so far, the signs point to him laying low in Jamaica."

"It's the worst, isn't it? The calm?" Mark says.

"I'm aware of that, buddy." I lean back and fish out my phone. "His twitchy fingers will force him to come out. He won't let go of that money, if it exists. Now would you excuse me? I'm going to call my sweetheart."

Mark stays cool. He knows I'm trying to provoke him about what he's missing out on.

Cass answers my call after what sounds like a few fumbles. I think she has her hands full.

"How are you, Cass?"

"I'm fine. Mom's back today, so Grace and I are flower shopping."

"Flower shopping? You're pulling my leg?" What is it with her and flowers these days?

"Well, she just sold our family home, and that house was full of flowers, unlike mine, as you know. I only have grass, mature trees, and weeds. I thought I'd cheer her up."

"Nice thought."

"Where are you, Sam?"

"I'm coming home."

"Best news ever." Just by hearing the lift in her voice, I know my girl is beaming. "I should've bought flowers for you too. The rose seeds haven't changed a bit."

"Give them time, Cass," I say. I know patience isn't one of her strengths. "Hey, is Ben with you?"

"He was here yesterday. He's out apartment hunting."

"How's the Sergeant?"

"He's okay, although he's been barking a lot. I guess because you're not here."

I ponder. That's a bit strange because usually, when I'm around he starts misbehaving. "I'll give him a good talking to," I say. "Hey, I'll be there for dinner."

"I'd better not burn the lasagna then?"

"I love crispy lasagna," I quip. "I'll talk to you later, okay? I love you."

"Love you more."

I hang up, unable to hide my smile. Perhaps I'm blushing too, because my partner cringes. I straighten myself, ditching my lovey-dovey face—a blushing SEAL is never a good look.

"Things seem to be going swimmingly well with you two?"

"I think I've finally cracked it," I say. "Next time, I'll teach you how. You and Ivy—"

Mark puts his hand up. "Shut it!"

"You'll be so jealous of us that you'll want to find the meaning of your life. And it's not work, I can tell you that."

"Since you're in an annoying mood, I'm gonna tell you this. Why don't you take time off?"

"Don't even try!"

"Listen, before you kill me," he says. "Now that your chance at love has been fulfilled, and we've got Lieutenant Recon contracting with Red Mark, maybe you can start focusing on Jack again. Go to Georgia and find out if the sidewalk boy is really Jack."

I sigh so deeply I almost growl—I haven't told anyone that I've just hit a roadblock on that lead.

"What?" Mark casts me a glance.

"That butcher shop—there has never been such a shop there, and none of the streets in Spring Hill looks remotely like the one in the photo."

"Crap."

"There are fifty-six known places called Spring Hill in the United States. Spring Hill, Georgia, isn't where Jack was, even though the photo came from the state's archive. Fifty-five more to go—and that's if the Spring Hill in that photo isn't some kind of an obscure location."

"You'll get there, Sam. I'll help you."

I nod. Of course he will. But this is between me and myself —and my girlfriend. "Thanks, buddy. I'll talk to Cass and see what she thinks."

"Teamwork, huh?" He smirks. Not very often Mark smiles at me candidly like that. He must be really impressed with my progress.

"Just like you and me, buddy—only better." I wink.

28

CASSIDY

"Where should we put the flowers?" I ask Grace.

"In Grandma's bedroom?"

"Good idea!"

Maximus greets us. He's been barking again. We could hear him even before we'd gotten near home.

"Maximus, down!" I say, and the mutt stands down, but his stare doesn't relent. His three paws fidget like he's about to bolt somewhere.

"Are you barking at the shed again?" I stare at the shepherd.

"Maybe he wants walkie walkie," Grace suggests.

"Yeah, I think you're right, honey. But it's dark soon, and I have to start dinner. Why don't you play with him in your room?"

"Okay."

I head upstairs with Grace, and Max follows. She peruses her bookshelf and tells Max, "Don't eat my books, okay?"

"Grace, do you really like this house?"

"Yeah," she answers, not really paying attention to me.

Instead, she pulls one of her favorite books, *An Atlas of Imaginary Places* by Mia Cassany.

"I know we've moved around a lot—but what do you think of Sam's house?"

This time Grace turns to me, eyes wide. "We're moving there, Mommy?"

"I want to know what you think first."

She puts her book down. "So I can be with Max all the time?"

"Yes. And with Sam, and me."

"How about Grandma?"

"Grandma can visit."

"Uncle Ben too?"

"Of course."

Grace pulls my hand. "So, when are we moving?"

"Soon. When Sam comes back, we'll ask him, okay?" I rub her back, pleased with her reaction.

"Okay, Mommy," Grace says. "Where is he anyway?"

"He's in Helena Forest, but he's coming home tonight. Well, I need to start dinner," I say with whatever confidence I can foster. "Be good!" I say to Max, who seems to want to pounce at me.

I put the flowers inside my mother's room, and I hear a knock on the door.

Did Sam forget his keys?

Soon Maximus bolts toward the door, growling—stranger alert. It can't be Sam, then.

My heart pounds when I see who's behind the door.

"Mr. Kelleher?"

"Cassidy," he greets me. "Call me Joseph."

Max keeps barking.

"Mom!" Grace yells.

"Grace, stay in your room. Max, upstairs!" I command, pointing at the stairs. "Go!"

Maximus duly follows my instruction.

"Mr. Kelleher, what are you doing here?"

"Joseph. I'm sorry to turn up like this. But... I've been trying to reach Sam. I know he doesn't want to talk to me, let alone see me—but I have something important for him. He moved, so I don't know his current address."

"Joseph, I don't think it's a good idea."

He sighs, ducking in regret. I can see the embarrassment in his stance. "You're right. I... um..."

When I told Sam that I couldn't find a bad streak in his father, I meant it. Now, the disappointment on Joseph's face is triggering regrets in me. In fact, it's more than disappointment. Perhaps he has reached past that—it's devastation.

He's a father seeking to redeem himself.

"I'm sorry to bother you, Cassidy. Have a good night." The man pivots, ambling along the driveway.

If he was my father—

"Joseph, wait," I call out. "Why don't you come in for a bit?"

His face lights up. "Thank you. I'm glad you two are still together."

I invite him to sit down.

"Would you like anything to drink?"

"A Fallen Angel?"

So he's done research on me. "Of course."

I open a couple of bottles and then sit in front of him.

"So you came all the way from New York?"

"Yes. And it's worth the journey. It's good to see you again." He sips the ale. "Cassidy, we've only met once, and ashamedly, it was the time when Sam and I were fighting."

"Well, you gatecrashed his party."

After I delivered the beer supply to Sam's creek house for his party that afternoon, I ended up staying on and, in the process, learning about the friction between the father and son.

I understand Joseph's desperation to mend his relationship with Sam, but his pushiness has made matters worse. He should've known better not to provoke his son by turning up at his house, during a party that he wasn't invited to.

That night, I remember they squabbled about Jack—the same argument that they're still having now about Joseph giving up on the search—and I saw the other side of Sam. The angry Sam. For my first night knowing my knight in shining armor, it was confrontational. But I understood, and despite the fight, I saw love between them—albeit lost in the animosity.

"I get it, Sam is mad at me. I was the one who lost Jack that night—I only let him go for a few seconds to take some photos. Then he was gone, just like that."

His mouth moves, trying to swallow back his tears.

"I deserve Sam's fury. But this isn't how I thought my family would be," he reveals. "Apart—full of hurt." He opens his wallet and takes out a photo. "Here, this was us, a few years before it happened—" He gulps. "Before the kidnapping. Sam was nine, and Jack was four."

I peruse the photo. Mr. and Mrs. Kelleher lean into each other, looking lovingly at their children. In front of them, Sam puts his arm around little Jack. Who would've believed that the father and son would end up estranged, disputing, while their mother is gone and their youngest son is still missing. Such is life.

"I gave up on Jack, but I had my reasons," the old man declares.

"And what are they, Joseph?"

"None of us was ever the same after Jack's disappearance. My wife fell ill, and Sam ran away from home pursuing his own quest to find his brother."

"He joined the Navy SEAL when he ran away, didn't he?"

"Oh, that was later. He ran away when he was fifteen, joined some fight club—that was how he earned his keep. It wasn't hard to find him—he was a minor then, so the hospitals always called me. Until he stopped going to the hospital altogether. I lost contact with Sam until I found out he was deployed to Afghanistan."

I nod, letting him continue.

"When the police told me there was nothing else they could do, I had to make a decision. I had to choose my fight—to go against the police or to take care of my family. I loved my wife."

He takes a moment to compose himself. Then he carries on. "It was impossible for me to leave her side, she was so fragile. She depended a lot on prescription medications, and I had to watch her every second she was awake."

Joseph pauses again.

"And I did lose hope, Cassidy," he concedes. "It was so farfetched to believe that Jack was still alive. They found his bloodied clothes, and there was no other lead for years—none. So I told myself I wasn't going to lose the only son I had left. Just like that, I gave up the fight and chose my living family instead."

He rubs his face as if flicking away regrets.

"In the end, I lost her. I couldn't mend her broken heart. She said she wanted to be buried next to Jack. So I used the plot that I bought for myself and marked it as Jack's to fulfill her wish. Then, my attempt to get Sam home failed too. He hated me even more, and I don't blame him."

"He doesn't hate you, Joseph."

"Oh, he did, and he still does. Every day I regret that decision. Had I gone on to continue my own investigation on Jack, I would've only lost my wife. She was the most beautiful, amazing woman. But I would've coped. I would've coped living without her. And I would've still had Sam—we would've worked together, father and son. And I wouldn't have been here fretting about this to his girlfriend."

"You can't blame yourself for that. It was an impossible choice!"

"And perhaps I would've found Jack too, and had him back in my arms."

"You said you had something important for Sam?"

"Ah, yes—"

"Mom! I'm bored! Max is bored too! He's chewing on the carpet," Grace complains as she walks down the stairs. But she stops when she sees my guest.

"Grace, honey," I reach out to her, and she leans on me, looking at the lanky figure of Joseph Kelleher. I introduce Grace to him, "This is my daughter."

"Hi, my name is Grace."

"Hi, Grace. My name is Joseph. I'm... um..."

I look at Joseph, and I give him a discreet shake of my head —I don't want to tell her yet that he's Sam's father.

"I'm a friend of your mom's."

Maximus soon joins us, pacing the room like he's about to go crazy. Right then, my phone buzzes.

"Sorry, I have to take this," I say.

"Mom, can Joseph play with Max and me?"

"Um... sure. Just in the backyard, okay?"

"Okay, come on, Joseph. Come, Max." Grace leads the way.

Once they're outside, I answer the call—perhaps almost miss it.

"Hey, you're busy cooking, I take it?" Sam says.

"Ah yeah. I am. I haven't burned the lasagna yet." The oven isn't even on! I quickly turn the dial.

"I'm not far. I just need to drop off a few things at Red Mark."

"That's fine."

"Hey, there's something I need to ask you tonight. Are you up for it?"

"Of course. Tell me when you're home."

"See you soon."

I hang up and walk straight to the backyard. Seeing Joseph and Grace playing with Max melts me—it feels like I've just met another family member that had been gone for a long time. But I know Sam won't welcome it.

I pull Joseph aside. "Look, I don't mean to be rude, but I think you should leave."

Joseph nods, ignoring the ball that Max has just dropped off at his feet.

"Come inside, Grace." I take her hand.

"Mom! We're just getting started."

"Joseph has to go, honey."

"Nice to meet you, Grace," Joseph says apologetically. Then he reluctantly plods to the door. "Thanks for having me."

"I promise I'll talk to Sam. You and him—it doesn't have to stay this way," I say. "He loves you. He just doesn't know how to do it after what he went through with Jack."

"I appreciate that. It'd be nice, but not at a cost, please. I'd rather stay on the outside and have you two stay together. Don't let me be your third wheel."

I close the door and head to the kitchen, putting in the Michael Angelo's Lasagna I got from the shop. When I said to Sam I'd cook dinner, he knew perfectly well that it meant heating up a prepped meal. But I must say, the frozen pasta looks pretty good. Even Lisa swears by it.

"Grace, have a shower. Sam will be here soon."

Grace is on her way back to her bedroom and obviously doesn't hear me. "What is it, Mom?"

"Have a—"

But there's a knock on the door, and it's Joseph.

"Cass, sorry, I forgot to give you this." He hands me an envelope. "Tell Sam he should look in Florida. Jack might've been taken in by a nun."

"You're back!" Grace steps out as I hold the envelope. "Why don't you stay for dinner?" she innocently says.

"I can't, Grace. I'm sorry." Joseph kneels in front of her. God! His posture looks so much like Sam's when my man tries not to tower over Grace.

"Will you come again and play?"

He takes her hands, and regret mars his face. "Next time, sweetheart."

In the distance, I hear a car purring. Max barks and I recognize his excited tone. There shouldn't be any cars traveling on this road at this time—unless you're coming home.

29

SAM

He's holding Grace's hand? That man is holding Grace's hand!

I park my SUV behind Cass's car. At least he still had the courtesy not to block the driveway, thinking it was his own home.

As I walk toward the porch, I can see Cass tensing up. Well, it's not her fault, not the least. That man should've known better not to turn up at my girlfriend's house!

"Sam!" Grace runs to me.

"Hello, Pup." I bend down, and as usual, she leaps into my arms. "Have you been good?"

"Yes. I read books and then played with Max and Joseph."

Cass comes to me, too, giving me a welcome-home kiss.

"Hey, sweetheart," I murmur, kissing her back.

"Grace, come on, inside," Cass says and tows the little girl.

I approach my dad. "Take a drive with me." The last thing I want is to lose my shit in front of my family. Hell yeah, Cass and Grace are my family now, and they don't deserve an unwelcome blast from the past.

I stop about five hundred yards from the house on a side

street with a trail where I usually take Maximus for a walk when we're around here.

"That's called stalking, Dad! You're a stalker!"

"Sam, calm down."

"And you're trying to play Grandpa with Grace? How dare you!"

"Sam, I've got something for you—about Jack."

"I don't want to hear it, Dad. I don't want to hear it. I just want you out of my life."

"You don't mean that."

"I thought I've made it clear, time and time again."

"I've been hoping you'd change your mind."

"Well, you can stop hoping now. Spend your energy thinking about yourself. And stay the hell away from my family!"

I turn back and drop him off at his car. I follow him as he drives along the road.

He stops, steps out of his car then marches to me.

"You don't have to escort me, son."

"I just want to make absolutely sure," I challenge him.

His car disappears into the night, and I return home.

I see a couple of empty Fallen Angels bottles in the living room. He really did try to cozy up to Cass. Shameless!

Cass and Grace are finishing their dinner.

"Sam, you're back!" Grace says, brandishing a milk mustache.

"Yeah." I wipe her lips.

"I can reheat the lasagna," Cass offers.

I rub her back and place a kiss on the side of her neck. "It's okay. I'll do that later." I'll grab a bottle of Fallen Angel and sit with my favorite girls.

"Did you rescue a kid in the forest?" Grace asks.

"Not this time. Mark and I were training some policemen."

"Like a summer camp?"

I chuckle. "Yeah, a summer camp for police, I guess."

"Alright, Grace, brush your teeth and get ready for bed," Cass instructs.

The girl reluctantly obeys.

Cass stoops behind me, arms hanging over my shoulders. "Ben made some cake for us."

Now that's something that'll go down well after a long hard day and an energy-destroying haunting. I take her up on her offer.

"You okay?" Cass serves me a big slice.

"I am now." I bite a chunk of the baking miracle. I'd befriend Ben just for this. "I'm sorry about my dad."

"You didn't punch him, did you?"

I sigh. "Almost. But I didn't."

"He didn't mean any harm, Sam. I'm sorry I couldn't say no."

"It's not your fault."

"Have you ever tried to sit down and really talk? I mean, a civilized talk?"

"The short answer is no."

She cocks her head. "And the long answer?"

Dismally, it's a no as well. I don't even have to answer. She knows.

"Mom, I'm ready!" Grace's head pokes over the balustrade on the second floor.

"Why don't you go upstairs and help her?" Cass suggests.

I thank her silently. After my dad's attempt to play Grandpa with Grace, I welcome a chance to bond with the girl, so I'm the one she's with before she goes to sleep tonight —not Joseph Kelleher.

I meet Grace at the landing.

"Are you going to tuck me in?" Grace anticipates.

"Yeah."

"Mom told me we're going to move into your house. Is it true?"

"If you want it to happen, then it is."

"I want to. Then I can play with Max all the time."

"How about me?"

"You too." She hugs me, wiping away my troubles. "When can we move?"

"I'll talk to your mom, okay? It won't be long."

"When we're in your house, can I call you 'dad'?"

My heart leaps. She wants to call me 'dad'? This time I don't care if I'm blushing red. *Grace wants me to be her dad.*

"Of course you can, Pup." I caress her hair. "But I'll ask your mom first."

"Okay. Good night, Sam."

"Night, Pup."

I wait for her to fall asleep. Cass passes by, gesturing to me that she'll be waiting for me in bed.

"Welcome home." She kisses me deeply when I join her. The best thing that happens tonight, well—after being asked by Grace to be her dad.

"Can we not talk about my father anymore?"

"I don't intend to."

I nod. "So, it's happening? You're moving in with me?"

"Grace told you?" she says. "We're going to start packing, I guess. Perhaps run a yard sale too."

"Smart move."

"So, you wanted to talk to me about something?"

"About Jack. About that photo that I found from a Georgia cold case."

"Was it really him?"

"Georgia was a dud." I adjust my pillow higher. "The

Spring Hill there doesn't look remotely like the one in the photo."

"But it doesn't mean that boy wasn't Jack." Her eyes look at me convincingly. "In fact, I think your dad found something. He left—"

"Sweetheart, I know you mean well, but I don't wanna hear it."

"Listen, Sam! He mentioned Florida. A nun might've taken him in."

I know Cass has a soft spot for my dad but is she really believing what that old man is saying?

As preposterous as it sounds, though, the location gets my attention.

"Florida? You sure?"

"Yes. He left an envelope. It's in the living room."

I grumble and head downstairs to find the envelope.

There's a photo in it, and I must admit the resemblance is staggering.

I take out the photo of the sidewalk boy. There's a window behind him, and *Spring Hill Butchers* appears in the reflection. There is a Spring Hill in Georgia, and there's also one in Florida. The two states share a border—it's not farfetched that the Georgia cold case where I found the photo might've spanned to Florida.

Damn, why haven't I thought of this before?

Jack's kidnapper allegedly had ties to the child trafficking syndicate. Florida is the gateway to Guatemala and Honduras. The need for drug mules is always high there.

I study the photo my dad left. Who's that nun hugging the boy?

A nun...

I recall Jack's kidnapper's pattern.

He usually took his victims to properties in a vicinity of a church.

Fuck!

This is real.

"Was he right?" Cass has followed me.

It irritates me that my father actually gave me the biggest piece of the puzzle yet. It's not the last, but it seems to be the right one.

It's now or never.

"I'm gonna go to Florida first thing tomorrow."

Before I apologize for leaving so soon after coming home, I see understanding rising on her face. She nods and then kisses me. "Go and find your brother."

30

———

SAM

I arrive in Spring Hill, Florida, the next morning. I've compared the current street views with the photo over and over throughout my flight, making sure that my thought isn't just a thought.

Walking on the street in person, I can't help feeling that I'm taking the same footsteps Jack did eighteen years ago.

I squat at the spot where that boy was photographed, staring at the opposite butcher shop. It has changed names, but the current owner told me that the youngest brother who used to run the Spring Hill Butchers is still around.

People pass me by, perhaps thinking I'm too well-dressed to be a homeless man begging for change. I wonder what Jack was doing then—if that boy was, in fact, him.

Leaving behind Spring Hill Street, I drive to the neighboring town to talk to the brother who ran the old butcher shop.

"Thanks for seeing me." I show him the photo of the sidewalk boy.

"Eighteen years ago, huh?" he says. "Yeah. This was our street, and it was our butcher shop, alright."

"Do you recognize that boy?"

The man puts on his glasses and draws the photo closer. "I don't know. I don't remember him. He must've moved around, I guess."

"Were there a lot of homeless kids back then?"

"Well, yes and no. They tended to show up, and then the next day, they're gone."

"Any convent or monastery around back then?" I show him the photo from my father—a boy being hugged by a nun. It is quite a close-up photo, but the background doesn't tell much. "We believe this was the same boy."

"Well, there's a big monastery in St. Leo. It could well be it."

"It's run by priests, though, right?"

"Oh, not all of it. There are nuns there. Well, at least there were back then."

It turns out my father wasn't preposterous after all.

Buildings like churches and monasteries often bring awe to those who visit them, but there's something about the St. Leo monastery that wrings my heart. I used to tell myself 'this is different' every time I had a new lead. But after two decades of investigation, I've never felt so grounded and pragmatically assured.

A young nun greets me at the abbey entrance.

"I'm looking for this sister," I say, showing her the photo from my dad.

"Oh, wow... this is an old photo. I'm not really sure who she is," she says. "Let me ask the Prioress."

After waiting for about ten minutes, the sister comes back and ushers me into the heart of the monastery.

"Please," she invites me in after knocking on the door of the office, tucked behind what looks to be a prayer hall.

The Prioress welcomes me, holding the photo in her hand. "May I know who you are?"

"I'm Sam Kelleher, from Montana."

"You've come a long way," she says. "This is Sister Laura." She taps a finger at the photo.

"Is she still here?"

"Yes. Are you her family?"

"I believe that boy she's holding is my lost brother." Articulating it sends chills to my core—chills of reality and worry. What if I'm wrong? I truly wish Cass was here with me!

"Sister Laura must be in the garden right now. She's tending to the roses, I'm sure," the Prioress says. She calls back the young nun who took me here and asks her to walk me to the rose garden.

A long silence through the journey to the garden ends with yet another stretch of silence. I stare at the nun crouching in front of a flower bed, plucking some weeds.

"Good morning, Sister," I say.

The nun turns her head to me. I freeze, doubting the realness of the situation. The woman must be in her seventies now, but I know it's the same person who holds Jack in that photo.

Sister Laura rises and unexpectedly gives me a hug as if she was my mother. I hug her back while thinking that those arms had once held Jack too. If this is all real, then I can take comfort in the fact that perhaps Jack was loved here.

"What a great day, don't you think?" the sister says, letting me go only to point at the sky and then the blooming flowers around her.

"Yes."

"What can I do for you, young man?"

This time I take out the photo of the sidewalk boy. I want to test if she recognizes him in a photo she might not have seen before. "Sister Laura, I believe this boy was in your care about eighteen years ago?"

"Oh... sweet Jack."

First, it's my weakening legs, then my shaking hands, and finally, I have to restrain my sob.

"You know him?" Sister Laura asks, appraising my reaction.

I compose myself, thinking that there are still things I need to verify. "So you called him Jack?"

"Yes."

"Jack who?"

"We never knew. When I found him wandering the streets, he was already an addict. His memory was pretty much non-existent."

That bastard! How could he do that to my brother?

Sister Laura takes my hand. "Come, I'll make you tea."

We sit down in the kitchen while she insists that I drink and have some cookies despite my loss of appetite.

Then Sister Laura explains, "Jack was mute for the first year that he was here. I'm sorry to say that he was really in bad shape. We used to call him Snowflake. He was so fair and delicate. He finally told me his name was Jack, but he couldn't remember anything else. It was as if he had been brainwashed."

"When you found him, apart from his drug addiction, did you think he was... abused?"

"He had bruises, but we didn't know if it was just because he fell down, or if he'd gotten into fights, or if someone had hit him—as in his parents or something."

One more thing I have to verify—which I almost don't want to. I've come so close, and I've been feeling all these over-running things that are perhaps clouding my logic. If the boy turns out to be someone else, it will break me.

But I have to.

"Did he have a birthmark?"

"He had a brown birthmark on his left shoulder. We used to joke that it was the shape of a little rabbit."

I close my eyes, trembling like I'm having a fit. I really, really wish Cass was here. After years of accumulating anger and despair, now that I've found the answer, somehow, I don't know what to do or how to feel.

"Hey... you've found him," the sister says and hugs me again.

I keep my tears tucked behind my eyelids. "Where is he now?"

"He joined the Marine Corps when he turned nineteen. I heard from him last month. He was in Afghanistan. Oh, there's a photo of him." She plods into a room, presumably her bedroom, and then returns to me with a postcard-size photo.

"Oh my..." I let out a chuckle.

My little brother. The last time I was with him, he couldn't ride a roller coaster because he wasn't tall enough. He's now a man. In his Marine fatigues, he looks menacing, perhaps even bigger and taller than me. But his face... it's unmistakably Jack.

"Thank you for looking after him." I hold the sister's hand.

"He was a godsend," she says. "What's your name again?"

"Sam. Sam Kelleher. I'm his brother."

"So, it's Jack Kelleher?"

"Yes. Jack Redley Kelleher."

There are so many questions—has Jack ever mentioned me? Has he ever wondered where home was?

But there's no time to waste. Everywhere in Afghanistan is a hot spot right now. I've got to get Jack out of there before the Taliban hits Kabul.

I call Mark, but he's not answering. We did get a new case this morning. The thought of my partner pressing on with the new recruit, and the possibility that he might need my help, is making me uneasy.

Then there's Cass and Grace. I don't want to leave them either.

I look at the photo of Jack squatting on the sidewalk. He is my little brother, and I've got to take him home.

Cass and Mark will understand. I'm sure they will.

Right now, guilt has no place in my life. I must go to Afghanistan.

31

CASSIDY

I can't remember the last time I felt this sick. Even lifting my hand is like moving a tombstone, so I've been putting off packing. Besides, with Sam being away, I don't think the move will happen anytime soon.

If I had a choice, I would've stayed in bed. But Grace has been badgering me, and my mother is at the brewery to keep the order going. So I drag myself out of bed.

The two acetaminophen tablets I took are no match to Maximus's constant barking, whatever he's up to!

"Max! Shoosh!"

"Moom! I can't find the *Imaginary Places* book!"

"You just read it." I go into her bedroom, sorting out the mess, looking under her bed, table, and chairs—which hurt my head even more.

"Mom, you've got to help me!"

"I am helping you."

"I want to read it."

Grace hasn't slept well. I feel it's got something to do with Sam not being around.

"Grace, I'll find your book. But now, it's nap time," I say, giving up on the search.

"No! I don't want to sleep!"

"Grace, please!"

The girl grimaces, scowling at me, but after a few moments of defiance, she tucks herself into bed. I think she finally runs out of energy.

"When is Sam coming home?" she asks, half yawning.

"I don't know, honey."

"Is he looking for another missing kid?"

"Yes." Although he's not a kid anymore.

"Now, sleep tight, Pup."

Grace cringes. "That's for Sam."

I've been calling her 'honey' since forever. I guess the SEAL Pup thing doesn't really suit my voice. "Okay. Sleep tight, honey."

I kiss her forehead and watch her sleep.

Then, my cell rings. I don't even try to contain my excitement. Without reading the caller's name, I know it's Sam. I'm hoping he's not too far from concluding his trip.

"Cass." The way he greets me is nothing like a man who's coming home. "I'm in DC."

"Oh? You have another lead?"

I hear Grace's bedroom door creaks open.

"Mom, is that Sam?"

"Oh, dear," I murmur. "Grace, go back to bed."

"Is that Sam? Mom! Please, I want to talk to Sam!"

Meanwhile, Max is still barking outside.

"Okay, talk to Sam while I get Max," I say. "Sam, here's Grace."

Maximus keeps barking.

"Maximus!" I yell, checking out what's happening in the backyard.

The Scotty shed door is open.

"What is it, buddy?" I round the shed and find two furry creatures hopping their way out of my sight. "You haven't seen rabbits before?"

But it is strange that the shed door is open. Maybe Mother forgot to close it.

"Mom! Sam wants to talk to you now!"

"I'm coming."

I put a padlock on the shed door and gather whatever energy I have to run inside. But soon, bile shoots up my throat, reminding me that my gut is far from happy.

While dealing with my vomiting, I hear Grace talking. "Yeah. She's in the bathroom. Throwing up."

After spitting out a few remnants of my vomit, I hurl myself beside the toilet seat, reaching for the flush.

"Mom! Quick! Sam wants to talk to you."

Laboriously, I push myself up.

"Here's Mommy." Grace passes the phone to me as I stumble my way out of the bathroom.

"So you're in DC, you said?" I ask Sam.

"Yeah." He stops short of explaining why. Instead, he asks, "Grace said you weren't feeling well, that you've been throwing up? Are you okay?"

"I'm fine, Sam."

"Have you... have you had your period?"

The way he asks the question hurts my gut. I can even say I'd rather have a stomach bug than hear it. Why does it sound like it would be a disaster if I hadn't?

"Did you regret it?" I deadpan. That day at the shed, we decided not to use protection. He said he was okay with it!

"No, I did not regret it, Cass."

"I'm not pregnant, Sam. I am having my period. I've been throwing up because of a bad piece of chicken."

He sighs.

He's relieved?

"Why the sigh?"

"There's a lot on my mind right now, Cass. I'm sorry."

"What if I was pregnant, Sam? Would you—"

"I would be happy. God, I would. But honestly, I'm relieved that you're not. Just for now. Just for now, Cass. Does that make me an asshole?"

"No." I sit on the floor, unable to stand anymore. "I'm sorry, Sam. It's one of those days when I'm just cranky for nothing."

"That time of the month, huh?" This time his tender voice returns.

"I guess so. I'm so sorry."

"It's fine, Cass."

Then I hear a public announcement.

"Sam, where are you?"

"Dulles."

"You're flying somewhere?"

"Cass, Jack has been deployed to Afghanistan. He's a sergeant there, and I've made contact with a friend in Kabul."

I can feel the skin across my cheeks tightens. Danger is home to him, and I'm starting to be okay with it. But going into a war zone—a real war zone?

"Sam! Are you mad? That place is a death trap!"

"Cass, you know I've been waiting for this moment for so long. I won't let this slip."

Sam has been searching for his missing brother for more than twenty years. Whatever happens, I'll need to be ready. But I never imagined this.

"You'll be a target there, Sam!" I'm not sure if I'm stating a mere fact or simply wanting him to change his mind.

"I can take care of myself."

"Why can't you wait till he gets home? The military is withdrawing everyone!"

"When you're in a war zone, anything can happen. One minute you're alive, the next you might be in pieces," he says. "You, out of all people, should know that."

My heart almost bursts.

He sighs. "I'm sorry. That was uncalled for." I can see him rubbing his forehead and cursing at himself.

"Sam?"

"I'm sorry, Cass. But you know what I mean. I can't risk it. I have to see my brother now."

"What if it's not him, Sam?"

"Without a shadow of a doubt, it is Jack. I swear to you."

"What if something goes wrong? What if..."

"What if I died?" he completes my sentence.

I bite back my desolation.

"If I died, it would be worth it," he says. "Cass, I swore on my mother's grave that I'd find Jack. Year after year. I won't be able to live with myself. I would die if it meant my brother could go home safely. And you..."

He pauses.

The silence stretches, and then he implores, "Please let me do this. With your blessing. Jack is my brother. He's a part of me that I can't let go of. I know damn well this is my last chance to see him again. And you're a part of me that I love with all my heart. So don't make me choose, Cass."

My heavy heart tells me to shake my head, but my whole body is filled with Sam's hidden tears. "Stay safe, Sam. I'm here for you."

"Thank you."

I let my tears fall. If anything happens to Sam, this will be the last time I hear him—over the goddamned phone.

"I wish I could hug you right now," he says as if reading my mind. "But you know we're special. Remember when you had that panic attack?"

"Sam..." Why is he bringing it up again now?

"We'd barely met. Yet you trusted me. You scared the hell out of me, but you trusted me. I need you to trust me again on this, Cass. Even when I'm not there to convince you. Please. I need you more than ever."

There is an adage. 'A distracted soldier is a dead soldier'—I don't want this to be Sam.

"I love you, Sam. You stay safe, okay?"

"You too. Ben is still around, isn't he?"

My brother must be close to landing in Jamaica's Montego Bay right now. "Yes, he is," I tell Sam, holding my breath. "Go and catch that flight. Grace and I will be waiting for you."

"You and Grace will be just fine. You're strong. And your daughter, she's even stronger than you. That's how it works. Right? The truth is, Cass, you don't even need a man to make you happy."

I don't need a man, but I do need Sam.

32

SAM

Kabul, Afghanistan—my old stomping ground. When I left the Navy, I never looked back, and I prefer not to talk about it. My military days have been far away from my mind until now.

The taste of sand is mixed with the smell of gunpowder, and the air is thick with the fume from jet fuel—it's a hell hole that I'm only willing to go back to for someone whose life means the world to me. And there aren't that many.

After being stuck at the city's airport and losing all contact because my phone decided to have a meltdown, I managed to get out and find my friend, a former interpreter embedded in my squad during my first tour here.

Rahim is now driving me to the US military compound. On every street, desperation is on display. Men, women, families—they're begging, crying, running. And then there are those who are left behind or simply too feeble to move.

"I can only go this far," Rahim says. "That's the gate. Call me anytime you need me. Don't go wandering by yourself."

"Thanks, Rahim. You're a true friend." I give him a firm handshake and run to the compound gate.

A soldier meets me there and then escorts me to a tent.

Marine First Sergeant Lydia Mayfair greets me. "Samuel Kelleher?"

"Yes, ma'am."

"You're very lucky to be here. How did you even get a flight?"

"I had contacts, ma'am."

"I didn't know Sergeant Benedict had a brother."

Before I left St. Leo, Sister Laura let me keep the photo of Marine Jack and told me that he goes by the name of Jack Benedict—since he couldn't remember his family name. St. Leo is a Benedictine monastery, hence the name.

"We got separated when we were very young," I explain to the first sergeant.

"I heard you were a SEAL?" she inquires.

"It was a long time ago."

"I bet. I also heard that you were one of the youngest in your class."

I smile shyly, hoping she'll stop her probing.

She says, "I'm sorry. I had to make sure that you were who you claimed to be, so I looked into your files. We couldn't take any chances."

"I understand."

"I didn't make it as a SEAL. I tried," she says proudly. "Maybe my daughter will."

"Never say never."

"Well." She clasps her hands as if she's nervous on my account. "Your brother would be very happy to see you. We haven't told him who you are yet. I thought you might want to explain it yourself."

"I appreciate it."

"Wait here," the first sergeant says and then disappears behind a partition. "Gunny, someone's here to see you."

My heart pounds as a figure emerges. I don't have to see the face shadowed by his cap. I know it's Jack.

"Sam Kelleher?"

If I closed my eyes hearing that voice, I would've said it was Dad—a younger Dad, perhaps.

"Yes, I'm—" My tongue twists mid-sentence, and my throat closes.

He looks at me as if he's ready to call a medic. "Yes? What can I do for you?"

I shudder in place, pressing my feet down, so I don't just give him a ramming hug out of the blue. That guy could kick my ass in one go, and I'd be done for.

"Sergeant Jack B—" My lips struggle to say the name, not because of my tight tongue this time. It's not his name! I simply look at his badge bearing the name 'Benedict,' and he acknowledges me.

"Yes. You are Sam Kelleher from D.C.?"

"Um... I flew out from D.C., but I live in Helena, Montana. Although I was born in New York."

"So, how can I help you? Something extremely important, I take it, that you've come all the way to this dump of a place?"

I shake his hand, only for my body to shake further from the contact.

Jack looks at me suspiciously. I bet I look like an amateur thief trying to pull off a heist that has gone wrong before it even began.

"Sister Laura from St. Leo told me you were here."

He scowls. "Sister Laura? Is she alright?"

"She's okay," I say. Then I take the deepest breath I can manage. "I'm your brother." My exhale halts, and I freeze.

Jack straightens himself. "Come again?"

Still reeling inside, it takes me a few seconds to answer him. "I'm your brother, Jack."

He takes off his cap, wiping beads of sweat. When he lifts his chin up, I'm astonished by how much of our mother there is in him.

"Um... well, this is awkward." His eyes skip from my face to the ground. "I... I didn't know I had a brother." He blinks a few times, then frowns as if assessing the possibility. Then he looks me in the eye. "Well, it doesn't mean that it's not true because as far as I know, my life started when I was twelve."

"Here," I say, showing a photo from my wallet. It's not Spring Hill, it's not St. Leo. It's the picture of us taken only weeks before that fateful night at the fairgrounds in Syracuse. I've got to let the picture talk because I can't anymore.

Jack's expression changes as if seeing a revelation. "I... I... So they weren't dreams..." he murmurs, clutching the photo. "Where's this?"

"Upstate New York. You were born there."

His head bobs a nod. "I saw this house in my dreams, but it always appeared hazy, very white, as if it was in the cloud. I never felt or thought it could be reality."

"Do you remember me?" I say, almost begging.

"N... well... not your face, but I remember someone used to wrestle me. He'd put his arm around my neck and then, yeah, wrestle me."

I choke as I laugh at his memory.

"It was you?" He eyeballs me.

I'm shaken with laughter while trying to hold back tears. I wish his memory goes beyond that—because I used to do more than just tease my little brother.

"Yeah, it would've been me," I concede.

His eyes shine with tears. Dare I believe he remembers? That I was 'that big boy' who always had his back?

As if there was a line connecting us, we're tugged together, and we engulf each other in an embrace. He knows. *He knows.*

My brother...

He's in my arms.

"What happened to you?" Jack says, looking down at me as we let go. "You used to be big!"

"I know. You've grown up!"

"Um... please, please sit down." He offers a chair to me.

I hear the familiar sound of a Chinook hovering above us, reminding me that I am in a war zone—but hell, it feels like heaven.

"So... what's your, or our, family name?" Jack takes a seat in front of me.

"Kelleher."

"Oh yes, of course, you said it," he scoffs at himself. "Well, it sounds a bit better than Benedict. I'm not sure if Sister Laura told you about it."

"Yeah, she did. We share the same middle name. Redley. It's our granddad's name. He was an ace in the Korean War. Sometimes Dad called us 'Reds.'"

"Sam and Jack Redley Kelleher," he mutters. "Our parents still alive?"

"Our father is. But... Mom passed away. Twelve years ago."

"I see." He takes a few seconds to gather himself, then he says, "I heard from Lydia you were a SEAL?"

"Yeah."

"So, the military ran in our blood? Was Dad too?"

"He was an Air Force pilot, but a back injury ended his career."

"And our mother?"

"She was a nurse at the military hospital."

Jack keeps nodding, obviously trying to keep up with all the facts thrown at him. Then he wrings his hands. "So, what happened to me?"

My gaze pushes and pulls at him. "You were kidnapped, Jack."

His lips part tentatively, as if wanting to say something—maybe that it couldn't be true. Most of all, I feel his pain.

I can't watch him suffer like that and do nothing, so I rise from my seat. But he holds out his hand, gesturing to me to stay put. Then he looks away.

Outside, vehicles move, people march, and commands are given. But inside this small space under the green tarp, it's dead silent.

I give Jack a moment. His back is to me, but I can see his jaw moving as if swallowing back his cry.

"You okay?" I say when he turns to face me again.

"Yeah. Go on, tell me everything."

I almost have to steel myself to restart. It's been so long since it happened, and now I know the story has a happy ending, but this part always hurts. Regardless, Jack has to know.

Syracuse, New York, twenty-two years ago.

Being a big brother is the best thing in the world. You have a cute, smaller ally who's willing to do whatever you tell him to with complete trust. But trust goes both ways. A big brother is responsible for that little life who depends on you for protection.

"Was fun seeing your car stall," Jack giggles as we leave the bumper cars arena. "You sucked big time."

"Hey! It was the car, not me!" I counter.

My brother tosses me a mischievous grin, and right then, I play-wrestle him. He retaliates. But unable to even stir me, he grumbles, and I let him go.

The Labor Day fireworks dazzle the sky over Syracuse's New York State Fairgrounds. The fair is swarmed with people who seem to have the same idea as us—escaping the city and making the most of the weekend.

"Stay close, Jack," Dad warns as my brother starts to wander away from us, checking out the milk bottle knockdown booth.

"I'm seven! I can walk by myself."

Dad takes hold of Jack despite his protest.

"I've got him," I tell my dad, holding on to my brother's hand lightly. I know it can be embarrassing to be held by your parent—especially when there are a lot of girls around.

"Dad, come on! Thunderbolt time!" I point at the roller coaster ride that has been coined 'the mother of all hell.' It boasts a three-sixty loop, and on a moonless night like this, apparently, you'll feel that you're moving in total darkness. The whole round takes only twenty seconds, but unlike other carnivals or theme parks, this ride goes twice—so effectively, this is longer than the Coney Island coaster.

"I want to as well!" Jack lets us know he's keen. And as if his voice isn't enough, he jumps up and down, neck stretched like a meerkat, desperate for Dad's attention.

I smile at Jack as we queue up. This will be the first time he'd ridden a roller coaster.

"Ready for this?" I ask my little brother as we're moving closer to the end of the line.

"Yes!" He tries hard to maintain his enthusiasm, but there's no denying his nervousness after passenger screams burst right in front of us.

I pull him close, circling my arm around his shoulder. "It'll be fun. I'll be sitting right next to you. Everything will be okay."

For five years, being an only child at the time, I was

used to being guarded by my parents—and my overeager German shepherd dog. Whether at school or a friend's place, while other kids were let loose, there was usually Mom or Dad watching me, either discreetly or embarrassingly.

Things changed when my brother arrived home one morning in a basket, wrapped in a blanket. People told me that newborn babies couldn't smile, but I swear Jack smiled at me as soon as I came to him.

Before he was born, the only thing that I persistently guarded was my one-eyed cat—mainly from my dog, who sometimes thought little Felix was an evil toy that was going to destroy our existence. Jack's presence invoked something in me, and I silently swore that I would take care of him—and protect him no matter what.

Suddenly, Dad pulls Jack out of the line. "You're not tall enough, buddy."

I glance at the board. *Min. height 50"*.

"Dad!" Jack protests, sulking.

I defend my brother. "Come on, Dad, Jack is probably just half an inch short. He'll be fine."

"No. He's only forty-eight inches. Next time, son." My dad keeps pulling him away.

I should quit, too, and join Jack, but I've been dreaming about the Thunderbolt for weeks!

My little brother purses his lips sideways.

"Jack, you'll join me here next year, buddy, I promise," I comfort him.

Kids on the line laugh at Jack, some calling him 'shorty.' One boy loudly mocks, "Pissing your pants already?"

Jack cowers, shielding himself from the laughter coming from all sides of the queue.

I turn toward the boy. He looks so adult. His jeans are way

too tight, which is apparently the fashion now. He's bigger, but no one makes fun of my brother!

"Do I see pink panties under your fly?" I challenge him.

"The fuck?" The boy pushes forward to get to me.

I'm twelve, but with my physique, people often think I'm fourteen or fifteen. I've started practicing Jiu-Jitsu, and I have a dream of becoming a pro-MMA fighter. Dad won't agree, but I'll find a way.

"Red!" My dad calls to me to shut it.

The boy goes back to his place.

But I'm not done. "I bet your fucking balls won't make it past the first loop!"

"Samuel!" my dad shouts, but I'm so far into the queue that he can't catch me. "I'll deal with you later!"

Meanwhile, the boy stays where he is. He doesn't even have the courage to look at me now. I take the front-row seat, and the Thunderbolt takes me to the sky.

We slow down as the coaster climbs the three-sixty loop, and when gravity sucks us down the circle, my life is complete.

At the end of the first lap, I see Dad and Jack waving at me, but the second time around, they're nowhere to be seen—as if they'd been erased from a photograph that I just took barely thirty seconds ago. They might've felt that cheering me once was enough, but uneasiness fills my gut, and it's not the by-product of the twisty ride.

My feelings get heavy when I still can't find them at the rollercoaster's exit. They've probably gone to the Ferris wheel, but it's unlike them to just leave me.

I circle the perimeter of the roller coaster. People's cheers and screams whooshing past me—ride after ride—but my dad and Jack haven't turned up. I further my search, checking the nearby toilets, rides, and games.

Until my feet take me to the Haunted Mansion.

There's commotion. A couple of policemen and the Fair's security people gather in one spot, covering something, or someone.

As I sneak closer, I discover that the someone is my dad.

Without Jack.

"Dad!"

His face is pasty, as if a white neon light had been shone on it. Even the dark of night can't hide the terror that racks his skin.

I run and hug him. "Dad?"

My old man stays silent.

"Mr. Kelleher!" One of the policemen appears to try to wake Dad up from whatever nightmare he's seeing behind his blank eyes. "Do you have the photo of your son?"

When Dad still hasn't answered, the other officer pulls me aside while paramedics escort him to a corner, away from the crowd. They keep saying that he's in shock.

What about me?

I'm in shock too! But I guess a big brother can't be in shock.

"Your dad mentioned your brother's name is Jack. What's your name, son?" the police officer asks.

"Sam. Where's my brother? What happens to my dad?"

"Look, your mother is on her way."

"Where's Jack?"

"We'll find him, okay?"

"Is he hurt? Is he..." I stare at the officer, mundanely following the outline of his thick mustache. "He's been kidnapped?"

"We don't know yet."

"He's been kidnapped!" I yell. This is what school has warned us about—stranger danger and all that. I can't believe it's happening to Jack.

I escape from the officer's grip, running the width and length of the fair, shouting Jack's name. This is what my dad should've done instead of just standing there like a petrified tree.

"Jack!" I cry out, entering the House of Mirrors.

Reflections and shadows surround me. A lot of them look like Jack, but I know my brother too well. I know the difference. He's not here.

The Haunted Mansion would be the last place that Jack goes to, but I go in anyway, as he might be lost and stumbling in there.

"Jack," I keep calling. "Come on, it's me."

Coming out empty-handed, I collapse. The guilt and regret are too heavy to bear. My desperation quickly turns into uncontrollable tears. My little brother is alone with a stranger somewhere, and he must be scared—I can feel it.

"Jack... where are you?" I cry into my hands. Perhaps the two inches that Dad fretted about wouldn't have mattered. Jack would've been safer with me on that roller coaster.

Moments later, another police officer finds me. He has come with my mother, who immediately gives me a tight hug.

"We'll find him, Sam," she whispers, holding back tears.

"Let's go, then!" I tug my mom's arm. "Let's find him."

"Let the police handle this," she says.

"No. We have to find him, now!"

"Let's go home, Sam," Mom sobs as she kneels in front of me.

Go home? Is that all we can do?

"They'll find Jack." She holds my hand as if she was going to lose me too.

I look at the police officer. They'd better! If no one finds Jack, I will!

THE CHINOOK RETURNS. It sounds closer to us this time, rattling our tent.

I ease my gaze at Jack as he tries to hide his tears.

"We tried to find you after that night," I tell him. "And the days, months, and years that followed. We tried everything we could."

The urge to tell my brother what our father had and hadn't done evaporates into the dusty air around us. It's not the time, and I'm not even sure now that there will ever be time.

"I really can't remember anything, Sam," Jack sighs.

"The police found your clothing stained with blood—your blood. Not long after, the investigation ceased, and you were presumed dead."

"So you never knew who took me?"

"No. He was never seen, never caught."

"The only memory I have before St. Leo was crawling from street to street. Cold. Dark, suffocating air. I was an addict, apparently, and I didn't even know how I became one."

"You must've been forced."

"Bastard!" he sighs. He releases his wringing hands and straightens his spine. "Wait... you said they found blood on my clothes?"

"Yeah."

"I have this scar on my back, likely from a knife wound." He rubs the spot between his shoulder blades.

"Did you escape from him?"

"I don't know, Sam." Jack grunts. He gets up, pacing in front of me. "Sister Laura was lovely. She was my hero. Still, I didn't feel that I had a life. Now I know why."

"I'm sorry, Jack. I hope... we can start our new lives together."

He stares at me. "You don't have to try so hard, brother. It sounds like you're proposing to me."

I join him in a laugh.

Brother.

He said it naturally. Despite his memory loss, I know deep down our bond is there.

Jack returns to his seat and leans back. "So, what do you do these days?"

"I have a rescue and protect company with my business partner, Mark Connor. He was in the Special Forces. Green Beret. We specialize in finding missing children."

"Impressive." His eyes ask whether it was because of him.

I simply smile.

"You're married?" he asks.

I take my phone out and shake it a few times in an attempt to wake it up. It seems to have recovered from the heat exposure, although I still have no reception. I show him my wallpaper—the photo I snapped at Grace's school.

"Your wife and kid?"

"My girlfriend and her daughter. Cassidy and Grace Winter."

"She's a knockout. You lucky bastard!"

She is, and more. With her help, I'd arrived here. If it wasn't for her kindness, her understanding of Dad, I wouldn't be here. I wish Cass was with me.

And somehow, I wish my father was here too.

"Sergeant Benedict." An officer enters the tent.

"I'll be right there," Jack says to the officer. He rises from his chair, putting a hand on my shoulder. "I've gotta go. Where are you staying?"

"With a resident."

"You know him well, yes?"

"I do."

"Okay. Here's my number," Jack says. "Keep in touch, and be careful."

"You too."

He doesn't need my protection anymore, but how my whole being yearns to give him just that—take him home with me *right now*.

33

CASSIDY

It took me almost a week to fully get over my tummy bug, but I haven't recovered from Sam's departure to Afghanistan.

If I was in his shoes, I would've done the same to find my brother. So I understand. But understanding doesn't make me forget that my man is going straight into a killing zone.

True to his promise though, Sam had called me a couple of times, followed by a few messages. He sounded upbeat despite apparently being stuck at Kabul airport.

But in the past couple of days—silence.

I've stopped watching the news, and with my mother's help, I keep my mind occupied by packing.

"How did you do it, Mom? Saying goodbye when Dad was still on active duty?" I plonk myself on the storeroom floor, sifting through a box, looking for things I may be able to sell.

"Well, you kids kept me busy, so I had no time to worry about your dad." She stops for a couple of seconds. Suddenly she scoffs, admitting it wasn't entirely true.

Only recently, I found out about her depression following Dad's death. She hid it well from us kids, but I remembered a period when I caught Mother crying a lot and thought she just looked so old—so old.

"You'd never get used to goodbyes or letting go," she says. "The worst thing you can do is to find a way to stop worrying because you can't. You just have to know when to put your emotions aside and when to let yourself be overcome by them."

I peruse some old books as I digest Mother's wisdom. I want to ask how, but I'd rather discover it myself with Sam.

Suddenly Maximus barks. It seems that he doesn't know how to co-exist with those rabbits.

"I'll take him for a walk. Max! Come on, walkie-walkie," she lures the dog. But Max seems to be in his own world, relentless in his barking.

"He's turning into a diva!" I mutter.

"I'll get him," Mother says, putting the leash on him. Soon, the pair make their way out.

I go back into the storage room, staring at piles of boxes that I still need to sort out.

Then I hear Grace scream.

It's not the scream that tells me she needs me.

It's one that tells me she *desperately* needs me.

"Grace!" I run up.

"Mom!" Her voice is coming from my bedroom. What has she seen?

"Hello, Cassidy."

My throat is clogged by panic and anger. I scramble to my closet.

"I didn't know you had a habit of hiding a gun in your bedroom. But hey, I've been watching you." The man shows off my Smith & Wesson pistol in his hand.

"Let her go!"

"I know you can use it, and you probably think I'm still the fool who doesn't know how to handle one."

I stare at his gripping hand. The gun is so close to Grace, and its thumb safety is unlocked. It's not the time to test his skill, or lack of it.

"Put it away." I stand in place, not wanting to prompt him to do anything stupid. "You know better than to play with it."

"Moomm... I'm scared," Grace trembles as the man holds her in his lap.

"Why are you scared, honey? I'm your daddy."

"Mom... please... please call Sam."

"Ahh... Sam," my ex sneers. "I've heard a lot about him. Sam, Sam, Sam. Where's he?"

I keep silent, observing the state of him. He's not drunk, and he's not on drugs either. He's just having fun with my fear—nothing new there.

I take a step closer, reaching out my arms. "Give me Grace, and we'll talk."

"I was so stoked when the brothers found you. I thought we could start again. You said it, before you ran away, that it was better that we parted—to give me time to reflect, and so we would be together again."

I did say that at the time, lying to his face to ease his rage and give myself a chance to run.

He rocks Grace as if trying to calm her down. His expression softens. "I've changed, Cass. I swear." Now he reaches out his arm, asking me to sit next to him. "Please."

"I will do as you ask, Harv. But let Grace go, and we can talk as adults."

"I'm ready to be the father and husband that you wanted me to be."

He hooks a finger into the gun's trigger guard, then lifts that hand, perhaps trying to persuade me that he's not a threat. Still giving me a clear view of what he's doing, he takes the gun to the side of his pants.

I would've moved to attack him, but he still has Grace firmly in his arms. He even kisses her—tenderly, lovingly. "Look at her. She's all grown up."

That is the face that I fell in love with—the face of a man that I thought would be mine forever. But I'm not a naïve twenty-year-old anymore, and I haven't forgotten what Ben told me about that scumbag rejecting Grace.

Harvey Whitlock is a man with a thousand masks, and I'm not going to be his fool this time.

He looks around my bedroom, babbling, "It's a nice house. But why Helena? You could do better!" Grace gyrates as he tries to kiss her again. He tightens his grip with one arm and rests his free hand on the gun handle poking out of his pants.

"Give me Grace!" I insist. My muscles clench seeing how close it is to my daughter.

Perhaps realizing I'm not entertaining his sweet talk, Harvey draws back the gun and points it at me. "Sit down!"

I have no choice but to do what he says.

"I have everything you need, Cass."

"You mean money?"

"Yes, and more. I still love you, and don't forget that Grace is my daughter, and I will never—never—stop loving her."

"Mom... is it true?"

A part of me is eager to say no. He doesn't deserve to be Grace's father! But I can't lie, and I can't afford to trigger Harv—whatever he might do to us. "Yes, Grace. This is your father."

Grace looks at him. Part of me is melting, part of me is fuming, but my response seems to soften Harvey. He lets Grace come to me.

"But I want Sam to be my daddy," she whispers.

Harvey blows out his frustration. "If I hear that name again—"

"What?" I challenge him. "You haven't earned anything to be Grace's father."

I stand up, shielding my daughter. My fist is itching to swing a blow on his face—just like what I promised myself—if only he wasn't holding a weapon.

"Sit down!" Harvey commands, the gun still pointing at me.

I take a seat, placing Grace next to me, as far from him as possible.

"I don't want to call him daddy," Grace whispers.

Harvey smirks cynically. "You think Sam is going to be a good father to you? Huh, Grace?"

Grace simply hides behind me.

His attention then lands on me. "I can see why you were attracted to him. A dashing slab of man meat. Does he remind you of your dad?"

I don't respond, and he carries on lecturing me. "Your life with Sam might look good on paper, like a fairytale—a hero comes home. But in reality, you'll be forever a widow."

"You hated me. In fact, you hated me enough that you didn't care whether I lived or died in the hands of the Seth brothers."

"It was your choice. Now you have another." The gun in his hand and his tone of voice tell me otherwise. He's set on taking us back. It's not my choice at all. "Come with me, and we can start again," he tries to persuade me again.

I bow my head, not wanting to answer.

"Of course, you can choose to be with Sam. And what will happen? You'll keep working your ass off, trying to make ends meet. You'll never be there for Grace because you'll spend most of your waking life at that bar of yours. You'll miss out on a lot of things—like Grace's swimming progress."

How dare he!

"We've moved on, Harv. You've gotta leave us alone."

Harvey calmly paces the room. "Your needs will never be fulfilled. You'll wonder how it used to be when you two were still smitten lovers. Where is he now? Where's your hero? Did you know that Seth has escaped?"

Just hearing the name suffocates me. I haven't had the severe nightmare that I used to have, but water is still scaring me, and even though it's no longer front of mind, the memory of that waterboard hasn't left me.

"Don't play with me!"

"I don't know if you keep up with the news. Should I tell you there was a fire at Montana State Prison yesterday?"

My muscles go rigid.

"The Department of Corrections hasn't released anything, but I know—I *know*—that there are two inmates unaccounted for. And one of them is Ambrose Seth."

"Then you'd better go. He'll be gunning for you."

"Oh, Cass. I hired him and his brother. I know how he operates. He might put a target on your man. Sam killed Denzel, didn't he? But every man knows what's bigger than revenge." He stoops to whisper in my ear. "Riches."

He lets silence linger as if giving me time to mull over his proposition.

Getting no response, he continues, "I've got what he wants. You'll be safe with me. Only with me. We'll start clean. No more debt." He reaches down his pocket and passes me a piece of paper. His eyes wander briefly to the Scotty shed.

That's why Maximus has been barking!

"You put that thing in my house?" I grouch.

So Harvey came to my house the first time—as the Seth

brothers told me—to hide that note, and then retrieved it recently.

"Well, technically not." He tips his head in the direction of the shed.

My drive to punch him heightens—if only Grace wasn't here. That piece of paper—those numbers—had led the Seth brothers to me, and I will never forget what they did.

"Cass, whatever happens to me, you will have the money. It's in a safe in Jamaica. I opened a few accounts—decoys, of course—but the third and sixth number sets are the correct safe IDs and passcodes."

"I don't want your money!" I toss the paper back to him. "And I don't want to know how you got it."

"It's two million dollars, Cass! Legit money that I've won from casinos and shares since you left. I've learned, baby. Every time I held that wad of cash in my hand, I thought of you and Grace."

"Fuck off!" I shouldn't have sworn in front of Grace, but this is just too much! His gambling addiction has never left him and will never leave him.

"We'll be a family again. I want that very much, Cass. Name a place, and we'll be there in a blink of an eye. I can give you what no other man can. Think about our daughter."

"Grace is just fine without your money."

"Where's your so-called protector? He's given up on you, huh? Surely, he knows about Seth's escape, yet he's still staying put in Afghanistan. I don't know what he's doing there—I bet it's got nothing to do with a missing child. No US diplomats are left there."

The fact that he hasn't mentioned Ben leads me to believe that Harvey doesn't know about my brother's trip to Jamaica. I think this scumbag is pouncing now because he found out

Sam was away—what better time to try to take my man's place!

"Leave!"

"Only I can protect you," my ex insists.

"If you want to protect me, give Ambrose Seth what he wants and send him into a trap. And let the police deal with the rest."

"Not that easy, Cass."

"Well, it is. Just leave. If you really love your daughter."

"Come on! Time to go." He pushes me with one hand, while the other points the gun at my back.

"Mooom..."

"It's okay, Grace. He won't hurt us."

"Move, or I will." He ushers me and Grace downstairs.

My phone is buzzing relentlessly on the coffee table. It's Mark, and I don't want to speculate why he's calling. Is it Sam? Or is he trying to warn me about Ambrose Seth?

"Let me answer," I say.

"Put it on speaker." Harvey stands next to Grace.

I do as he says. "Mark."

"Cass, Ambrose Seth. He escaped. Go to Red Mark headquarters. Now! I'll meet you there."

I tremble at the news—but in a way, I'm relieved that he's not calling to tell me he was sorry for my loss. "Have you heard from Sam?"

"I sent him messages, but he hasn't replied."

"Okay."

"He's alright. You know that, Cass. He's probably just held up."

Before anyone can say anything else, the window shatters. I shield Grace as Harvey curses, and the next thing I know, he's on the floor, bleeding.

"Cass! Cass! What's happening?" I hear Mark yelling through the speaker. "I'm coming!"

The figure of Ambrose Seth looms in front of me.

"Useless prick!" He kicks the motionless Harvey.

"I know where the money is!" I shout at him, relentlessly shielding Grace. "You can have the whole two million."

But he sniggers. "That can come later. Right now, my priority is your boyfriend. I want him to claim you. Only then can I claim him. You know what I'm talking about, don't you?"

So the man has chosen revenge over riches.

Against my ex-husband, I might have had a chance, but Ambrose Seth isn't someone who will entertain some cheap bargaining. Nonetheless, I have to try for the sake of Grace.

Ambrose notices the phone on the coffee table. Without hesitation, he throws it to the floor and destroys it with his foot.

"I'll leave my daughter here, and I'll come with you."

"Mom... don't, please..." Grace weeps.

"It's okay, honey," I whisper to her. "Grandma will be back soon, and Mark will pick you up."

"Do you know the mistake I made when I tried to take you the first time?" Ambrose sneers. "I underestimated that girl. So, both of you, out!" He swings his gun wildly as if he's about to release random shots.

Without resisting, I follow his instructions.

Just as we step out the door, another car zooms in. Soon shots are fired, and there's nothing I can do but cage Grace in my embrace.

Who's shooting who? I have no idea...

34

SAM

I spend the night with Rahim and his three brothers. They decide to stay put in Kabul despite the mass exodus, not wanting to leave their mother and sister, who live at the other end of town.

After one of the brothers fiddled with a small satellite dish on the roof, I've finally got mobile reception.

My phone keeps beeping, signaling missed calls from Mark—whatever they're for. At least I know he's alive. I should reply to him, but with the dicey phone reception, my priority is to call Cass while I can.

But after trying three times, my calls remain unanswered.

I groan, feeling uneasiness surging within me. And when I see Ben calling me, my blood curdles. Something very wrong has happened!

"Sam—you've gotta—back—"

"Ben! You're cutting out!"

"Get down here!" he yells. "—Seth—Cass—"

Ambrose Seth has Cass?

The call gets disconnected, and I immediately run to the

roof, hoping to get better reception. I know I shouldn't be doing this, but I'm desperate.

I call Ben back. "Ben!"

"Sam! Where the fuck are you?"

I realize Rahim and his brothers have joined me, rifles in their hands, guarding me. Those men are the epitome of loyalty in this hell. I acknowledge their presence with a sincere nod.

"I'm still in Kabul. Look, Cass hasn't answered my calls."

Ben's voice roars in my ear. "Kabul? You shitting me, man? You're in fucking Afghanistan?"

"Ben! What happened?" I know he's more than annoyed.

"Get your ass back here! Seth has Cass and Grace."

"Fuck!" My rage explodes as loudly as a blast. I feel like kicking something. "How? Where were you?"

"Hell, where were *you!*"

"You're supposed to protect her while I'm away. That was the deal."

"Damn you, Sam! The deal is, *you* protect her. Not drag your ass to some IED-invested graveyard!"

"Ben, don't. Just don't!" I take a deep breath. "We can sort our shit later—just you and me, however you want. But you've gotta get to them now. Call Mark!"

The reception is unusually clear. I can even hear Ben sighing. "He's been shot."

35

———

SAM

It's the dead of night, but this Afghan war, and my own war, know no time nor day. How the hell did Ambrose Seth get out? How could he even get near Cass and Grace? I don't dare to think about how Mark is doing.

"I've got a flight for you, departing in two hours," Jack says.

"Thanks, brother."

"Get them back. I know you will." Jack pats my shoulder.

"Come with me, Jack. Get out of this shithole. I know you can."

"Of course I can. I was offered a seat weeks ago."

"So?"

Jack lowers his gaze, resolute. "I'm gonna be here until the last soldier has been evacuated."

I huff—fear, agitation, and impatience all roll into one. "Jack…"

"I volunteered to stay 'til the end. I've given priority to my men who have families back home—young families."

It hurts to let him go, but he's a Redley, he's a Kelleher. Of course he will stay behind if that means others can escape.

I pat his shoulder. "Take care, Jack."

"You go and kick that bastard's ass!"

I give him a curt nod. "If not, I'm sure she would." Perhaps I'm saying it to console myself. Cass and Grace against Ambrose? The odds are terrifying.

"You two are made for each other, then," Jack says.

"Semper fi, brother. I'll find you. I swear, I'll find you again."

He opens his arms and pulls me into a hug. He's not so little anymore, I should know that, but to see him so resolved and determined, I'm in awe.

"Godspeed, Sam." He turns me around, forcing me not to look back, and when my feet refuse to move, I feel a Marine slap land on my back.

GUNFIRE, kerosene-filled air, the mad rush of people, cries, screams—like a bad memory, it has passed, and I'm back in peaceful Helena.

Peaceful for everybody else, maybe. In my current world, though, the war rages on.

Worse still, as if a beautiful passage of life has been snatched from under my feet, I'm without Jack. It hurts to know that his name, and the casual 'brother' calls, will have to move to the back of my mind.

Right now, though, only three names matter: Cass, Grace, and Mark.

Ben Winter waits for me at the hospital entrance. He's pacing between pillars, his hand moving as if he's clutching something.

"How's Mark?" I ask him nervously.

"He's been sedated. The bullet got his lung."

"Jesus!" I wish I had taken that bullet. My partner must've

been in a dire situation, desperately protecting Cass and Grace.

"I still want to kick your sorry ass, Kelleher, but let's find my sister first."

"Did Mark say anything?"

"No, he was unconscious when Mom found him. She'd just come home from walking Maximus," Ben says, leading the way into the ward.

"And you?"

He breathes hard, his lips flatten. "I just came back from Jamaica, looking for leads on Harvey."

"For Christ's sake, Ben!" I knew this guy was way too brash. He's too green to be a Red Mark.

He adds, "He's been seen at a couple of banks. He didn't open normal accounts, but safety boxes."

"Fuck..."

I do want to have our fight right here, right now, but it's not the time.

We keep walking. Ben's hand is still moving nervously. It appears as though his index and middle fingers are clipping something. Seeing the direction of my eyes, he blurts, "I'm trying to quit!"

"Huh. There's never been a better time, then."

"There's never been a worse time!" he frets, slowing his pace. "He's in there." He gestures at an open door at the end of the hallway.

I walk into the room—surprised and heartened to see Ivy Cavanagh by Mark's bed.

"Sam..." Ivy whispers and gives me a quick embrace. Soon her attention is back on Mark. "I came here as soon as I heard."

"Thank you. It means a lot."

"The doctor managed to get the bullet out. I guess now it's

just... wait and see." She pulls up the sheet to cover more of Mark's chest. "He'll pull through. I know he will."

"Of course," I say. The alternative is not an alternative at all!

She gently puts her hand on top of Mark's, but her gaze is on me as if asking for permission.

"I'm sure he would appreciate it," I quip.

Ivy stretches her palm and fingers as if wanting to engulf Mark's whole hand. She stares at his pale face. "I love him," she blurts.

My heart jolts against my ribcage. How I wish my friend were awake.

But then she scoffs. "There, I've said it. But I guess you already knew." Now she's watching her own hand. I know that hand is desperate to do more than just perch there.

"Tell it to him then."

"I know the law of love as well as the law of this state," she says coldly. "You know I won't tell Mark that. We don't have a chance—an I-love-you will only hurt our case."

"Ivy, give it time. He'll see, I swear, he'll see."

Ivy shakes her head, withdrawing her hand. "Sorry. That was silly of me." She gives her full attention to me, saying, "You go and get your girls. Don't worry about Mark. I'll stay here with him."

"Okay."

Barely twenty-four hours ago, I said goodbye to my long-lost brother. Now, how do I leave a friend? A wounded friend who defended my family?

I hold his hand. "Hang in there, buddy. I owe you one, and you'd better be alive when I'm back!"

Ivy reassures me with a soft nod. "I'll call you if anything changes. I'm sure he'll be okay."

With her by his side, I'm sure he will.

I turn around, but just before I leave the room, she calls me. "Sam, wait!"

I swivel, and I'm greeted by a startled Ivy. Her hand is in his, and damn, my partner is squeezing it!

Mark mutters. It's unclear what he's saying, but it does sound a hell like 'Ivy.'

"Told you you've got a chance," I quip.

"I'm here, Mark," Ivy says. "And Sam is here too."

He mumbles something as I come closer.

"I think he wants you," Ivy says.

"Take it easy, buddy."

But Mark persists. He really wants to tell me something. I place my ear over his mouth.

"Tripoli."

"Mark... did you say Tripoli?"

His eyelids shudder. "He called Tripoli." His voice is crisp this time, but as soon as he exhales at the end of his sentence, he slips back into unconsciousness.

My mind is pulled in all directions. I don't know what that name means, but maybe I'll find out later.

I rush out to meet Ben. "So what do we know?" I ask him as we make our way out of the ward.

"Cass's phone was destroyed, but I managed to get her sim card out. I sent it to a friend, and he retrieved the recording of her last call with Mark."

"Let me hear it."

Ben takes out his phone and plays the recording. Mark is frantically trying to get Cass to drive to Red Mark, but then all hell breaks loose.

"Son of a bitch!" I curse at the voice. "That's... that's her ex?"

"Yes, that's Harvey Whitlock, alright. And he's dead."

Mixed emotions rouse inside me. I can't imagine what would be on Grace's mind, witnessing her father's death. Her memory of him might've been faint, but surely, she understood what happened. I just have to trust that Cass would've done everything she could to shelter her daughter from any distress.

At the same time, I'm glad the son of a bitch is gone. Because one, he won't ever bother Cass again, and two, it saves me from having to deal with him. He was the root of it all—and I couldn't have been held responsible for what I might've done.

The playback continues. This time, the voice of Ambrose Seth makes my blood boil.

Right now, my priority is your boyfriend. I want him to claim you. Only then can I claim him.

"Fuck..." I think hard about where to start. This hospital lobby is not the best place for me right now. "Mark just told me a name. Tripoli. Does that ring a bell?"

"Who the hell is Tripoli?"

"Does Ambrose have a Marine friend?" Somehow the nickname reminds me of a line in the Marine Hymn—*the shores of Tripoli.*

"Don't think so. Army and Marines aren't usually best friends, are they?"

"Well, if both or one of them is an ass, then yeah. No one gets along."

Ben ponders for a moment, then he says, "In that prison fire, two were unaccounted for. Could the other person be Ambrose's accomplice?"

"Who's that other person?"

"The identities of the escapees are kept confidential."

"Well, we know one of them is Ambrose." I look at Ben as if trying to find an answer in his eyes. While it's not there, I think I know someone in this very hospital who will be able to help. "Come with me!" I motion to him.

We march back to Mark's room as fast as a hospital allows us to. I pull Ivy outside.

"Look, I really need your help," I say to her. "The identity of the prisoner who escaped with Ambrose Seth during the fire—please tell me who he is."

"Sam... I can't."

"Ivy, you're the attorney general of the state of Montana. Of course you can!"

"Sam, you know—"

"Please. We think that other person is Ambrose's accomplice."

"Is he a Libyan immigrant, by any chance?" Ben interjects.

"How did you know that?" Ivy frowns.

"Tripoli!" I say, my eyes acknowledging Ben.

For that work, I might just take back my words. Mr. Winter certainly belongs in Red Mark—he's got to be our next recruit, but with some tough love and a serious boot camp.

"I'm not all brawn, you know!" Ben quips, perhaps realizing that he's impressed me.

"Mark must've heard Ambrose making a call to Tripoli. The police know all locations and properties linked to Ambrose, so it's likely that he needed a new place to hide."

"Tripoli's place," Ben says.

"The police have searched his house. It was empty."

"Ivy, I would've done this myself, but—" Between the two of us, Mark usually does most of the information digging. Now I feel like I've lost an arm. "Maybe he has an old friend? Or any possible rental? Could you find out?"

Without hesitation, the attorney general makes a call. A few moments later, she gives us the answer. "A house in Wolf

Creek. It belongs to his old boss. Apparently, they were close. It's for sale, so it's currently empty."

"I owe you!" I turn around.

"Wait!" She stops me. "The man has an uncle who rents out a farmhouse in Coulter Point. You might want to check that one out, too."

I give her a peck on the cheek and then gesture to Ben to keep up with me as I dart out of the hospital.

"You've got a gun?" I ask Ben as we decide to split up to cover the two possible locations.

"Not on me."

I toss him my second gun. "Whatever you do, don't get shot. No Taekwondo kick can repel a bullet."

"What do you know, Kelleher?"

I might've lost an arm without Mark, but I must admit—even though I still hate Ben's guts for hunting Harvey Whitlock behind my back—I'm finding a partner in him.

36

———

CASSIDY

All of the windows in this room are covered with plywood. Grace is sleeping on my lap while Ambrose Seth watches from his armchair right in front of me.

If it wasn't for Mark, I would've likely lost Grace. In a panic, Ambrose used us as a human shield, and I swear, he could've shot my daughter anytime then. Mark opened fire, I'm sure only to get Ambrose off Grace, but he paid the price. I don't even know if he's still alive.

Since we got here, Ambrose hasn't said a word—I don't even remember seeing him blink. The bullet Mark lodged in his shoulder doesn't seem to bother him too much. His executioner's eyes remind me that he has no limits, let alone compassion. My ordeal when I was in this man's hand plays in my mind.

"Take me with you and leave Grace here," I brace myself to bargain with him. "Let Sam pick her up. And you can do whatever the hell you want with me."

His brows arch sharply as if what he's hearing is so idiotic he can't even laugh. The man stands up for the first time since he forced me to stay put on this old sofa. His phone is firmly in his grip. I'm sure he's about to call someone.

"You should know a thing or two about gambling, huh, Cassidy? From your dear dead husband?" He walks closer to me, only to turn around and pace the room. "You hold on to your trump card for as long as you can. And your Grace is just that—my trump card."

Silence falls once more. I can't see out, and I was blindfolded on the way here, but I can hear and smell farm animals. Even this room looks like a part of a farmhouse. I know Ambrose isn't stupid enough to take me to a place where there are people around, but I hope I'm not too far from civilization.

Grace suddenly stirs. She stretches and smiles, looking at me. But when she notices her surroundings—dim and strange —she cries.

"Honey, it's okay. Mommy's here."

"I want to go home!"

"We will soon," I say. But my daughter keeps crying.

"Shut her up!" Ambrose orders.

"Calm down now," I whisper and hold her close. I look straight up at Ambrose, who's towering in front of me. "She needs to go to the bathroom. Now."

"She'll just have to wait, or feel free to wet that old junk!" He points at the sofa.

"I need to go too," I insist. "Come on. You've held us for hours now."

Ambrose takes out his gun and points it at me.

"Look away, honey," I say to Grace, keeping her chin on my shoulder while I'm facing my captor.

"Move!" he commands, allowing me to stand up. He then steers us out of the room to a small toilet right next to the kitchen. He follows us like a shadow, stopping me from looking out the only open window in the house. But I catch a glimpse of what's in the distance.

"Thank you." I enter and close the door.

"Be quick!" Ambrose yells.

When I said we needed to go, I didn't lie. But I do have something else in mind. What I saw from the window confirmed my suspicion—there is a paddock, and another house.

"Are you done?" I ask Grace.

"Yes. But I want to go home."

"We will, honey," I reply as I relieve myself.

Before I flush, I spy on Ambrose through the gap in the door. He's making a call, but his voice is soft. I can't speculate who's at the other end—it could be that Tripoli guy he called when he took us. At this stage, I don't really care. What counts is that his attention doesn't seem to be on me or Grace—or his gun.

I open the door slowly. Ambrose will soon know the way I gamble. I don't have a trump card, but I have my brain and a toilet lid in my Sarah Connor arms. I signal to Grace to stay in the toilet. With all I've got, I swing the moldy piece of ceramic against the back of his head.

My weapon breaks in two, and the big man falls with a thump—his phone and gun are stuck between his belly and the floor.

He's still moving while my hands are rummaging through his pockets, looking for his car keys. But they're not there, and I already know he's not the sloppy type who'll leave them in the ignition. The keys could be anywhere!

A hand snatches one of my wrists as I withdraw.

"Grace, run!" I yell as I desperately elbow Ambrose's bleeding head. I keep him face-down so he can't draw the gun that's still stuck under him. Feeling his resistance, I attack the area of his shoulder that had been damaged by Mark's shot.

This time Ambrose wails in pain. As soon as he lets go of me, I whack him again with what's left of the toilet lid.

He's down, and I have no time to check if he's still alive—I bolt out, knowing Grace is already outside.

"Come on, Grace!" I carry her while I keep running. I have no interest in finding out what Ambrose is up to. There's nothing but a dirt field around the house, so I simply head toward the paddock on the adjacent property.

Past the paddock, there's another farmhouse.

"Hello!" I scramble around the house, hoping for someone. Most farmers in Montana know how to shoot, so I'm counting on it. But the house is empty. I pick up the only phone I can find.

"Shit!" There's no dial tone.

I leave through the back door. If I have to carry Grace while I hike, it will slow me down, and no doubt Ambrose will catch up.

Then I see something that might just be our ticket out.

"You still remember how to ride?" I ask Grace as we run to a stable.

She gives me a confident nod.

Ambrose Seth claimed to know me well as a spouse of his 'client.' But I don't know if his knowledge stretches as far as my barrel racing days. Sooner or later, he will come to this farm. But my hope is that he will check the house first and then the barn—one of those will be a place someone would naturally hide in.

I huff a sigh of relief to find a mare staring back at me.

"Hey there," I say and pat her. "Good horse."

I snatch a saddle and reins nearby. Without wasting a

second, I gear the mare up. My hands tremble, and I can't put the belt into the D ring fast enough.

"Mom... quick."

I hear it. A vehicle is approaching.

"I'm almost there, honey."

After checking that everything is secure, I swing Grace up onto the saddle. Watching my surroundings, I quietly tug the horse out of the stable.

"You okay?" I ask Grace.

"Yeah."

I'm still walking alongside the horse, using the stable to conceal us—anticipating Ambrose might arrive anytime now.

"We're gonna go fast soon, okay? Move forward, honey. I'm gonna sit right behind you," I instruct Grace. "Hold on."

I wait until we reach a row of trees. Once we're in the shadow, I mount the horse and guide her to canter into the forest.

37

SAM

"No fucking way!"

I toss my phone onto the dashboard, unable to reach Ben. I can't believe that useless thing refuses to turn back on—I thought I'd gotten it fixed in Helena.

I keep driving north while trying to switch on my phone again. This time a voicemail notification beeps as soon as the system loads. It's not from Ben.

Samuel Kelleher. We meet again. Do you still remember what I said the last time we met? Blood for blood. Come to Coulter Point before sunset. I haven't decided what to do with the little girl, but Cassidy... well, you'll either watch her die or find her dead. I prefer the first—

The message is cut short by a ruckus. Something breaks, and the man doesn't even seem to have a chance to say anything in response. Then rustling noises ensue as if the phone was rubbed against a rough surface. Everything else comes out muffled—but there's definitely a struggle.

Grace, run!

Then the message ends.

My heart stops. That was Cass—loud and clear.

"No..." The sigh is squeezed out of me by anguish.

The message only arrived about fifteen minutes ago. If anything, I hope Grace did manage to run. But I'm pretty sure Ambrose still has Cass.

I quickly dial my interim partner. "Ben!" I pray that my phone won't let me down again. "He took them to Coulter Point. Where are you?"

"I'm almost at Wolf Creek."

I check my satellite navigation.

"You go ahead and check out Wolf Creek," I decide. Ambrose could well be heading there with Cass now that something has happened at Coulter Point. That prick might be determined to make it harder for me now. "I'll continue on to Coulter Point. Grace might've been left behind there."

"What do you mean left behind?"

"Your sister fought Ambrose—or at least tried to." I pause.

"Sam! What happened to her?" Ben yells.

"I don't know. Ambrose left me a message, but it was cut short. I heard Cass telling Grace to run."

"Jesus Christ!"

"Cass might still be there at Coulter Point, Ben. But be prepared. Ambrose might head your way."

As soon as I hang up, I replay the message from Ambrose.

The third time I listen to it, just before the message ends, I hear a faint crash, followed by Cass's half-grunt. Dare I think that she managed to subdue Ambrose?

In danger, her first choice would be to keep Grace with her. When she told Grace to run, she must've been adamant that she could get back to her daughter.

Cass is still there!

I speed up.

When I'm close, I stop a hundred yards before the house in question, approaching the gate on foot. There's no car, although I notice tire marks everywhere. The house is empty too, but now I know what the ruckus was. Cass seems to have hit Ambrose with a cistern lid! My badass sweetheart. She's an expert in restoring peace, but she knows how to stir it when it's called for.

I follow the footprints from the back door—leading to a farmhouse nearby. A phone headset is dangling off the hook. She *was* here.

And I see a stable. There's no horse inside, and the gear is gone. It could be abandoned, but I can smell that an animal has been kept in here. Knowing her, a horse would be her choice for a getaway ride.

I rush back to my car and follow the tire marks. They disappear when it hits the road, and it ends at a T-junction. I turn left. Pass a river, I stop. I'm about three hundred feet above it, but I see something in the distance. I put on my binoculars.

"Shit..." It's Cass, and she's riding fast. For her to come pretty close to the water means she knows Ambrose is on her tail, and she has no other choice—although I can't see him.

I make a call to Ben.

"She's not here," Ben replies.

"Your sister is riding with Grace along the Coulter River. Head toward the bridge and wait there," I instruct.

"She's on horseback?"

"Yes. She's half a mile northeast of Wolf Creek Bridge. I can't see Ambrose, but he might try to cut her off at the bridge."

"I'm on my way!"

"I'm on her side of the river. Ambrose might well try to

flank her. We both know your sister won't cross the water, so I'll stay on this side and get to her."

"Got it."

"If you see Ambrose, shoot him," I instruct.

"And if he flanks her from your side?"

"I'll come between him and Cass, then kill him."

I can almost hear Ben gritting his teeth, but I'm sure he's glad to hear what I said.

I add, "If anything happens at my side of the river, cover for *her*. You hear me? *Her*."

I don't care if Ambrose gets me. I don't care if the son of a bitch cuts me up, skins me alive, or drinks my blood—as long as Cass and Grace are safe.

I take my SUV off-road, heading down toward the river until I run out of path. Ahead of me is a trail riddled with fallen trees and loose rocks. I hear a vehicle coming from over the debris-filled hill.

Worries crowd in.

Ambrose is going to flank Cass. He's got a clear run from where he is while I'm stuck here.

With the terrain ahead of me, I have no chance of pursuing him on foot, no matter how fast I run. I've made split-second decisions countless times, but only *this* one counts.

The river.

Cass's nemesis could be my ally today, and it helps that she's downstream from me.

I was a SEAL. Water is my home. If my instincts are right, Ambrose is coming to recapture Cass. If he'd wanted to kill her right now, he would've stayed on higher ground; there are plenty of vantage points he could use to shoot her.

I prefer the first—he said in his message. He wants me to be present when he kills her.

As long as Ambrose doesn't know I'm around, there shouldn't be anything else that will trigger him to unleash the unthinkable on Cass or Grace. Soon enough, he will get a mighty surprise from me.

38

CASSIDY

The trail ends here. It feels like I've been holding my vomit for hours as I rode alongside the river. We're now up against harsh slopes and rocky terrains. The horse won't make it there, and if we go on foot, it will be hell for Grace—I won't let her go through that.

Ambrose is close. I can hear his car—probably driving on the road above.

Either I turn around or face my nightmare.

"Mom! He's coming."

Shit!

My adversary is closer than I thought. Ambrose Seth has driven his car off-road, and now he's coming down, straight at us. Only the terrain slows him down. But it's a matter of time.

I've got to cross to the other side, where we will be on higher ground, and then disappear into the wooded area—not out here where we're exposed.

"Mooom!"

I have no idea how deep the water is, but judging by the pronounced ripples, I think the horse will negotiate it without having to get us to dip too low.

I kick-on the mare. While I know she will give everything she has, she feels my emotions. The horse spins around in place.

"Easy, easy," I say to the mare and try to reposition her so she's facing the river.

With one hand holding Grace and the other holding the reins, I have to rely on the horse's willingness to get in the water and run steadily. I kick-on her belly one more time, controlling my breathing. The horse moves, and this time she descends into the water.

"Hold on, baby!" I tell Grace. But my little girl knows what to do. She's riding better than I am. Sam was right, Grace is stronger than me, but at the moment, I need to go on for her.

The water goes up to the horse's thighs, as the sound of Ambrose's car gets louder.

I cluck to encourage the horse to keep going while steadying my breathing.

My mouth feels foul. This is more than I can take. I'm not facing my nightmare, I'm in it, and I'm wide awake. But it's not about me. I'm doing it for Grace—and Sam. I won't rob my special people of their happiness just because a heartless prick wants me. I need to be alive for them.

The mare jerks and whines, disturbed by the noise of the car engine, revving madly as if it was about to blow up. Grace and I hold on, and we finally get to the other side. But gunshot sends our horse berserk. I turn my head, catching a glimpse of Ambrose's bleeding face. He's shooting low—I think he's aiming at the horse.

Much as I try to calm the mare down, she insists on going away from the forest, toward the plains. That will make us an easy target. I need us to get behind the trees and disappear.

I manage to settle the horse, but I sense she's one gunshot

away from throwing us off. We have to go on foot, or we will be immobilized with broken bones.

"Grace, lean forward, lean forward," I instruct. The horse is agitated but is steady enough for me to dismount. Once grounded, I snatch Grace off her back and cocoon my daughter with every inch of my body. The horse soon bolts away as one more shot blares across the valley.

Staying low, I scramble desperately to take cover.

Now Ambrose is about to cross.

"We'll be okay, honey," I say as I zigzag my way up the riverbank, making my move as unpredictable as possible. But Ambrose seems to have stopped firing.

There's silence for a while. Then I hear a gun cock.

"Close your eyes, baby," I say.

Expecting Ambrose to arrive at my heel, mocking a goodbye to me and putting a bullet in my head, my heart stops when I see a frame emerging from the water.

No, it's not the ghastly figure that has been haunting me.

It's Sam, facing my nightmare head-on while Grace and I are shielded behind him.

No one would have anticipated that, I guess stealth is the main weapon of a SEAL, and he's using it to surprise and destroy Ambrose Seth.

"Keep your eyes closed, Grace."

"Mom... what's happening?" Grace cries as I shield her.

"We're okay, baby. Sam is here. Just stay still for now."

Ambrose's body crashes into the water as Sam hurries on toward him. I swear my man was declaring something to the dead prick—whatever it is.

I check every inch of Grace. Apart from her drenched clothes and shoes, and messy hair, my daughter seems to be in good shape.

After removing Ambrose's gun and checking his pulse, Sam pivots toward us.

He pulls Grace and me into his embrace. He places his face right in front of mine, whispering, "You alright, sweetheart?"

Water drips from his hair, flowing to my cheeks. My eyes take some soaking, but it doesn't stop me from looking into his gray diamond eyes. The feeling of safety is even stronger. This is a rescue that I will tell my future children and grandchildren. I might've been too proud to be a damsel-in-distress before, but boy, I admit it's good to be in a hero's arms. As long as the hero is Sam.

He then takes Grace up on his hip. "You okay, Pup?"

Sam examines Grace as thoroughly as I did.

"She's okay," I whisper to Sam, who is doing another round of checking on his SEAL pup.

Suddenly, I hear another voice.

"Ben?"

"Where has he been?" Sam quips.

"Uncle Ben!" Grace yells, but she's still clinging to me.

"Cass... you okay?" Ben rushes to me as if there isn't anyone else around. Even Grace is a little surprised by his sudden, solid hug. I remember this sensation when Ben turns into a hell of a protective brother, like the time in Black Crow River.

"Yeah," I tell my brother.

Ben kisses me, checking me at the same time—for signs of injury, I'm sure.

"I'm okay," I assure him.

He ruffles my hair playfully, then turns to Grace. "You okay, Grace?"

"Yeah," she murmurs.

Ben then glares at Sam but ends it with an admiring gaze.

"You trust me yet?" Sam tests my brother.

Ben raises his brows, restraining a smile.

"You wanna go to Uncle Ben?" I whisper to Grace. I really need to check on Sam. He looks okay, but I need to make sure nothing of him is broken under that black tee.

"Come on, pumpkin. Mom and Sam will need to talk," Ben says.

"I'm a SEAL pup, not a pumpkin."

"Is that right?" Ben gives Sam a quick look, to which Sam responds with a proud nod.

"I want a drink," Grace says.

"Okay, come on." Ben stretches his arms to her. "You don't want to see Mom and Sam kiss again, do you? You said it was gross?"

Grace smiles shyly, releasing her grip on me, and lets Ben takes her.

When the two walk away to a nearby tree, I kiss Sam as I pat his torso, looking for any kind of wound.

"Not even a scratch," Sam brags.

"Tell me it's over?"

"It's over."

I kiss him again and then take the time to admire his arms under his wet long-sleeved T-shirt. He takes off his top. "Is that better?"

I smile, resting my head against his pecs.

"I'm proud of you," Sam praises, turning his head toward the river.

"I almost pissed in my pants, but hey, I made it."

"That's my girl."

"Your cowgirl," I correct him.

He chuckles. "We'll have time for that." Then he picks me up and carries me in his arms.

I kiss Sam. Passionately.

He is the father that Grace deserves. And his lips have never felt so comforting.

I touch every inch of his face, trying to convince myself it isn't a dream. He's alright, he's out of Kabul safe and sound, and he got to me in time.

"How does it feel to be a knight in shining armor?"

He shakes his head. "No, I'm not your knight in shining armor."

What he says seems to contradict what's spread in front of me. His bare torso, still wet from the river and his sweat, gleams under the sun. I guess he doesn't need armor to shine as a hero.

He gives me a side smile. "I'm just a man who stands between you and hell."

I trace his lips with my finger, warning him that an even harder kiss will follow. "Hell yeah, you are."

39

CASSIDY

Pain shared is pain halved; love shared is love in abundance.

Sam and I still boast about our not-even-a-scratch victory over Ambrose Seth.

And as summer turns to fall, Sam and I begin our lives as a full-fledged couple, with Grace happily absorbing the attention, care, and love from the both of us. After what she'd gone through, we're determined to make sure she grows up a healthy girl—body and mind. With her ongoing therapy, and the whole Winter and Red Mark families rallying around us, I know Grace will be just fine.

My other hero, Mark, has fully recovered from his surgery. Grace has gotten a lot closer to him. She didn't see much of what happened when Mark got shot, but I'm sure she knows he saved her. Mark has even babysat her a few times. Actually, Mark is an excellent 'manny.' Sam still teases him about his 'kiddy connection' sometimes, just to remind his partner whom he learned it from.

Tripoli was recaptured by the police. He was spotted spying at Coulter Point, perhaps wondering what happened to his partner in crime. Apparently, Ambrose promised him ten grand for starting the fire at the prison and lending him the property.

Following Ben's tip, Harvey's money was found in Jamaica, and it was seized by the Feds. Only about fifty thousand dollars was left in the safety box. No one knows where the rest of the money went or whether the two million he claimed existed at all. I think Harvey did have it —it wouldn't have been the first time he possessed that kind of money. Perhaps the casinos he won his fortune from (and their associated agencies) got their hands on it before the Feds.

Today we're preparing for a picnic in Sam's backyard following news that Jack had been booked on a flight out of Kabul. We haven't got further confirmation, but if the original plan still stands, Jack will be in Helena this afternoon.

"You shouldn't have gone over the top like this." Sam steals a chicken wing from a tray I place next to the breadbasket— my own buffalo chicken.

"Well, I've gotta make an effort if one day I'll become Mrs. Kelleher."

"Oh, Cass! Even if you burnt the kitchen, I would still marry you."

"Hmm... then I wonder why you haven't asked me yet." He hasn't popped the question, but I found him touching my ring finger a lot in the past couple of weeks.

"Patience isn't your strength is it?" he teases me. He pulls me over so I lean on him. "You had your nightmare again last night?"

"Yeah," I admit. "But it was brief, and it didn't get to the most gruesome bit. Thanks for holding me." I remember waking up in his arms.

"You don't have to say thank you, sweetheart."

"I didn't scream that loud, did I?"

"No." He rubs the top of my palm. "And I notice it has become less frequent."

I give him a nod. "I'm still working on it. But when I'm awake, I can think about Dad fondly now."

"Good." He lands a light kiss on my lips.

I lick the buffalo sauce he's transferred onto me. "I think it tastes pretty good," I comment.

"Not bad at all. You're on fire, lady." He smacks my bum.

"Well, speaking about fire, could you bring the heaters out?"

"Radio!" Sam gets up, pinching another piece of chicken as he heads to the storage shed.

"Grace, watch Maximus, okay? Don't let him near the ham," I say.

"Okay, Mom."

The sun shines momentarily before it hides behind the clouds.

I set a couple of potted plants from Mother on the table. The bright white contrasts nicely with the blue tablecloth. My roses aren't ready yet—I've seen leaves sprouting, but it'll be months before I'll see flowers, apparently.

Smiling, I bow down to smell the jasmine, amazed by how much things have changed. One by one, my fears are being erased. Nothing dramatic, but slowly and steadily. Patience isn't my strong suit, but Sam is a good teacher of that.

"You okay?" I ask Sam, who's looking at the watch nervously.

"Umm... no. Not really," he confesses as he turns on the two heaters, one at each end of the table. "What if he changes his mind? What if something happened in Kabul? The Marine Corps has been pretty sketchy with their updates."

"He'll be here," I assure him.

Not long after, I hear a knock at the door.

"Could you get it, please?" Sam begs.

"Why?" I tidy up his polo shirt collar. "You've met him once."

"Exactly, *once*. What if he changes his mind about me?"

"Think about it as a follow-up date."

"What the hell does that mean?"

"What did you do on our second date?"

"Well, we fucked," he says innocently. "Nothing could go wrong then."

I punch his biceps. "Okay! I'll get the door."

When I peep out the window, I see a man in uniform—standing tall, as if he is on duty.

Uneasiness fills me. What if Sam was right? That something has happened in Kabul?

But if it was a death notification, there would be at least two officers. I don't even want to look for the other, if there are, in fact, two of them.

But I have to.

After searching with my eyes, I'm sure the man is the only one at the door. And he's a hell of a hunk.

"Hi, are you Jack?" I greet him. He removes his cap, and I recognize that face—I guess the forensic artist that Sam had commissioned did a pretty good job.

But that's not it. There's a flash of Sam in him. That's why he looks familiar.

Although noticing the Marine's name badge, now I'm not so sure.

"Hi, yes, I'm Jack." He glances down at his badge. "An old name. My brother didn't tell you?"

"Um... no."

"The Sisters who adopted me never knew my family name, so it was decided that I should be a Benedict—as they're from a Benedictine monastery."

"I see. Good to know."

"You must be Cassidy." He returns my smile with a grin worthy of a GQ cover. With his dark blue eyes, chiseled jaw, and soothing low voice, this man is quite a charmer! Lucky for Sam, I've made up my mind about who I love. Otherwise, I might've jumped ship.

"Good to finally meet you, Jack."

Jack then bends down to hug me. The contact is making it all too real. My emotions surge—this is Jack Kelleher, the brother that Sam had fought hard to find for almost his whole life. I'm close to bursting into tears, as if I felt what Sam would've felt. But Grace arrives behind me.

I nudge her forward, introducing her to Jack. "This is my daughter Grace."

"Hi, Grace." Jack somehow feels the need to squat so he's on the same level as her.

"Say hello to Jack," I say.

"Hello, Jack."

"So nice to meet you. You look just like in your photo."

Sam must've shown it to him.

"You're tall!" Grace quips. "Like Uncle Ben."

Jack's eyes widen, perhaps thinking he has another brother.

"My brother," I clarify.

The Marine crouches even lower as if guilty of towering over the little girl. "Yeah, I guess I am tall."

"Come on in," I say. "Your brother is in the back. He's nervous, so be gentle."

"I'll try my best."

"Sam, Jack is here," I call out.

Foreword and formality go out the window. The two brothers run to each other, colliding in a fierce embrace. The thumping sound of them patting each other's back affirms the reunion is complete.

"You made it, brother," Sam trembles.

"Wouldn't miss it for the world," Jack replies.

They smile at each other. Sam always says Jack looks like their mother. But right now, I see two men mirroring each other—in happiness, brotherly love, and the lost time they're trying to make up for.

Jack looks around the backyard. He even takes the time to pat Maximus, who's eager to size up the new stranger. Noticing Maximus's missing front paw, he asks, "That dog served with you?"

"No. I adopted him. His handler didn't make it," Sam answers. Then he reaches out his hand and pulls me beside him. "You've met Cass."

"Yes. And Grace too." Jack nods at my daughter, holding his laugh as she's trying to get Maximus not to jump up at him. It looks like the dog is trying his old antics—leaping with his one paw up, only to purposely fall on his human, so he gets a hug.

"Come on, Max, down!" Sam helps her out.

"You've done well," Jack comments.

"Come and sit down, gents. Beer?" I offer.

"Gotta say yes!" Sam urges. "It's her own brew."

"Wow, in that case, you've done *really* well," says Jack, winking at Sam. "Of course I'll have one."

"Here we go," I say, passing a bottle to Jack.

"Thanks." Jack has a sip and gives me an aha look. He then scans his surroundings again. "Is our father here?"

Nervous heat climbs over me. I look at my watch—this is getting a little too close.

Sam bows his head. "Um... I didn't think it was a good—"

There's another knock at the door. Sam immediately shifts his gaze to me. "He's here?"

"I invited him," I say nervously.

Sam rubs his face with both hands, and lines form on his forehead. He darts to the door.

"Sam!" I call out. Then I tell Jack, "Please wait here."

My insides are in freefall. The last thing I want is for the two men to be fighting again.

When I get there, the door is already open—and you can hear a pin drop.

I freeze, unable to step further. I watch with wide eyes as Sam hugs his dad. It's silent, yet there are a lot of things said between them.

A moment passes, and the two men face each other.

"I never abandoned you, Sam—not your mom, not your brother," Joseph Kelleher sobs. "I accepted what the police told us then, that Jack was dead. Because I had to take care of your mother—and you. She was really sick. It was impossible for me to keep searching or fighting against the police while she depended on me. I did love and care for her with everything I had. Clearly, it wasn't enough."

Sam sniffles, nodding furiously as if recalling the moment he lost his mother.

Joseph places his hand on Sam's shoulder. "Yes, she died from a broken heart, and I'll never forget that, Sam. I lost her, but I wasn't going to lose you. You're my son."

"I'm sorry I've been so harsh on you. You must've felt alone as much as I did."

Joseph Kelleher shakes his head, but his fatherly gaze is calm. "No. I always feel that the two of you are still with me. And I survive because of that."

Sam cringes, between smiling and crying. I lean on the door jamb, unable to stop my weeping. A true father will never abandon his child, and his love will never fade. For what Sam has gone through, I'm glad he can now experience that love—without inhibition, without complications.

"I found him, Dad," Sam sobs. "*We* did."

Joseph trembles, shaking his head in disbelief this time. Nevertheless, his wrinkled face shows jubilance that I've never seen before on the old man. "How was he when you saw him?"

"He was fine. He looks just like Mom," Sam chuckles. "But he's—get this—he's taller and bigger than me."

The father and son laugh away their tears.

Then, realizing my presence, the old man raises his eyes to mine.

"I guess you've met Cassidy." Sam guides Joseph inside.

Joseph hugs me. "You've kept your promise," he whispers, kissing my forehead. There's a part of me that wishes he was my dad, but this is more than perfect. "I'm glad my son found you."

"Hey, hey, she's mine," Sam protests and pulls me back for himself. And he gives me the sweetest kiss, apparently to affirm his claim.

Joseph glances out to the backyard, and his spine straightens. "Sam... is that... is that... Jack!" Joseph cries out as he scrambles to where Jack is. "It's you!"

Jack stays in place. For the big guy to look so petrified, I can't imagine what's going through his mind. But soon, his long arms reach out to Joseph—he knows deep down who that man is. Meanwhile, Sam doesn't waste any time joining them.

"Remember our dad?" Sam says as if feeling the need to introduce Joseph. "He didn't let you on that roller coaster because you weren't tall enough."

Jack cackles, wiping a few tears as they break the hug. "God... I really don't remember, but I believe you."

"My Reds," Joseph says.

I prop my back against a tree, enjoying what's unfolding in front of me.

Grace is in Joseph's arms now, giggling as Maximus steals a piece of ham from the old man's hand. I've told my daughter who he is, and she's stoked that she'll have someone to call 'pop-pop' (apparently 'grandpa' was reserved for my father, even though she'd never met him).

Tears soon turn into laughter as Sam tries to demonstrate how he used to wrestle his brother. Jack plays along and becomes a willing participant, even though he could easily bring Sam down.

Sam glances at me, and I simply smile back at him. He may be unbreakable, but I know his heart can hurt. Right now, he's whole. No matter how much life tries to break him, his strength shines through, not because he's black and blue, but because he's here—with me.

I'm ready for life with him. Whether it's calm or storm, whether he's near or far, my soul will riot no more.

40

SAM

I arrive at Red Mark headquarters to check on the progress. The command center is almost finished. We're just waiting for a set of digital screens to be installed. But truly, I'm here mainly to check on my partner's progress, whom I know is meeting with Ivy Cavanagh this morning.

My hope to see those two all over each other, or better still, to find Mark's office blinds all shut, is dashed. Instead, I find my partner sitting straight in his chair while Ivy is on the other side of the table, explaining something to him.

What the hell is wrong with that guy? He needs to be unconscious to show love to her?

It looks like the meeting's over. Ivy gets up, and as usual, she gives Mark a friendly hug and a small peck of the cheek. And that fool is just standing there like a salesman having his first transaction.

Ivy greets me as she passes me by. "New suit?"

"Yes." Which I'm possibly about to ruin. "What do you think."

She smirks. "Don't break a heart today. See you, Sam."

I catch her as she steps out of the building. "Is everything okay?"

"Yes. We'll introduce you to the new chief of police next week."

I nod meaninglessly—we both know my question has got nothing to do with that. I then angle my head toward Mark's office. "Please be patient with him."

Her face crumples. "Two years is a long time to hold on to unrequited love."

"Mark has a big heart. And you know what? When a big heart is frozen, it takes a long time to thaw."

She smiles painfully. "That's a good one, Sam. Good one."

Beyond the expression on her face, there's a message that I think she wants me to read—but I'm at a loss to uncover what it is.

With her chin up, she then says, "Maybe it's better this way. I'm no good for him. He doesn't even know who I really am."

"No, he doesn't. But I do know—you two are good for each other."

She shakes her head. "You don't know me either, Sam."

Ivy rushes to her car, leaving without a backward glance. That woman carries her stoicism as closely as Mark does. Their love for each other might just remain unresolved, but honest to God, I can't see my partner with anyone else.

I join Mark inside his office. "How long are you going to keep this up?"

"Keep what up?"

I roll my eyes. "Goddamn! You squeezed her hand in that hospital."

"Don't hold it against me. I wasn't aware of anything!"

I stare at him, refusing to accept his answer. In fact, he's got to know what Ivy told me that night. "She loves you, Mark. She told me, and you've got to do something about it!"

He releases an exhale. "Love is a beast, Sam. I don't want it to destroy what we have now. I'd rather stay friends with her than lose her altogether. Look what happened between me and Rena."

Being stood up at the altar by your fiancée really hurts. For that to happen after being together for almost a decade, that's gotta hurt even more. Mark isn't one to sulk over anything. This time, though, he lets his sorrow show. Perhaps that night at the hospital did change him somewhat.

"It doesn't have to be that way," I assert.

He taps his fingers on his desk. "She's holding a secret, Sam. I don't know what it is, but—a woman with a secret is a woman who'll break your heart."

Perhaps he knows more about Ivy than I thought.

He adds, "Still, I respect and adore her. If we did become lovers, and that secret tore us apart, I would end up hurting her—because I'm done getting hurt. And I don't ever want to hurt her."

I soften my stance. He's endured enough teasing from me. Clearly, it's not just him being stoic or apathetic about love— he simply wants to guard his affection—and above all, to protect Ivy.

"I'll let you off this time. But you know I won't give up on you two," I warn—lightly but seriously at the same time. I've got to stop my partner from achieving his goal of being a bachelor forever.

Mark tosses me a side smile. "What have you got there?" he asks about my bulging side pocket.

I pull out a jewelry box, showing him what's in it. "What do you think?"

Mark analyzes the ring. "It's beautiful. So you didn't take your dad's offer?"

"No. I think Mom's ring should go to Jack."

"That's a nice thought," he agrees. "So it's going to be a big night tonight?"

"Yeah. Ben is going to babysit Grace."

"Speaking about Ben... could you possibly ask him to come here maybe the day after tomorrow? If all goes well with you and Cass tonight?" He winks.

Son of a bitch!

"You don't think I can pull it off?" I gripe. "Well, I think it'll be better if the invitation comes from you, my friend."

"Okay," Mark agrees. "So, where are you taking her for dinner?"

"Dinner? That'd be your choice, wouldn't it, Mr. Terrible-At-Dating?"

"Well, I know a thing or two about organizing unforgettable dates, you know," Mark maintains.

"Well, I'm gonna take her somewhere, doing something that she's terribly good at and I'm terribly poor at."

"Poetry?"

I smirk and leave my partner be.

I HEAR Cass running down the stairs as soon as I knock on her door.

"Hello, handsome," she greets me but then cocks her head. "You told me to wear something comfortable, and you're wearing... a suit?"

"Trust me on this, okay? By the end of the night, you will be glad about what you're wearing, and you'll laugh like hell at me."

"Sounds perfect." She links arms with me.

"How's the packing going?"

"We're almost there."

I let my mouth curve into a smile. I can't wait to have her and Grace at the Woodhouse. I'm already imagining all the trouble we'll create.

We take a drive north and arrive at our destination an hour before sunset.

"Sam? Are we..." She takes in a three-sixty-degree view of the ranch.

"Yes. Our stable isn't quite ready. I thought this was a nice spot."

"Are you sure about this?" she says. "Didn't you tell me you were afraid that you'd kill... the horse?"

"Well, this horse is quite a giant, yet he's very gentle."

Cass runs to a stable, where we're greeted by the ranch owner, a guy with the strangest English accent. Apparently, he used to breed Clydesdales in Scotland. "He's yours, young lady," he hands over Cass's ride. "This is Rusty. He's the dominant one, even though he's smaller than Bosco over there."

While Cass mounts Rusty like a pro, Gordon has to spend a few minutes helping me up. "Remember our practice," he says. "Just trust the horse."

"Okay..." I say like I'm about to put my life in someone else's hands.

I told Cass I wasn't her knight in shining armor, but at the moment, she looks at me as if I am, despite my clumsiness. I'm sure it's all because of the suit. Not that she won't like me in proper riding gear, I know seeing me in a suit gets her hot—that is exactly my intention.

"Where are we going, Mr. Kelleher?" Cass asks as we hit the trail.

"Rusty knows where to go."

I look ahead and welcome the fresh, clean air pressed close against my cheeks. The golden hour is approaching, and the sky is magnificent. Lines of red maple and black birch run alongside us as we press on.

"How long is the ride?" Cass asks.

"About half an hour."

"Fifteen minutes, I'll race ya!" And without warning, she kicks-on Rusty.

"Cass, no, Cass!" I shout as Bosco follows suit.

I almost close my eyes, readying myself to break a bone or two before I even get there, but Bosco slows down. He's still trotting, but this time I feel the rhythm, keep my balance, and get to the end of the trail in one piece.

Miss Kalispell Barrel Racing Champion is already there waiting for me at the top of a ridge. Smiling proudly, she comes to me and holds my horse, allowing me to jump down safely.

"Hello, handsome," she flirts, ditching her jacket. Then she glances at the blankets and pillows spread behind her—which Gordon has prepared for me earlier. "If you let me lead, I will strip you buck naked right now."

Sounds fucking irresistible, but I have to ask her properly.

I lift her arms overhead, stopping her from ravaging me. Then I secure both her wrists, cuffing them with one hand. "There'll be time for that. For now, enjoy Peril Ridge," I murmur, turning her around to face the sunset. I let her arms go and hug her from behind, pressing her back against my chest.

"What a stunning view," she sighs.

I trail her arm up and down a few times with my fingertips. Then on the last stroke, I rub the shank of the ring against her skin. Feeling the cold platinum, she jolts.

"Sam?"

I swing myself in front of her, then I kneel. "Cassidy Winter, will you marry me?"

A wide smile spreads across her face. "Sam Kelleher, of course I will!"

As strong as she is, she pulls me up and imposes her lips on mine as if she has to do it before the sun goes down.

She then appraises the twinkles in the stone. "Gray diamond?"

"My eyes will always be on you," I murmur as she admires the ring. It looks amazing on her.

Cassidy Winter—she's the only one who can break me, and I'm only too happy to pick up the pieces and do it all over again.

Finally, I scoop her up, take her in my arms, and whisper, "Let's make babies!"

She wraps her hand around the back of my neck as she reaches up to my lips. I know she can't wait to have me.

I let her down on the layers of blankets.

"How do you want me, sweetheart?" I whisper.

THANK you for reading *Her Unbreakable Protector*.

Grab the next book, **Her Devoted Protector**, and find out if Mark is finally able to put his past behind him and take a chance on Ivy. What danger awaits when the secret she's been keeping puts her position as the attorney general under threat?

And... will Ben finally join Red Mark?

Curious about how Maximus plays cupid with Sam and Cass? Pick up **the series FREE prequel**, *Montana's Bravest*. It's a quick read that will also give you a glimpse of Red Mark's early days.

Join my newsletter for release updates, free books, and more ➜ alessakelly.com.

ALSO BY ALESSA KELLY

****Redmark Rescue & Protect Series****

Download the FREE prequel to the series, MONTANA'S BRAVEST

Two ex-military men and former bodyguards Sam Redley Kelleher and Mark Connor live and breathe danger to protect others. Discover the start of their journeys in this prequel novella.

Her Unbreakable Protector (Sam's story)

He risks death to reunite families. She's terrified of getting too close. When her past takes her hostage, can these soulmates survive a fatal bullet?

Her Devoted Protector (Mark's story)

She loves him madly. He bears a hidden wound. Can their simmering passion survive secrets, betrayals, and brutal crime lords?

Her Steadfast Protector (Tyler's story)

She's living in a nightmare. He's haunted by the ones he couldn't save. When everything goes wrong, can they find comfort in each other's arms?

Her Faithful Protector (Jack's story)

When the woman who keeps him grounded is taken by her ruthless ex, an emotionally scarred US Marine races to save her life and their love...

**** The Fearless Lovers Series****

Download the FREE prequel to the series, **STAYING FOR YOU.**

Burning for You: From Enemies to Fearless Lovers

He's a simple farm boy at heart. She's a big-city girl. Thrown together by revenge, will their explosive chemistry endure a hostile takeover?

Fighting for You: From Strangers to Fearless Lovers

She's ready for a soulmate. He's sealed away his heart. When attempted murder brings them together, can they survive long enough to find love?

Longing for You: From Secret to Fearless Lovers

He's a notorious mercenary boss, she's a no-nonsense oil tycoon. When legal entanglements take them on a collision course, will they rise to beat unsurmountable odds?

The Hartley Brothers Series

Hold Me Forever

She's a traumatized survivor. He's a closed-off veteran. Can two lost souls find safe harbor together?

Cherish Me Forever

Two wounded hearts. When unexpected love comes within their grasp, can they learn to trust before it's ripped away?

Standalone

Protecting Her

He's a disgraced ex-cop. She's on a mad quest for justice. When they're trapped in a deadly game, can they escape into each other's arms?

Join my newsletter for release updates, free books, and more ➜ alessakelly.com.

Her Unbreakable Protector: A Rescue & Protect Romance Suspense Novel (Red Mark Rescue & Protect Book 1)

www.alessakelly.com

© 2023 Alessa Kelly

ISBN

ePub: 978-1-922363-24-4

Paperback: 978-1-922363-26-8

THE MEANING BEHIND THE RED MARK LOGO

Red Mark is named after its two founders, Samuel Redley Kelleher (nicknamed Red) and Mark Connor. The fox is their mascot; it's a resilient and resourceful animal with sharp tracking instinct, and one of the most protective in the canine family.

For all the courageous military spouses and partners